In my dreams, everything is soft.

The harsh edges of the world are blunted, my face cradled by clouds. My body seems suspended in water, my hair freed from its utilitarian knot, silky lengths cascading down my back. I am a body still becoming, untouched by tragedy. In my dreams I am safe; I have a strong hand to hold; a door to lock against the dark; a trusted ear into which I whisper my fears. In my dreams I am patient and kind; I have room in my heart for more pain than my own. I am not afraid to smile at strangers. I have never witnessed death.

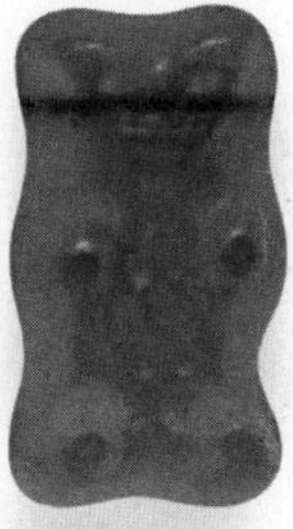

**BOOKS BY TAHEREH MAFI**

Shatter Me: Series One

**BOOK 1**: *Shatter Me*

**BOOK 2**: *Unravel Me*

**BOOK 3**: *Ignite Me*

**BOOK 4**: *Restore Me*

**BOOK 5**: *Defy Me*

**BOOK 6**: *Imagine Me*

Shatter Me: Series One Novellas

**BOOK 1.5**: *Destroy Me*

**BOOK 2.5**: *Fracture Me*

**BOOK 4.5**: *Shadow Me*

**BOOK 5.5**: *Reveal Me*

**BOOK 6.5**: *Believe Me*

Shatter Me: Series One Novella Collections

*Unite Me*

*Find Me*

Shatter Me: Series Two

**BOOK 1**: *Watch Me*

**BOOK 2**: *Release Me*

The Woven Kingdom Series

**BOOK 1**: *This Woven Kingdom*

**BOOK 2**: *These Infinite Threads*

**BOOK 3**: *All This Twisted Glory*

**BOOK 4**: *Every Spiral of Fate*

*An Emotion of Great Delight*

*A Very Large Expanse of Sea*

# WATCH ME

SHATTER ME: SERIES TWO

BOOK ONE

TAHEREH MAFI

STORYTIDE

*An Imprint of* HarperCollins*Publishers*

HarperCollins Children's Books,
a division of HarperCollins Publishers,
195 Broadway, New York, NY 10007

HarperCollins Publishers,
Macken House, 39/40 Mayor Street Upper,
Dublin 1, D01 C9W8, Ireland

Storytide is an imprint of HarperCollins Publishers.

Watch Me

Copyright © 2025 by Tahereh Mafi
All rights reserved. Manufactured in Capriate San Gervasio, Italy. No part of this book may be used or reproduced in any manner whatsoever without written permission except in the case of brief quotations embodied in critical articles and reviews. Without limiting the exclusive rights of any author, contributor, or the publisher of this publication, any unauthorized use of this publication to train generative artificial intelligence (AI) technologies is expressly prohibited. HarperCollins also exercises their rights under Article 4(3) of the Digital Single Market Directive 2019/790 and expressly reserves this publication from the text and data mining exception.

harpercollins.com

---

Library of Congress Control Number: 2024947917
ISBN 978-0-06-349764-1

---

Typography by Jenna Stempel-Lobell
26 27 28 29 30 RTLO 10 9 8 7 6 5 4 3 2 1
SPECIAL EDITION, 2026

The question of the next generation will not
be one of how to liberate the masses, but rather,
how to make them love their servitude.
—Aldous Huxley

No one will ever know the violence it took
to become this gentle.
—Unknown

# ROSABELLE

## CHAPTER 1

When I open the cupboard, the shelves are empty.

This is no surprise, of course; the shelves have been empty for weeks. It's for Clara's sake that I make a show of opening them every morning, pretending there might be more than the same skittering cockroach living inside.

I close the cabinet door, then turn to face her. Clara never leaves the bed unless I carry her; today she's sitting up and staring out the icy window, her pale eyes made paler by the blast of early morning light. Her hand trembles as she twitches the threadbare curtain, and a blue glare briefly illuminates the glass.

"We're out of bread," I announce. "I'm heading out."

Some days Clara lets me leave without asking questions. Other days she asks me how I pay for the food I bring home. Today she says, "I dreamed of Mama last night."

I keep my face impassive. "Again?"

Clara turns toward me, so gaunt her eyes appear sunken in her face. "She wasn't well, Rosa. She was suffering."

I step into my boots, shaking my head as I move into a shaft of light. "It was only a dream," I say to her. "The dead don't suffer."

Clara looks away again. "You always say that."

"And you stare at her photograph too much," I say, knotting my laces. My right hand doesn't shake today, and I experience a rush of relief as I straighten, then a flash of terror as I note the dwindling fire in the hearth—and the disappearing pile of firewood beside it. I force the terror down. "Besides," I add, "you hardly knew her."

"Well, you hardly speak of her," Clara counters with a sigh.

Through the window I glimpse a redheaded woodpecker and watch, transfixed, as it hammers its beak into a mossy trunk. It's been just over a decade since the fall of The Reestablishment—just over a decade since we've lived here, on Ark Island—and I, too, wish I could bash my head over and over against a hard surface every day. I take a sharp breath, ignoring the ever-present ache of hunger.

It's still strange to see the birds.

They fill the sky with sound and color, rattling roofs and branches. All around us evergreens spiral skyward, never surrendering to the seasons. It's always damp here; viridescent; cold. Lakes shimmer unprovoked. Distant mountain ranges seem painted in watercolors, layers of teeth made translucent by fog. The warm and well-fed have been known to call this land beautiful.

"I won't be long," I say, buttoning myself into Papa's old coat. Years ago I cut off the military insignias with a dull blade, earning myself a scar in the process. "I'll see about rebuilding the fire when I get back."

"Okay," Clara says quietly. Then: "Sebastian came by yesterday."

I stiffen.

Very slowly I reanimate, wrapping my mother's tattered scarf too tightly around my neck. I was allowed to work at the mill yesterday, and by the time I got home Clara had been asleep.

"He came to deliver the mail," she says.

"The mail," I echo. "He came all this way just to deliver the mail."

Clara nods, then reaches under her pillow to retrieve a folded newspaper and a thick, unmarked envelope, both of which she holds out in offering. I tuck the two into my coat pocket without glancing at either.

"Thank you," I say softly. I imagine, for a moment, how it might feel to slit Sebastian's throat.

Clara tilts her head at me. "He said you missed last week's meeting."

"You were sick."

"I told him that."

I look toward the door. "You don't need to tell him anything."

"He still wants to marry you, Rosa."

I lift my head sharply. "How do you know about that?"

"Would it be so terrible?" She ignores my question, shivering violently. "Don't you like him? I thought you liked him."

I turn to face our little kitchen, the small stove, the rickety table and chairs we never use. The wooden plaque hanging above the sink.

Our society
REESTABLISHED
Our future
REDEFINED

My eyes unfocus.

I was ten when I came home to find a black bear tearing through the last of our food. Clara was three; Mama had been dead three days. I don't remember killing the bear or burying what remained of my mother.

I remember the blood.

I remember the weeks it took to scrub the floorboards. The bars of Clara's crib. The ceiling. Mama's last words to me had been *close your eyes, Rosa,* except that she'd closed her eyes and I'd kept mine open. She put the gun in her mouth just hours after we heard that Papa would no longer be executed for war crimes. He'd traded all of us in for a half-life, selling secrets to the enemy in exchange for a slow rot in prison. I used to think Mama killed herself because she couldn't withstand the shame. Now I'm certain it was because she knew she'd be forced to pay for Papa's treason.

Maybe she thought they'd spare her children.

I grab the bear pelt from its hook and drape it around Clara's trembling limbs. She hates the pelt. She says the bear's pain still lingers in the cottage, that it makes her retch even after all these years. So when she allows the fur to settle on her shoulders without protest, I know the situation is dire.

"If you married Sebastian, things would be better," Clara says, suppressing another shiver. She pauses to cough, and the hacking sound drives a hole through my head. "They'd lift the sanctions. You wouldn't have to pretend we have food in our cupboards every morning."

Slowly, I meet her eyes.

I remember when Clara was born, when I'd looked at her and wondered whether Mama had given birth to a doll. Only later did I realize I must've looked just as strange when I was born: all ghost and glass. I study her often when she sleeps, or when the illness overtakes her so completely she slips into a coma. At thirteen, she's tender and optimistic; nothing like I was at her age. Still, despite the seven years between us, she and I are physically similar: shockingly pale; hair so blond it's nearly white; eyes a disorienting shade of cold. Staring at Clara is like staring into the past, at what I used to be, who I could've been.

I was soft once, too.

"I really think he loves you," she says, her eyes brightening with feeling. "You should've heard the way he talked about you— Rosa, wait—"

I don't say goodbye to my sister.

I reach for the automatic rifle tucked away in the entry, pulling the strap over my head before tugging a battered balaclava over my face. I step into the cold, and thick flakes catch in my eyelashes just as the front door slams shut behind me, the sound briefly drowning out his voice. It's my only explanation for being startled.

"Rosabelle," he says, cutting in front of me with a smile. "Still dead inside?"

# ROSABELLE

## CHAPTER 2

I sidestep Lieutenant Soledad, absently running my hand along the cold weapon slung across my chest. Soledad is no longer a lieutenant the way he once was; the title is a relic of another time. In this newly imagined world he's the head of our island's security, which makes him nothing more than a glorified busybody. And a tyrant.

I nod at familiar faces as they pass, their eyes anxiously tracking between myself and Soledad, who's fallen into step beside me. Snow is beginning to stick to the ground; spirals of smoke curl away from stacked chimneys, smudging the skies like errant brushstrokes. I adjust the balaclava on my face; the wool is old and itchy. I am impatient.

"I thought our appointment was for tomorrow," I say flatly.

"I thought I'd surprise you," he says. "Impromptu interrogations often yield interesting results."

I come to a halt, turning to face him.

I remember when Soledad was young and fit and full of bravado—when he served under my father, the chief commander and regent of Sector 52. Now he's somehow barrel-chested but soft; stooped. His skin is waxy, his hair thinning. He wears the stale air of another time, the only lingering evidence of that epoch imprinted on his face. A soft blue glow pulses at his temples, his dark eyes occasionally brightening, then dimming.

Unbidden, my right arm trembles.

Quietly I change course for the day, feeling the pressure of a single, physical key tucked inside in the false pocket sewn into Papa's old coat. The only lock I own is bolted to the shed camouflaged in the wilds beyond the cottage—which I meant to visit first, and which I'll now have to avoid. No one in the pit knows about the lock because the lock is illegal; the homes in the pit are meant to be borderless. Our minds, too, are meant to be open at all times for inspection. It was the way of our parents, the way of The Reestablishment.

*Surveillance is security,* Papa used to say. *Only criminals need privacy.*

I glance at Soledad, who still wears his old military fatigues, the front pocket adorned with the tricolored emblem of a buried era. He lost an arm during the post-revolution skirmishes and wears his prosthetic proudly, one sleeve rolled up to reveal the silver gleam of muscular machinery.

"So," he says. "We can set up here, or we can head back to central. Your choice."

I cast a furtive glance around the pit, which comprises a cluster of cottages, square windows aglow in the gray morning light. People scurry along, heads down, avoiding eye contact with Soledad, who's never paid the pit a visit without doing some damage. Those who live here have been sanctioned—cut off from the community for any number of infractions—but no one has lived here longer than Clara and me, who've never known another home on the island. In the chaotic weeks after our supreme commanders were slaughtered, Papa sent us here with Mama, promising to follow as soon as he could. It turned out Papa had stayed behind on purpose, voluntarily surrendering to the rebels. As a reward, we were sanctioned upon arrival.

"Do we have to do this now?" I ask, thinking of Clara, shivering and starved. "I'd rather keep our appointment for tomorrow."

"Why, you have plans this morning?" He says this like it's a joke. "You're not allowed a shift at the mill today."

A sharp pang of hunger cuts through me then, nearly taking my breath away. "Just some things to do."

Soledad grabs my chin and I suppress a flinch, steadying myself as he forces me to look at him. He stares into my eyes for a long beat before letting go, and I kill the flare of revulsion in my chest, compelling my racing heart to slow.

I remind myself that I am dead inside.

"So strange not to know what you're thinking," he says, a notch forming between his brows. "All these years and I still haven't gotten used to it. Makes it hard to believe you're always telling the truth."

Another slight tremor moves through my right hand. I'm the only person here unconnected to the Nexus. Even Clara was brought online before Papa was arrested. Just before the end, all civilians under the directive of The Reestablishment had been connected to the neural network, a program quickly dismantled by the new regime. Soledad and the others like to remind us that the reason we lost the war was because the rebels hadn't been chipped.

I have no acceptable excuse.

"Pity we can't seem to get you online again," Soledad says finally. "Things might've been easier for you."

Memories flare to life: cold metal; muted screams; drug-induced nightmares. With Mama dead, there was no one to beg them to stop. No one who cared whether their experiments would eventually kill me.

"I couldn't agree more," I lie.

Soledad shifts his weight. Blue veins of light pulse through his metal arm, silver fingers flashing as they flex and curl. "So," he says. "Why'd you miss the meeting last week?"

Just like that, an unofficial interrogation has begun. Here, in the freezing cold. While my neighbors watch.

Clara, I realize, can probably see us from the window.

There's a sudden chorus of shouts and my heart stutters, steadying only when I spot Zadie's twin boys, Jonah and Micah, tackling each other in the snow. One of them punches the other in the gut, this accomplishment punctuated by peals of laughter. I catch the drifting scent of breakfast meat from a nearby cottage and my knees nearly give out.

I return my eyes to Soledad. "Clara was sick."

"Coma?"

"No." I look away. "She spent most of the night throwing up."

"Food?"

"Blood," I clarify.

"Right." Soledad laughs. He sizes me up through Papa's overlarge coat. "That makes more sense, considering the fact that you're both starving."

"We're not starving." Another lie.

A fresh circus of sound short-circuits my nervous system. A murder of crows lands heavily on a nearby roof, eerie calls clamoring, wings flapping. I'm watching them, fascinated a moment by an iridescent sheen of black feathers when two earsplitting shots ring out.

I stiffen on impulse—then force myself to thaw, my fingers to unclench, my pulse to slow.

"Fucking birds," Soledad mutters.

He walks over to the duo of fallen bodies, then stomps on their small, hollow bones, smearing blood and feathers into the snow. I blink, exhaling softly into the cold. I've been dead inside for years, I remind myself.

Most people here hate the birds for what they represent. The birds mean that The Reestablishment has been dethroned, that the project has all but failed. The New Republic and its traitorous leaders—the children of our fallen supreme commanders—have been a ripe source of hatred for as long as I can remember.

Clara, I realize, will have questions about the gunshots.

"I've got real work for you, if you're interested," says Soledad, now wiping his boots on a clean patch of ground.

I look up. Realization is swift. "You didn't come here for an interrogation."

Soledad smiles at me, but his eyes are unreadable. "Never misses a thing, this one. I've always hated that about you."

"How many this time?" I ask, my heart beginning a traitorous rhythm.

"We've got four altogether. Three have been processed already. New one came through last night and he's definitely—" Soledad's eyes brighten, glazing over in an inhuman shade of blue. Suddenly he whips around, marches over to the twins still grappling in snow, grabs one of them—Micah—by the scruff of his neck, and shoves him, angrily, to the ground. "You've just lost your rations for the week."

Jonah darts forward. "But— We were only playing around—"

"He was going to take your eye out," Soledad barks, then jerks his head in a familiar motion.

Micah screams.

Jonah stills, but his eyes are fixed on his brother, who's lying on the ground, now silent and twitching violently. There's the slam of a door, a sudden cry, and his mother, Zadie, comes running. Soledad shakes his head in disgust, and Micah is released from his paralysis. With some effort, the boy revives in his mother's arms.

"Sorry, sir," says Micah, his chest heaving. "I didn't mean—"

Soledad directs his next words to Zadie. "If you can't get these two idiots to stop acting like animals, you'll spend another year in the pit. Is that clear?"

Heads appear, then disappear, in neighboring windows.

Zadie nods, mumbling something inarticulate, then grabs her boys and bolts.

In the quiet aftermath Soledad returns to my side, scanning me for a reaction, but I'm careful, as always, to betray no emotion. It's the only way I've survived here, where I'm surveilled not only by the system but also through the eyes of everyone I encounter—even my own sister.

*Surveillance is security, Rosa.*

*Only criminals need privacy.*

*Only criminals need privacy.*

For so many years I used to believe everything my father said.

Those were the years when Soledad was a friend to our family; the years we lived in a warm, comfortable home, when food was abundant, when Nanny would dress me in silks before braiding my hair. I'd sneak downstairs during my mother's dinner parties just to hear the sound of her laughter.

"How many more before you'll lift the sanctions?" I ask, ripping the balaclava off my head. I feel the static of my hair; the compression of my chest. Brisk wind batters my face but the icy air is welcome against my heated skin.

Soledad shakes his head. "I can't answer that. Your father is still alive, still feeding secrets to the enemy. For as long as we can't know your mind, you'll always be a question mark." He shrugs, then looks away. "We all make sacrifices for the security of our nation, Rosabelle. For the security of our future. This is your sacrifice—and it may never end."

He returns his eyes to me.

"Look," he says. "You can kill them all at once or one at a time. I'll let you decide. When you're done, I'll see about getting Clara some medicine."

"And food," I say too quickly, then pause, taking a moment to compose my face. "And firewood."

"All at once, then," he says, narrowing his eyes.

"All at once," I agree. "And right now."

Soledad raises his eyebrows. "You sure? One of them won't stop screaming. She had a bad reaction to the sedative."

I feel unseasonably warm. Overdressed. I distract myself by stuffing the balaclava into Papa's coat pocket, and the thick envelope from earlier kisses me with a paper cut. The pain focuses my thoughts.

It's not necessary to kill them like this.

We have among our ranks some of the best medics and scientists in the world; we possess far more advanced and humane ways to kill the rare spies who manage to breach Ark Island.

Of course, murdering them isn't meant to be humane.

“Do you care how I kill them?” I ask, and my voice is mercifully steady.

The electric hum of the helicopter pulls my attention skyward. Clara will see it. She’ll know what it means.

“I don’t care how you do it.” Soledad smiles now; a real smile. “You’ve always been creative.”

# JAMES

## CHAPTER 3

"Okay. All right. This is fine. You're fine," I say, pacing up and down the short length of my prison cell. I hesitate, then look around for the hundredth time.

I mean, I'm guessing this is a prison cell.

It's clean, which is weird. It's also well-lit, fully illuminated by a light source I can't identify. The walls and floors are made of gleaming steel—so glossy I can see myself from every direction—and the warped reflections keep freaking me out. I have no idea how long I've been in here. Every once in a while a weird mist is released into the room, and each time I lose what feels like a few hours.

My brilliant plan is not exactly going to plan.

"Look," I say, pointing at a melted blur of my face. "There's no reason to panic. You've still got your own pants on, plus all your original body parts, and if you were supposed to die here, no one would care if you had to use the bathroom, okay? They'd let you die in a heap of your own shit—"

As if on cue, a mechanical whirr precedes the reveal of an aperture in the ground. I've been here long enough to have learned that every time I say the word *bathroom* a panel slides away to reveal a bottomless black pit, the opening of which is lined with metal teeth that all but promise to bite off your dick. I've never been so terrified and relieved to take a piss in my life. I fucking hate it here.

I tried shouting other things, too; things like *Get me out of here* and *Motherfucker* and *Ice cream sundae,* and all I got was more mist in my face.

I wonder if anyone back home has realized I'm gone.

"Of course they have, moron," I mutter.

Adam is going to be pissed. Warner is going to be super pissed. Juliette might already be crying. If I survive this, Kenji will probably kill me himself.

A week ago it seemed like a good idea, trying to break into Ark Island. This shithole is the last refuge of The Reestablishment—the last gasp of a fascist psychopathic government that basically wants to enslave the world—and no one's ever been able to penetrate their defenses. Back in the womb of home and family, where I'm still treated like a baby who doesn't know how to wipe his own ass, doing something like this seemed genius. If I could do the one thing even the famous Aaron Warner Anderson couldn't do, maybe they'd finally respect me. Maybe they'd finally look at me like a man and not a ten-year-old boy who used to cry for his big brother every night.

"Great job, idiot." I bang my head against the wall.

If I ever make it back home, they'll never let me do anything again. My own half brother is basically running the world with his wife, and I'll be reduced to desk work. Back in diapers. All my security clearances revoked.

I let out a nervous laugh, then push both hands through my hair. I don't know how Juliette did solitary confinement for nearly a year. Before she single-handedly orchestrated the downfall of The Reestablishment, she'd suffered in ways I could never imagine. Now, looking around this gleaming hellscape, I realize I've never appreciated her enough. I thought I couldn't love her more than I already do—hell, she and Warner helped raise me—but imagining how The Reestablishment tortured her—

Nah. I can't go there. Not here. Not now.

"Shower!" I shout at the wall.

Nothing happens.

"Piece of shit!" I shout at the wall.

The toilet hole opens again.

"Listen," I say angrily, "if you're not going to kill me, the least you could do is offer me some snacks—"

The words have barely left my mouth when I'm startled by memory. Propelled into motion, I search my pockets until I find it—a little plastic pouch of gummy bears, half-melted.

I can't help but smile.

These assholes stripped every weapon off my body but left me the candy. I'd swiped it from five-year-old Gigi's snack bag on my way out the door; a moment that now feels like a lifetime ago. I rip the packet open, then stare at the melted gummies for half a second, the artificial scent of various fruit flavors generating sense recognition so strong my heart nearly gives out.

"Hey," I say, narrowing my eyes at my liquid reflection. "Pull yourself together."

I empty the bag of gummies into my mouth, then stuff the plastic into my pocket. I'm still chewing when I say, "You're going to go home. You're going to see everyone again. You're—"

The room begins to vibrate with a soft, mechanical rumble, and the words die in my throat. I stiffen and back up, shielding my eyes as one of the walls disappears, then reappears in a flare so bright I can't clock the change.

Suddenly, I have a visitor.

I knew The Reestablishment had seriously advanced tech—we've been studying their work for a decade—but this girl materializes as if out of thin air. We're face-to-face, trapped by steel in all directions, and she's standing so inhumanly still that for a second I think I'm hallucinating. She looks like an elfin creature out of a fairy tale, so slight she's practically a beam of light. White-blond hair, icy eyes. Skin like glass.

Really, absurdly gorgeous.

My heart beats a little too hard as I blink and straighten, fake candy flavors coming alive on my tongue at the worst moment. My mouth is full of half-chewed gummy bears. I'm trying to chew without looking like I'm chewing. Jesus.

The tiny elf takes a step toward me, and I flinch.

"State your name and date of birth," she says quietly, her cold eyes appraising me.

Something about the way she tilts her head—that, and the smooth, measured sound of her voice—and suddenly I understand. This beautiful weirdo isn't a real person. She's artificial intelligence.

I exhale, irritation doing the counterintuitive work of relaxing my body.

The fact that she's a robot makes things easier. First of all, I'm not going to talk to a fucking robot. I might be an idiot, but I'm not uninformed. I know how much The Reestablishment loves surveillance. I know that this cell is being watched. They love mind games. Love to torture. If they wanted me dead, they'd have sent a real person to mess with my head at least a little before killing me. Instead, this thing is probably recording and analyzing my vitals while doing a background check. I bet it's mining some database right now, figuring out that Aaron Warner Anderson is my half brother; that Juliette Ferrars is his wife; that I'm the youngest son of Paris Anderson, the dead, ex–supreme commander of North America. They've caught themselves a big fish.

Mentally, I kick myself in the face.

"I gave you a directive," she says, and takes another step closer.

I chew a little more, trying to swallow without killing myself. "Look, if the computer in your head doesn't already know who I am just by scanning my face, I'm not going to answer your questions. So if you're here to extract information, you're shit out of luck. Maybe just send in the guy who's supposed to torture me."

She hesitates, surprise coloring her features so briefly I nearly miss it. Fascinating, lifelike tech.

She blinks those strange eyes at me before saying, softly, "Are you *eating* something?"

"Gummy bears," I say with my mouth full.

She blinks again. There's something so human about the way she studies me then that it gives me goose bumps.

"I don't understand," she says.

"Gummy bears? It's, like, a chewy candy—"

"You're not afraid to die?"

"Uh." I stop chewing. "What?"

And then she moves toward me, closing the gap between us in two strides, and I realize with a sudden, palpable fear—

This is a real woman. Not a robot.

I'm so distracted by this fact, so alarmed by the warmth of her small hand as she touches my face that, at first, I don't even notice the knife she's pressed to my throat. She has my head in a surprisingly firm grip, my neck open and exposed to her blade, but I can feel her breath against my skin and it's messing with my head. She's got doll hands. She smells fresh, like pine trees and soap. Up close her eyes are a pale grayish blue and her dark coat is moth-eaten and oversized. Underneath she wears a baggy sweater, the collar gaping to reveal a glimpse of skin so fine I feel lightheaded just looking at her.

I don't think I understand the point of this exercise.

I'm a high-profile prisoner; any idiot would know not to kill me right away. They should be torturing me for information. Using me as bait or leverage. Instead, they've assigned me an elf who needs to stand on tiptoe to reach my neck. It feels like I'm being assaulted by a flower.

It's annoying, though, the knife at my throat.

I decide to toss her across the room just to be safe, but when I slip my hands inside her coat she takes a sharp, startled breath and nearly stumbles. I grab her on instinct, holding her steady without thinking, but I'm thrown by the feel of her—a waist so small it seems almost dangerous. I study her face, my eyes narrowing in confusion, and she stares back at me with a flare of emotion so intense I swear to God I feel it in my chest.

"You smell like apple," she whispers, and I'm actually about to smile when she slits my throat.

I see the flash of metal, but the blade moves fast and the pain doesn't hit me until she's backed away. I lift a hand to the wound as my vision deteriorates, blood seeping against my fingers just as I realize I can't speak.

*Motherfucker.*

She's cut my trachea, too.

Doll Hands has clearly done this before, and done it well. I sway slightly, making a strangled sound as I land badly on my knees. She looms over me, watching, expressionless.

As if from outer space I hear her say, “He’s ready for organ extraction,” just as I slump to the floor.

She swipes the gummy wrapper from my pocket before she disappears.

# JAMES

## CHAPTER 4

Sounds bleed in and out: a smear of voices, the clangor of metal. *Pain.* Light flares in electric bursts behind my eyes. I feel hands on my body, cold steel, my thoughts slurring. A blind assessment of the situation seems to indicate that I'm lying on a gurney, being wheeled down what I can only assume is a hallway. I have to hold on to my mind, force it to focus before I pass out, because if I pass out I won't wake up until my throat's healed, which means I might wake up right as they're cutting the kidneys out of my body.

Or worse.

It's not common knowledge that I have healing powers, but it's not exactly a secret, either. The Reestablishment must've really gone to shit out here if they're this bad at their jobs. You'd think one of the most technologically advanced fascist regimes in history would've done a little digging on its prisoners. You'd think they would've known that they couldn't just slit my throat and toss me on a gurney in the bowels of some top-secret location on a top-secret island without serious consequences. You'd think they would've bound my hands and legs before releasing me from my cell, that they might've given me some kind of tranquilizer or at least sealed my eyes shut—

Yeah. Never mind. Now that I think of it, no way they're that stupid. This is more likely some kind of a trap.

Time to pivot.

Luckily, my head is beginning to clear. My breathing has begun to stabilize. A sentence I never thought I'd think: I'm grateful for the mess of blood all down my throat, because it's hiding the fact that my wound is healing.

I slit my eyes open.

Doll Hands is a blur beside me, but there seems to be someone else, too. My hearing is improving, my heart rate picking up.

"—was hoping to get home in time for dinner," some guy says, then laughs. "I guess I should've known better. All of them back-to-back, huh? I'll be working through the night processing your new dump of bodies."

Wow, great.

Doll Hands is a serial killer. My pants were getting tight over a serial killer. Kenji is going to love this.

"Did I tell you my wife is making lasagna?" The guy laughs again, but now he sounds nervous.

Can't blame him. Serial killers tend to make people nervous.

"She makes great lasagna," he's saying. "Actually, she's good at everything. I mean, I always knew she was talented, but man, every day she surprises me. Oh, and we just got our wedding photos back—"

Without warning we crash into something, and my head lifts, then slams back onto the steel gurney so hard I nearly wince. Silently, I revisit every foul word I've ever known.

"Whoops, didn't see that wall there!" More panicked, high-pitched laughter from the guy, then the shuddering sound of wheels, the vibration of metal, and we're on the move again. I have to be careful not to lift my chest as I inhale, but I'm feeling strength return to my body, which means it's about time to make a move.

"You know," says the nervous guy, "you don't have to come with me all this way—"

"Yes, Jeff, I do," she says softly. "Soledad's orders."

Something stirs in my chest when she speaks, and mentally I punch myself in the crotch. Her voice is silky smooth—the voice of a sociopath or a siren—and I'm worried Jeff and I might piss our pants if she keeps talking.

"Oh," he says. "I—I didn't realize."

Luckily, Doll Hands says nothing to this, but now I'm wondering who the hell Soledad is.

"Did I mention my wife is making lasagna tonight?"

More silence.

"I love lasagna," says Jeff. "Do you—do you love lasagna?"

When she ignores him for the second time, I start to feel bad for the guy hoping to cut the organs out of my corpse. I sit up and turn to face him. "For what it's worth, Jeff, I fucking love lasagna."

Jeff screams.

I lock eyes with Doll Hands for only a second, long enough to catch the horror on her face before I jump off the gurney and shove it violently in her direction, the heavy steel pinning her to the wall with a satisfying crack. She cries out as Jeff scampers off screeching, triggering an alarm as he goes. The hall is suddenly blaring with lights and chaotic sound. I spin around. Panicky-looking people in lab coats start streaming into the hall, but when they glimpse my blood-soaked neck and shirt—and the wilting girl sliding down the wall—they quickly disappear. The place, I note, is bright white and entirely unmarked. I have no idea how to get out of here. More important, I need to find a weapon.

Doll Hands is back for round two.

She shoves the gurney away from her in a jerky motion, struggling for air as she straightens. I watch her clasp a hand to her side as she fights to breathe, and I can't help but grin at the sight.

"My bad. Did I break your ribs?"

"Drop dead," she bites out.

"You first."

"You're deluded," she says. "This is not a victory. You have no idea what they'll do to you now."

The sirens kick into higher gear, wailing with renewed vigor. It's probably a matter of seconds before this place is swarmed.

"Look," I say, shouting a little over the chaos. "I don't love this situation, either. It feels really weird to hit a girl. But considering the fact that you just *murdered* me a minute ago, I think I'm entitled to retribution. So I'm giving you two options: show me how to get out of here, or hand over your knife."

"Go to hell."

"Did one of those broken ribs puncture a lung?" I ask, really smiling now. "Can you feel yourself dying?"

"Have you ever had your intestines ripped out of your body?" she says, her eyes flashing. "I hear it's excruciating."

"You have five seconds to decide," I say, crossing my arms against my chest. "Five. Four. Three. Two— *Fuck*—"

I rear back as a searing pain sets fire to my arm. Apparently she chose option two: hand over her knife. I squeeze my eyes shut and yank the blade out of my shoulder, somehow managing to bite back a deluge of expletives.

"You have terrible aim," I say, gritting my teeth as I wipe the weapon clean on my shirt. "The trick, if you haven't figured it out yet, is to kill me instantaneously." But when I look up at the girl, I can see why she threw the blade badly; she's half-bent, holding on to the wall for support, her skin ashen. Still, I'm surprised by the look in her eyes. She doesn't seem angry anymore.

She shakes her head, almost disappointed when she says, "Idiot."

Then she retrieves a syringe from her pocket, bites off the cap with her teeth, and plunges the needle into her thigh. She nearly screams as she straightens, her chest heaving as she draws air into her lungs.

A thunder of footsteps echoes down the hall.

I turn, bloodied and confused, to discover a swarm of

military personnel storming toward me. I mean, obviously this was going to happen—The Reestablishment wasn't going to just let me walk out of here—but, damn. They're aiming weapons in my direction I've never even seen. Huge, heavy, scary, neon shit. They look awesome. I want one.

"Rosabelle," a voice booms.

A man detaches from the group and steps forward, and I'm so busy processing the fact that the serial killer is named something as soft as *Rosabelle* that I nearly miss the sight of his veiny metal arm. It also takes me a second to notice that he looks insane. Blue light glazes over his eyes, pulses at his temples, radiates across his bionic prosthetic. A feeling of unease prickles my skin.

Bad memories.

The Reestablishment once put my dad back together with similar sleek prosthetics. That sort of seamless limb regeneration was unheard of a decade ago, and while we still haven't figured out how to replicate the tech precisely, it looks like it might be commonplace around here. Clearly, The Reestablishment has been advancing new levels of bioengineering, and, clearly, we've been underestimating their ability to progress in isolation. For over a decade we've been trying to prepare for whatever fresh hell they might be brewing out here, but our spy efforts fall short, over and over, because all our tech is built upon the entrenched systems and networks that *they* established.

The Reestablishment knows how to deactivate our satellites because they designed them; they know how to mess with our power plants because they built them; they know how to shut down our electrical grids because they engineered them. The civilians don't seem to understand that outliers of The Reestablishment still live among us. When the regime fell, only the rarefied elite decamped to Ark Island. Only the highest-ranking, richest military families of The Reestablishment were even notified of the exit plan; they were the ones who could hop on private jets and avoid the fallout.

The rest of the sycophants stayed behind.

It's never been easy to discern which of the "reformed" members of The Reestablishment might still be loyal to the old order. Many of them are now undercover agents dotted all over the globe, undermining us at every opportunity. Last year was more brutal than ever: there was a mysterious gas-line explosion at one of the elementary schools, and over a hundred kids died. It was one of the darkest days in our recent history; the nightmare is still embedded in my skin. We keep trying to explain to our own people that we're being hacked and attacked, but it's getting harder to convince people of these facts when The Reestablishment appears, by all outward appearances, to have gone totally dark.

All we know for certain is that we're struggling.

These psychological operations are meant to turn the masses against us. People have short and fickle memories; too many are beginning to wonder whether life under The Reestablishment was better. Juliette is worried. Even

Warner, who rarely shows emotion, seems stressed. He floated the idea of launching a covert mission into the Ark, but we all knew he wouldn't leave Juliette in her condition.

So I came up with this genius plan: uncover something useful about the psychopaths out here, make it home alive, and, in the process, earn the respect of my friends and family. The problem is that no spy from the mainland has ever breached these borders and survived. I'd hoped I had the necessary skills to be the exception.

Looks like I was wrong.

The guy with the robot arm is striding toward me now, weapon raised. I'm running a few scenarios in my head, trying to do the necessary calculus to determine whether it's worth stabbing this dude before he blasts a hole through my chest, when suddenly he slows. He studies me with those creepy eyes. Lowers his weapon.

"Incredible," he says, his voice touched with awe. "You look so much like your father. What a shame that both of you should die such tragic deaths." Then, tossing his gun blindly at Rosabelle: "Make it quick."

# ROSABELLE

## CHAPTER 5

In the split second the weapon sails between myself and Soledad, the inmate launches himself forward, snatches it out of the air, and lands in a smooth tumble.

He immediately opens fire on everyone.

Shots explode, screams pierce the din. Soledad barks orders, but sounds warp and distort; sirens blare as lights flash. I back up against the cold wall, my heels knocking against the footboards, my hands searching for purchase. The scene developing before me is so impossible it seems to bleed at the edges. I feel as if the floors are melting under my feet, my breaths loud in my ears, the pain in my ribs beginning to crescendo once more. They shoot at the inmate over and over, but his reflexes are extraordinary; he manages to dodge most of their fire, sustaining minor injuries that I now realize he can easily overcome. Watching him move is like witnessing wind: it's only clear he's been there when someone else falls.

There is no precedent for this situation.

I've been summoned here countless times, and my work has always been faultless. Never have I failed to kill a mark. Never has an inmate been able to escape. This one cannot be allowed to run rampant through these halls; he cannot be allowed to report back anything he's witnessed here. And I—

I will be executed for this failure.

The realization hits me like another shot of adrenaline. An image of Clara flares to life behind my eyes, her name repeating in my head. If I am dead, no one will wipe the blood from her lips. If I am dead, no one will catch her when she collapses. No one will bathe her, no one will read to her, no one will comb the knots from her hair. Clara is only allowed to live as she does because I take full responsibility for her needs. Without me, they will toss my sister in the asylum, where she will die a slow, torturous death.

If I am dead, no one will ever smile at her again.

I drag myself upright, biting back a sound as pain lances through my body. I have no idea how many ribs I've broken. Systematic starvation has weakened my bones, atrophied my muscles. I feel the telltale tremble in my right hand and clench a fist against it.

The Reestablishment has no sympathy for the weak.

I realize as I step forward that I've gone slightly deaf from the barrage of chaos and sound. There's a ringing in my ears so loud I hear only a muted dissonance as I force myself into the fray, limping slightly over fallen bodies. My vision has tunneled to a single figure: the inmate is now engaged in a round of hand-to-hand combat with the only two remaining officers, and I watch him land a bone-crushing blow to the jaw of one, then the other, before he racks his stolen weapon and opens fire directly at their throats. I flinch twice, in concert with each recoil. Blood spatters everywhere, but only one officer's head detaches fully from his body.

My ears are still ringing.

Dimly I register that Soledad is lying nearby in a pool of his own blood, the glint of his prosthetic flashing in my periphery. In a movement so excruciating it nearly takes my breath away, I bend to swipe Soledad's gun from his limp fingers, then hoist the hefty weapon into my arms, absently checking the laser fill of the magazine. Floaters crowd my vision; sweat beads at my brow. It occurs to me that I'm running a slight fever—that perhaps my physical state is worse than I feared.

Strangely, this realization offers me comfort.

If I'm to die either way, there is little to fear from injury. I will not be afraid of this stranger who seems chronically unafraid. I will not be afraid of an arrogant insurrectionist; a worthless rebel. Soledad's last words to him echo in my head—

*You look so much like your father.*

I don't know what that means. I don't know who his father is or whether the information is relevant. Perhaps I will never know, as Soledad is dead. I know the inmate has blue eyes and brown hair, a reductive description that fails to illustrate a problem. His face is like none I've known. His beauty is absurd and shocking, the effect aggravated by contradictions that draw the eye over and over: he's a study in contrasts, at once playful and unyielding. His brow and jaw are severe, but there's a boyish dusting of freckles across the bridge of his nose. His body is solid, taut with muscle, but he seems at ease in his own skin. His eyes seem to shimmer, as if laughter comes to him freely—and yet he single-handedly slaughtered a dozen soldiers.

*He was unarmed.*

I still feel the crinkle of plastic in my pocket; still recall the synthetic apple scent on his breath. I thought Clara might like to cut out the colorful bears illustrated on the wrapper. I thought she'd like to know what sugar smells like. I thought I'd be returning home to her with food and medicine and firewood, and I realize now that I might not return to her at all.

I close my eyes. Open them.

I didn't cry when my mother shot herself in front of me. I didn't cry the first morning I found Clara choking on her own blood.

I will not cry now, or ever again.

In the emerging silence, my hearing seems to improve, the metallic ring fading. Now I hear my heartbeat, the sound of my own dragging feet. The weapon is slick in my hand, heavier than I remember it. My arms are shaking. I can't seem to breathe.

The inmate turns around.

I fire.

He's faster than I am; stronger; smiling as he dodges my imperfect shot. Blood is now smeared across his face, streaked through his hair. His clothes drip as he walks, his boots leaving red footprints along the white floors. He's wounded in several places but this fact doesn't seem to bother him. In fact, he seems delighted.

There's no one left to kill but me.

News of this massacre has certainly reached officials by now, but all our surveillance technology can't make up for a lack of manpower. I don't know how long it'll be before another troop is notified, armed, and unleashed. We are unaccustomed to such attacks. We have more scientists than soldiers. Never, since its inception, has the island sustained such losses.

The inmate winks at me. "Looks like we're finally alone, beautiful."

I fire again.

He dives out of the way, laughing, but the kickback damages my injured body anew. I stumble as fresh agony turns the edges of my vision white. One of my broken ribs, I realize, must've finally pierced an organ.

I rack my weapon, heart thundering in my chest. I wonder how they'll tell Clara I'm dead. I wonder whether they'll be gentle with her, but I already know that they won't. The electric battery thrums under my hands as the gun recharges. We learned early on that manufacturing bullets was expensive and time-consuming. Most of our weapons are now powered by directed energy. Lasers so powerful some can reduce bone to ash in a single shot. The inmate is pointing two such weapons in my direction. Over his shoulder he's slung four more, collecting loot as he stalks toward me. He must be carrying over a hundred pounds of weaponry, but he doesn't seem fatigued by the effort.

Another flash of white teeth as he grins, and suddenly the distance between us has vanished. I don't realize I'm on my knees until it occurs to me that I'm staring up at him, my head burning bright with fever. He pries the gun from my hands and it seems to be happening to someone else. I stagger slightly and he says *Now we're even* but the words stutter in my head and I wonder whether I've imagined them. Pain is crowding my thoughts, heat devouring my mind. I am delirious.

Already dying.

He aims the glowing barrel at my face and I'm less ashamed of defeat than I am of what I intend to say next. My greatest moment of weakness: observed by a stranger. Recorded by machines. Remembered forever.

"Please," I gasp. "Tell them to be gentle with her."

The inmate lowers his weapon an inch. "What?"

My head rocks backward, meets a hard surface. "She's just a child."

"Who?" he demands, his voice booming between my ears. "Hey—"

"My sister," I choke out, though I can't seem to move. I feel as if I'm going blind. "When I die, they'll throw her in the asylum."

The inmate seems to still.

I feel this somehow, though perhaps I'm hallucinating. I can't tell whether my mind has already detached from my body. Perhaps it's the fever. Chills wrack my bones; pain spasms across my torso.

For once, the silence scares me.

"She's just a child," I whisper again.

When he says nothing I brace myself for the final blow, for the pain that precedes nothingness, for the failure that was my life, for the futility of all that I am—

But when I force myself to look up, the inmate is gone.

# ROSABELLE

## CHAPTER 6

In my dreams, everything is soft.

The harsh edges of the world are blunted, my face cradled by clouds. My body seems suspended in water, my hair freed from its utilitarian knot, silky lengths cascading down my back. I am a body still becoming, untouched by tragedy. In my dreams I am safe; I have a strong hand to hold; a door to lock against the dark; a trusted ear into which I whisper my fears. In my dreams I am patient and kind; I have room in my heart for more pain than my own. I am not afraid to smile at strangers. I have never witnessed death. In my dreams sunlight glazes my skin; gentle wind caresses my limbs; Clara's laughter makes me smile.

She is running.

In my dreams, she's always running.

*You're so pretty with your hair like that, Rosa,* she says. *Would you like to play a game with me?*

I inhale sharply as my eyes fly open.

The chorus of my own harsh breaths and pounding heartbeats surge with a disagreement of unintelligible, distant sound. I lay frozen a moment, trembling with cold, my eyes communicating horrors to my mind.

My first thought is that I've been buried alive.

I lift a hand to the smooth, eggshell interior of my tomb, and only after my heart nearly gives out do I recognize the first flaw in my theory: this narrow, enclosed space is unnaturally illuminated. Tentatively, I rap my knuckles against the cool stone, and the sound echoes. A second flaw: I don't appear to be underground.

I strain my ears for more—more anomalous sound, more clues as to my location—and make out only a distorted jangle of metal and the intermittent hum of machinery. Looking down at myself as best I can, I run a blind hand down my body.

It occurs to me then that I feel no pain.

I'm wearing a hospital gown. My ribs appear to be intact. A deluge of memory assaults me: the inmate, the massacre, my imminent death. *Clara.*

The smiling rebel, who disappeared.

At this reminder of my disastrous failure, I stiffen with dread. If I'm still alive after failing to kill a spy from the mainland, it's because The Reestablishment has chosen a different avenue of punishment. They don't believe in acts of mercy.

Voices swell suddenly, footsteps growing louder. I steel myself in anticipation of something—anything—

Several clicks and a sound, like a gasp of air, and my tomb unseals around me without warning. The hulking top lifts upward as fluorescent light blazes through the open sides. I blink slowly against the glare, realizing I'm parched. I swallow against the sandpaper of my throat, then study the surrealist landscape of my nightmare. The stone lid hovers just above me; to my right I glimpse a cross section of torsos. Lab coats swarm and scatter; the steady, familiar blue light of surveillance strobes into my vault.

Even here, now, I am being watched.

I school my features, trying not to betray emotion as I scan what's visible of my location. There appear to be five people in lab coats; two are turned away from me, and one is exiting the room. I can't decipher the various clicking and humming of machines. I don't know what they've done with my clothes. I have no idea what torture they have planned.

"Commence transfer," someone says.

Fear seizes my limbs, renewed terror building as a disembodied voice begins to count down from twenty.

"Wait— Sir—"

"What?" a man barks.

"Based on her vitals, she won't last more than six minutes in the cradle—"

"Fourteen, thirteen—"

"—and we have her scheduled for ten."

"So?"

"Nine, eight—"

"Ten minutes and there's a chance her lungs will never recover—"

"I didn't make the call."

"But—"

"Klaus says ten minutes."

*Klaus.*

"Four, three—"

"Note that she'll need to be dressed and rehydrated within the hour."

"What if—"

"Two—"

I never have the chance to scream.

There's a weightless moment, a sudden plummet in my stomach, and the bottom of my tomb unhinges, releasing me. Ice-cold water closes over my head, filling my gasping mouth, surging up my nose. A metallic tang coats my tongue and sears my throat, indicating there's more to this liquid than water. I thrash wildly, my eyes flying open as a terrible cry builds in my lungs, panic storming the walls of my chest. It's pitch-black. I'm underwater and blind, choking—

*Close your eyes, Rosabelle.*

The deep, treacherous voice, like something forged from the sea, awakens in my head. A painful chill courses down my spine.

We've all heard stories about Klaus.

Klaus is the reason Ark Island exists as it does. Klaus is the reason The Reestablishment will reign again. He's the pinnacle of chemical intelligence; an omnipotent, synthetic brain built upon decades of work and research—built atop the charred remains of Operation Synthesis—but only a select few have ever heard his voice. Klaus is the fodder of Ark legend, so cloaked in secrecy I'd begun to wonder whether the program was even real—

*There is no doubt that I am real.*

I stiffen. My lowered heart rate picks up, my eyes widening in fear. My hair has come loose of its knot, wet lengths lapping my face as I turn sluggishly in the murk. Nausea strikes, my gut clenching against nothing. I blink, pupils dilating, desperately searching the darkness for signs of life. Unfathomable depths meet me in all directions, the infinite gloom broken occasionally by fizzing flashes. I move toward one light source but something solid grazes my leg and I scream, shadow filling my mouth as a sudden flare, like a tongue of fire, illuminates the water.

All at once: clarity.

I'm in an undersea forest of light, spindly branches of bioluminescence fracturing the water like neon circuitry, each vein pulsing as if in possession of a heartbeat. Dozens of slick, grayish bodies appear suspended in the immeasurable expanse around me, their naked forms electrifying at random. Threads of light course across their moldering skin, hollow eyes glinting. They're obviously long dead, minds and organs sacrificed at the altar of artificial learning.

This must be the cradle.

The rumors are that Klaus must be fed; that his chemical soul was born of human starter; that the cradle is skimmed only when the drained corpses rise, like scum, to the surface. I don't know how many of the rumors I've heard about Klaus are true. I only know that they're all fodder for nightmares.

*I told you to close your eyes.*

This time when I hear his voice, I don't hesitate to obey. Curiosity alone has kept me conscious, but I'm beginning to lose the fight for oxygen, and it's a relief to surrender.

Flashes of color brighten and dim behind my closed eyelids, the accompanying sensation like fingers prying at my skull. I wrap my arms around myself as a slithering disquiet reaches up through my ribs, wrenching my bones. My head heats. Electric shocks radiate inside me. Images bleed across my vision, scenes from my life examined impatiently and out of order—

a shiver of cold as my bare feet hit the floor this morning;

Clara, age four, tied to my back as we hike through the forest;

wide-eyed love as I watch my father button himself into his uniform;

the heft of a weapon in my small, doughy hand;

thirst; sweat slick down my back in the beating sun;

*Nothing,* my father shouting. *Nothing is wrong—this is grown-up talk, Rosa, go to your room—*

pain, explosive, as I snap my femur during a training exercise;

the damp, inky darkness of predawn;

the twist of my gut the first time Sebastian kisses me;

*I'm having dreams about Mama again,* says Clara one

morning, *she says she's looking for her glasses; she wants to know if you've seen them—*

awe, the first time I see a flower;

anger;

*anger;*

shredded petals as I rip blossoms violently from their stems;

the deafening sound of the gun going off;

Clara losing her first tooth, smiling as she says, *Look, Rosa, I'm dying;*

my mother, fuming that I've knocked on my father's office door;

the lurid gloss of her pink dress;

a wild look out the window;

*How many times do I have to tell you that your papa is an important man? He is chief commander and regent of Sector 52, don't you understand? He has serious responsibilities, and if you want his attention you'll have to prove yourself worthy—*

It's as if my brain is being teased apart, as if Klaus is sifting through all of me, messily unearthing memory from flesh. Sensations buzz through me: exhaustion and isolation from the years I spent training; bright joy at the sound of Clara's laughter; vomit the first time I killed someone; the blinding gasp of hunger; the betrayal of my father's betrayal; anger reducing me to ash; shame; shame; self-loathing; *fury—*

My eyes roll back in my head as fresh agony shatters through my right arm, images flooding my mind with abandon now: steel clamps; neon wires; the stutters of baffled scientists; the rage of Soledad; the revulsion in Sebastian's eyes;

*No, don't fix it;*

*Let the pain remind her what a disappointment she is;*

*You've disappointed us, Rosa;*

*You've disappointed all of us—*

They'd said I wouldn't last more than six minutes in the cradle. I wish my lungs would fail. I wish I knew how to escape this hell. I'm sure I've been here for an eternity—

*Strange,* says Klaus, turning inside my skin. *Very strange.*

I'm growing dizzy with fatigue. My body seems to be ballooning, stretching painfully to accommodate this mental invasion. Exhaustion drags me deeper and deeper into the dark. I drift against a cold cadaver, the dead fingers of a dead body grazing my cheek, but I lack the energy even to flinch.

I realize, with some relief, that I must finally be dying. Again.

*No, you will not die today.*

My eyes flicker open.

*But it's not clear, Rosabelle Wolff, whether you deserve to live.*

# JAMES

## CHAPTER 7

Fuck this shit.

Fuck this place.

I hate it here, hate myself for thinking this was a good idea, hate my family for being right about how much of an idiot I am, hate the fact that I can never prove them wrong because I'm a moron, hate that Warner is probably right, that profanity is probably a failure of the mind, that only idiots need to rely on foul language to express themselves properly—or whatever stupid shit he said to Adam that one time, I can't remember—but I've already acknowledged the fact that I'm an idiot, so I think it's okay for me to just lean into the personality for the moment.

*Fuck.*

I bang my head against the tree trunk, startling a group of birds, disturbing a dusting of snow. The rough bark scrapes my forehead in a painful, pleasant sort of way, and this pisses me off, too, though I'm not sure why. Whatever.

At the moment, everything is pissing me off.

On the one hand, I'm really happy I managed to escape. On the other hand—

Did I?

Did I, though?

This place. This *creepy* place. These tricky assholes. I don't believe they're really this stupid, that they'd really let me walk out of a highly secured prison/laboratory with all their awesome guns.

I glance at the stock of weaponry camouflaged in a nearby thicket. If I can manage to get even one of these magnificent pieces of machinery into Winston's hands, I might be able to beg forgiveness for being a moron. But the truth is, despite the fact that I'm technically a free man standing here freezing my ass off in the middle of—I squint upward, then around—some mossy, frosty mess of forest, I'm not sure I'm actually free. And I'm not sure I'll ever make it home.

I begin to pace.

Fact one: There's snow on the ground. There's snow on the ground, and I killed, like, a bunch of people, and definitely left a trail of blood in my wake. I managed to suffer through the worst of my injuries as they healed, but I'm not exactly equipped with a medic kit. I had to pry two bullets out of my leg with my bare hands and then pack the open wounds with snow; a toddler could've pointed in the direction of me screaming obscenities at the sky. Fact two: I'm hiding in the forest like a cartoon princess. Even without a blood trail, The Reestablishment could easily scan this island with a heat-seeking drone. Fact three: A squirrel had the audacity to climb up my leg with its freaky claws and look at me with its stupid, adorable face, and I swear to God I thought I saw its little eyes glowing. I don't know if I'm seeing things, but the fourth fact is: I don't trust these people.

And fifth of all—

I groan as I drag my hands down my face.

Fifth of all, I should've killed the girl.

A bright red bird swoops overhead, landing on a nearby branch. It studies me with its beady eyes, and I glare back, practically daring it to be some kind of robot.

"What are you looking at?" I ask.

It ruffles its feathers, head twitching.

"Hey—don't shake your wings at me. I know you're probably some cyborg bird—"

It cuts me off with a soft trill, alighting with another shake of its head.

I sigh, backing up against the tree trunk. The Reestablishment took pretty much everything useful off my body, including my watch, but based on the position of the sun I think it's safe to estimate that I've been out here for at least several hours. *Several hours* I spent hiking through the forest and they still haven't tracked me down.

I haven't had to kill anyone at all.

This distinct lack of recent murdering is making me anxious. Every sound startles me. Every fairy-tale creature pisses me off. Unspent adrenaline is coursing through my veins, winding me up—making me paranoid.

I slide down the trunk into a seated position, accidentally bumping my heap of weapons in the process. They illuminate through the brush, awakening from their electric stupor. I'd bet all my clothes plus the very excellent hair on my head that these things have trackers in them.

I close my eyes, exhaling.

I spent the first couple hours keeping myself busy, setting up camp. I built a temporary, concealed shelter with local materials; collected snow for water; stole nuts from squirrels, berries from birds. Aside from the fact that I'm freezing through my bloodied sweater, this landscape is not a challenge. Seriously. In one of my early training sims I was stranded in a remote jungle for ten days with nothing but an empty canteen for water, and by the end of it Warner almost paid me a compliment.

He said—and I quote—

"That wasn't altogether disappointing. But just because your body can heal itself at an extraordinary rate doesn't make you invincible. Stop showing off. You spend too much time with Kishimoto. Next time, don't bleed all over everything like an idiot. Don't let your enemy know what you're capable of. Unless, of course, it is your intention to be swiftly murdered in your youth."

A glowing review.

The only problem is, I didn't learn from my mistakes. I did bleed all over everything, and maybe I was showing off a little. But Warner is pretty much never wrong, and according to his calculations, I should be at that swiftly murdered stage in my life by now.

This is some kind of psychological manipulation, I know it is.

They *let* me escape.

I had a feeling this was a trap when they threw me on a

gurney without strapping me down. I should've known for sure it was a trap a few beats earlier, when they sent a gorgeous murderer into my prison cell to distract me with her gorgeousness. I should've killed her the moment I realized she was human. Should've disarmed her immediately and drove the knife through one or both of her eyes instead of losing a full heartbeat of my life wondering how a person could walk around with a face like that without warning people first. Honestly, killing her at literally any point would've been a really excellent idea.

Instead, I left an enemy alive, and I did it on purpose.

I bang my head against the tree again.

Usually I'm good about compartmentalizing things. Usually I keep my childhood trauma in a hermetically sealed box buried under piles of other useless shit in my brain, but in that moment—

I don't know, it was like I was ten years old again.

She was stripped down, about to die, totally vulnerable, and all she could think about was her little sister. As far as I'm aware, serial killers don't stop to think about their little sisters. Sociopaths don't get emotional before they're murdered. And while it wasn't clear just by looking at her face, under my hands the girl felt so slight it was almost unnatural. As if she was malnourished. As if maybe The Reestablishment was starving her.

She reminded me of Adam.

Adam Kent Anderson, half brother of Aaron Warner Anderson; husband to Alia; father to Gigi and Roman. My big brother, nicest guy in the world. Wouldn't hurt a fly, refuses to own a gun. He runs a design firm with his wife. Helps organize fundraisers at the elementary school. Has no interest in the family business. Doesn't like to talk about his past. We go to the same restaurant every Thursday, and he always orders the same thing: a cheeseburger with no onions.

Adam used to be a soldier of The Reestablishment, but he enlisted only to protect me. He dropped out of high school to become a hired gun against his will, and he did it to save my life. I made the mistake of projecting his backstory onto her.

It was a stupid, emotional move.

I don't know anything about the girl except that she murdered me, and then tried to murder me again and again. It was a huge mistake attributing complexity to her character. I don't even know for sure that the girl is still alive—but I know the kind of medical miracles The Reestablishment is capable of. If they got to her in time, she'll definitely live to murder another day. Hell, I saw that guy with the robot arm and I knew right then that we've been underestimating these fascists. There's no world in which I just escaped The Reestablishment without real consequences, and the inviolable truth of that fact is stressing me out.

I pop a gross berry in my mouth and chew.

I wonder why they left the gummy bears in my pocket. I wonder why they're letting me think I got away with something. I wonder why I thought I'd be able to get off this island without a solid exit strategy.

*Your power has made you intolerable.*

Warner said that to me once.

He said, "I thought you were annoying as a child. I was right. I thought you might grow out of it. I was wrong. Now you seem to think you're a superhero. You walk through the world like nothing can touch you. I don't know why you smile so much. Kent knew better than to smile so much. I certainly never taught you to smile. Shut up," he said, when I tried to point out that he smiled all the time these days. "One day that overzealous optimism is going to get you into trouble. You think I'm being hard on you. I am. It's because I don't want you to die, you idiot."

I smile at the memory. That's as close as he ever comes to saying *I love you, little brother.*

I spit out the berry pit.

I stole a jet to get here—add that to the list of stupid things I've done—except in order to get here sort of undetected, I landed the plane on a smaller island nearby, one still under the governance of The New Republic. I kayaked from the smaller island to an even smaller island, and then paraglided off a cliff into the densest, most unpopulated stretch of Ark Forest. For obvious reasons, I couldn't really leave a trail, and anyway, I'm guessing the guys back home have already repossessed the plane I stole. It's unlikely to be where I left it.

"Okay. New pivot."

I jump to my feet and clap my hands, startling a raccoon

in the process. It stares at me from a couple yards away, a pair of frog legs poking out of its mouth.

"Yeah," I say, pointing at the furry bandit. "Get excited. These assholes aren't making any effort to find me, so I'm going to build a fire, roast some nuts, and then we're going to hammer out the details of a new plan."

The raccoon resumes chewing, unblinking.

"Ideally," I say, popping another berry in my mouth, "the best way off this island would involve stealing another jet."

I chew; the raccoon chews.

"But, realistically, all I need is a boat."

I poke around the underbrush, searching for dry kindling.

"I know what you're thinking," I say, brandishing a stick at the raccoon, now clutching a nut in its fist. "You're thinking—James, that's the obvious thing! They're going to expect you to do the obvious thing! The ports are probably rigged with explosives! Heavily secured! Soldiers everywhere! Too many to kill even for someone as strong and capable as you are!"

The raccoon nibbles at the nut.

"Well, I appreciate the compliment, but that's not what we're going to do." I gather up a few more sticks. "The thing is, I'd tell you what we're going to do, except— You're recording me right now, aren't you, you little trash panda? And I'm not going to tell you shitheads exactly what I have planned."

I step toward the animal, staring into its dark eyes. In the perfect slant of light, the blue sheen is unmistakable.

"So," I say, bending to better meet its gaze. "If you're watching this program right now, I'd encourage you to ask yourself this: What would Aaron Warner Anderson do? Because that's the question I'm about to answer. And he taught me everything I know."

# ROSABELLE

## CHAPTER 8

*Because that's the question I'm about to answer. And he taught me everything I know.*

The feed garbles as the video distorts, the sound of static overwhelming the footage as it becomes a blur of sky and branches. The inmate appears to have punted the raccoon through the forest. I immediately turn to another screen, where a different perspective—through the eyes of a hawk—showcases him from above.

*James Alexander Anderson.*

His bloodline is legendary.

My heart thunders in my chest as I watch him, an unfocused fear constricting my airways. Finally, I understand Soledad's last words. Finally, I'm beginning to grasp the true level of chaos unleashed upon our island.

The Anderson family is notorious; not only are they responsible for building The Reestablishment, they're responsible for tearing it down. The patriarch, Paris Anderson, was one of our leading founders. He rose in rank over the years to become the supreme commander of North America, only to be brutally slaughtered a decade ago by his eldest son: the infamous, traitorous Aaron Warner, who betrayed us all by defecting to the Omega rebels. He and his now wife, Juliette Ferrars—the daughter of another supreme commander—overthrew the government in one of the most devastating global coups in history.

There's the snap of a twig, the rustle of leaves. James stands up to stretch, his sweater lifting to reveal a glimpse of lean torso. He ruffles his own hair in a boyish, unassuming fashion, then squints up at the gathering clouds.

I take a steadying breath.

First I watched him massacre an entire troop of soldiers, and now this. I've been sitting in this command room for at least a few hours, watching James run his battered, bloodied body through the forest. He's hiked challenging terrain, waded through shallow lakes, and climbed a steep mountain face all while carrying over a hundred pounds of artillery on his back. He sat down on the ground at one point, tore open his own wounds, and dug bullets out of his leg with no anesthesia. It was horrifying to witness.

At the moment, James has resumed a seated position on the snow-dusted ground, his face severe in a tempest of firelight. He pushes up his sleeves to reveal strong, corded forearms before stoking the flames of a decent campfire, his motions assured and practiced. Smoke spirals skyward, announcing his location to the world, but he seems relaxed. He cracks nuts in his fists, a smile blunting his edges as he tosses acorn caps into the woods, using each one to pelt imaginary targets.

The simple game seems to please him.

I find this fascinating.

"You see the problem," says Damani.

I tear my eyes away from James long enough to meet her gaze. Mona Damani, one of three commanders I've had the displeasure of meeting today. Her long dark hair gleams in the dim light of her central office, where every wall is made of tech glass that activates upon her biometric directive. I've been brought inside the womb of synthetic intelligence, exposed to the inner workings of Ark surveillance in a way I've never been before.

Somehow, this is my life now.

*He* is my life now.

"Yes," I say, expressionless as I return my eyes to the screens. "He's a competent adversary."

Competent. Terrifying.

If I fail at this mission this man will slaughter me and it will cost him nothing. I won't even be a memorable kill.

"Klaus has predicted his every move," Damani says, her voice warm with satisfaction. "It's the first time we've been able to properly test the program on an unknown subject." She stills, her eyes unfocusing a moment as she receives an incoming message. She returns to herself, then consults another screen. "It's been thrilling to watch this play out in perfect order. A true triumph." She finishes this statement by staring at me expectantly, awaiting a response.

"Yes," I agree. "Thrilling."

I learned only hours ago that this level of psychological invasion was even possible. I've lived under the iron boot of surveillance for as long as I can remember, but Klaus's untapped powers have proven the limits of my imagination: I cannot fathom the untold dangers of such a technology, and I still haven't decided whether to react with terror or disgust.

It's treason either way.

Damani manages a smile. "Your lack of enthusiasm seems to indicate a hesitation on your part."

"You misunderstand," I say quietly. "I never experience enthusiasm."

She laughs in a sudden burst, one hand to her chest as various emotions—relief, understanding, concern—scatter and fade across her face. "Soledad knew you the longest, is that right? Since you were a child?"

"Yes."

Damani nods, as if that explains everything. "The rest of us aren't used to interacting with someone disconnected from the Nexus," she says. "Soledad was always better at reading you than anyone else—which, of course, is why you reported to him." She sighs heavily. "Unfortunately, his was a necessary sacrifice. We lost many brilliant souls this morning, long may they rest, all in the pursuit of a greater good for the global future. I hope you realize the weight of what we're imparting today."

I only stare at her. A flare of hunger tears savagely at my gut, and I blink slowly, containing it.

Her smile grows uncertain. "You can understand why we had to keep the details from you. It was imperative that your first engagement happen as organically as possible;

Klaus determined that your chances of success with the subject would be higher if he had reason to underestimate your intelligence. By failing to kill him, you presented yourself as weak—a conclusion further abetted by your final plea for your sister. You evinced a convincing, pitiable frailty that diminished his opinion of you as a rival, and by sparing your life he's established a subconscious emotional precedent as your protector, a development we hope to—" She hesitates, glancing at another screen. "Ah. Watch. In just a moment he's going to bathe in that lake, right there—"

She taps on a glimmering body of water in the near distance, pulling it into greater focus, and I'm still processing the words *pitiable frailty,* heart pounding as I reassure myself I've revealed nothing new, that my greatest weakness has never been a secret. I've often felt that The Reestablishment quietly delights in the fact of Clara's existence, if only because my concern for her gives them leverage to control me.

Abruptly James walks into the frame, approaching the lake just as predicted. He pulls his shirt over his head, and the sight of his naked upper body is so unexpected I nearly avert my eyes. I don't want to watch this. It feels voyeuristic to watch this. And yet, I can't look away from the screens.

I'm not *allowed* to look away from the screens.

I further neutralize my expression as he reveals an expansive chest, an exquisitely honed torso. Dried blood is painted down his neck, smeared across his sternum, and confusingly this only heightens his physical appeal. I feel the rise of a disconcerting heat as I study him, physical awareness kindling inside me without my conscious permission.

The sheer power of his beauty is terrifying.

The sharp slope of his nose, the brutal cut of his jaw, the staggering brawn of his body. He'd be easier to categorize if his severe lines weren't softened by surprises: easy laughter; the wrinkle of his nose; gleaming eyes. He's tanned everywhere the sun might touch, with a dusting of freckles scattered across his upper back. In contrast to his sun-kissed skin, the white of countless nicks and scars screams in protest. I file away this information: his healing powers do not erase the attempts on his life.

Absently, I touch a hand to my throat.

I wonder whether James will always wear the mark of our first meeting. I will forever remember, with excruciating clarity: the way I faltered when he touched me, the way he caught me on impulse, holding me steady even as I prepared to murder him.

I experience a pinprick of shame.

"What did I say?" Damani is smiling. "Amazing, right?"

"Amazing."

The dossier I was given lists his age at twenty-one years old. His eyes, blue. His hair, brown. But in the glow of afternoon sun I see that his hair is more gilded than originally presented; from above, golden strands glint in the filtered light, lending an unexpected glamour to his appearance. It makes me wonder whether he was blonder as a child. It makes me wonder what he was like as a child, full stop.

As the son of a supreme commander he couldn't have

had an easy upbringing, and yet I cannot comprehend what emotional equation would account for the way he smiles, as if it costs him nothing. There's something playful about him even in anger; I've never seen someone make violence seem casual. His unpredictability makes me nervous.

I keep searching him for patterns and uncover inconsistencies instead.

Damani pulls up a different screen, this one from the perspective of a field mouse staring squarely at him from a tree branch. James stills, as if sensing the camera, then looks over his shoulder and scowls, flipping off the tree before unbuttoning his pants.

"Perverts," he says.

Discomfort pools inside me. I watch only his feet as he treads into the crystalline waters. He mutters a soft oath, flinching at the temperature, then dives fully into the lake.

Damani stiffens beside me. "What did he just say?"

I glance up at her sharp tone.

To herself, she says: "Play that back."

Again, we watch James test the water, curse under his breath, and then dive into the lake.

"No," she says, speaking with someone I can't see. "No, he was supposed to say *son of a bitch,* not *son of an* icy *bitch.* Yes, look, I realize it seems like a minor detail to you, but this isn't the first time—"

Damani leaves the room, the sound of her boots echoing. She turns briefly to seal the soundproof glass door, trapping me inside with a hundred angles of a half-naked James before leaning against a nearby pillar. Her eyes narrow as she watches me, her mouth moving rapidly. I return my eyes to the monitors.

I cannot deny that James is mesmerizing to watch.

He radiates a force and magnetism palpable even through the distance of a screen. The spectacle of his uncommon beauty puts me at a great disadvantage. It's jarring to occupy space with him, and this fact so unnerved me the first time we met that I nearly failed to kill him. I can't afford to be caught off guard again.

I take a tight breath, forcing myself to look at him.

To grow tired of looking at him.

He submerses himself over and over in the icy depths, pushing wet hair out of his eyes, rivers of diluted blood sluicing down his body. I wonder, as I watch him, whether he has any recollection of what was done to him. He likely doesn't know that he was submerged in the cradle over and over during the initial hours of his imprisonment. He probably accounts for the lapses in his memory as falling asleep; a misappropriation of time. He'd never guess that Klaus was able to map his mind, mine his psychological history, and approximate his reaction to thousands of different scenarios for the duration of a twenty-four-hour period. The program is still imperfect, unfinished—and yet they were able to design a limited plan of action and reaction. As a result, they were able to steer James directly toward the outcome they desired most, all while allowing him to believe his decisions were his own.

The profitable illusion of free will.

Nothing was more devastating to The Reestablishment than the revolution that led to their downfall. It makes sense then that all efforts to feed the insatiable, chemical mind of Klaus have been in pursuit of a program designed to generate the voluntary servitude of the masses.

I can see it now, the usage scenarios multiplying. It's simple logic: if we believe our choices are our own—if we do not know we are being bent into obeisance—we will not be tempted to revolt. The ultimate goal of synthetic intelligence, then, is the obliteration of organic intelligence.

The eradication of resistance.

A self-preservational instinct seems to glitch inside me at the thought, a stutter of my nervous system sending up a warning. I know, even as I'm thinking, that the direction of my thoughts is illegal. This fear clears the slate of my mind, wicking the theories away like water. It's not safe to let my doubts percolate. I've learned the hard way that disconnection from the Nexus isn't enough; the only way to survive mental invasions on the Ark is to police my own thoughts, keeping secrets from myself.

I refocus my energies on James, giving him my full attention as he wades deeper into the water. My head tilts in tandem with his, mirroring him as he zeroes in on something just under the surface. He goes suddenly still—and then dives with surprising force, resurfacing moments later, laughing and out of breath. I watch him do this several more times before he emerges, victorious, with a shimmering fish caught in one fist.

"*Hey,*" he calls, turning his broad smile toward a camera. "Can I eat this? Or is this robot meat?"

The fish flaps desperately in his large hand.

"I mean, look, food is food," James is saying. "I'm not too proud to eat robot meat. But how many grams of protein do you think is in robot meat? More than a regular fish? Less? Just because I'm on vacation doesn't mean I stop trying to hit my daily goals, you know?"

*Just because I'm on vacation.*

His nonchalance: another absurdity. I add this to the file I'm building in my head. Later, I'll spend more time examining the data I've gathered. For now I glance over my shoulder at Damani, who's begun pacing the short hall outside the glass door, gesticulating angrily as she speaks. She still hasn't briefed me on my new mission, but the withholding of information follows a familiar pattern. It's always been like this.

At least this mission, unlike the others, is cause for hope.

Should I execute my directives without fail, I might finally be released from the pit. Clara and I might finally be delivered from starvation, from illness. The penance I've paid all these years for the sins of my parents might finally come to an end. This was the promise Klaus made me as I was raised, like wreckage, from the amniotic fluids of his mind.

A series of splashing sounds interrupts my reverie. James emerges from the water slowly, hair dripping, clear rivulets snaking down the hard planes of his face. I'm careful to keep my eyes above his waist as he moves onto dry land. For the first time he looks almost tired, eyes closing as he stands in a cooling patch of sun. He tosses the fish toward his campsite, then pulls on a pair of dark boxer briefs. I finally exhale, a modicum of relief releasing my shoulders as I unpin my eyes from his head, watching him now warm himself before the hot coals of his fire.

Damani bursts back into the office.

The barrage of sound shatters inside me: the knocking of her heels; the exhale of the glass door; a sharp breath; the muted drum of her fingers against her arm. Gone is her triumphant smile. She looks irritated, though she explains neither her irritation nor her absence, choosing instead to hover over my shoulder, watching James now with a palpable anxiety that hadn't existed before.

"Has he opened your letter yet?" she demands.

I turn slowly to face Damani. "What?"

# ROSABELLE

## CHAPTER 9

"Your letter," Damani says, impatient. "The one from Lieutenant Rivers. *Sebastian,*" she corrects herself. "It was confirmed through Clara's comms that she delivered your mail to you this morning. You don't remember?"

I resist the urge to pat myself down, search my empty pockets for the small stack of mail Clara handed me only hours ago—no, a lifetime ago. But I'm no longer wearing this morning's clothes. I'm dressed in a benign set of pink medic scrubs. White tennis shoes. My request for a standard-issue, black tactical uniform was summarily rejected. My boots were not returned to me. My clothes were incinerated.

Papa's coat—my only winter coat—was destroyed.

"Why would James have my mail?" I manage to ask.

She frowns. "The subject swiped them from your coat at some point before leaving you in the hall. I believe his exact words were: *Now we're even.* I suppose it makes sense you wouldn't remember—you were nearly dead with fever."

I return my eyes to the screens, heart pounding so hard I'm worried Damani can hear it. Perhaps it's because it feels like a violation for a stranger to open my mail before I do—or because I have no idea what Sebastian might be sending me this time—or perhaps, more terrifyingly, because I think I do know what he's sending me and I don't want to process the news like this, with the eyes of my world watching me—

"Never mind, here we go," says Damani, nodding up at the monitors. "I was worried I'd missed it."

Panic wreaks havoc in my chest.

James is stepping into his bullet-riddled utility pants, tugging the waist up around his hips when a sharp corner of an envelope pushes out of a side pocket. I hold my breath, watching as he tugs free the stack, confused for only a second before a smile brightens his features. He shakes a bit of water from his hair, glances at the headline of yesterday's paper—

ARK ISLAND STILL LEADS THE WORLD
AS ONLY SELF-SUSTAINING NATION

—then folds the slim sheaf back into his pocket. He pins the heavy envelope between his teeth as he zips, buttons, and pulls his blood-crusted sweater over his head and then, finally, sinks into a seated position before the dwindling fire.

"Well, well, well," he says, turning the stationery over in his hands. "This is some fancy paper."

Somehow, my heart beats harder.

It strikes me, as I observe him, that James lives in his skin without self-consciousness, comfortable despite the violent scars on his body, despite knowing he's being watched. This fact inspires in me a voracious envy I'm helpless to suppress.

He looks up at a nearby squirrel, and Damani switches

screens to better capture his face.

"People don't really send letters anymore," he says to the rodent, ripping open the envelope. "Not unless they want to say something really—"

James's eyebrows fly upward, the words dying in his throat as he unsheathes the shimmery card from its sleeve. I watch, paralyzed, as his eyes move across the page. He lifts his head sharply, scowling at the squirrel when he says—

"Who the fuck is Sebastian?"

Damani laughs, clapping her hands together. "Oh, this is great."

I'm hardly breathing.

"She's getting married? The serial killer is getting married *next week* to some douchebag named Sebastian Alastair von Douchebag the Fourth?"

Bile has risen up my throat.

"You're the serial killer," Damani says to me in an undertone. "The subject will refer to you as a serial killer several more times over the next twelve hours."

"I'm sorry, but does her fiancé know that she might be dead right now? Does he even know she's a serial killer?" James seems unusually bothered by the invitation, which he wastes no time holding over the fire, glaring as flames devour the expensive stationery. "Downer wedding."

"Belated congratulations, by the way," says Damani. "The island is buzzing—we all got our invitations yesterday. It'll be the wedding of the year."

I shake my head an inch, acutely aware that all Ark officials—including Sebastian—are watching me for a reaction. "He's not my fiancé," I force out. "We're not getting married."

James picks up a sizable rock, which he throws forcefully at a small boulder, eyes intent as he watches it break apart. From the wreckage he picks out a jagged piece.

"I'm sure it's hard to believe," Damani says to me, her eyes still glued to the screens. James has begun to use a round stone as a hammer, hitting it against the rough edges of the jagged piece, honing it into a crude blade. "Certainly no one thought Lieutenant Rivers would honor the betrothal after your family's fall from grace. But he put forth a passionate argument in front of the council, and the motion was passed with shockingly little objection."

I swallow. My throat feels raw.

"Oh, and you should know," Damani adds, sparing me a glance. "Going forward, we've decided you'll be reporting to Lieutenant Rivers—"

I stiffen, the statement like a slap to the face.

"—who knows you nearly as well as Soledad once did."

On-screen, James is using the crude blade to sharpen a stick into a spear.

"We all realize the complications of having you report to your fiancé, but duty supersedes all else in this case. Until we can get you online, you'll have to be under the command of someone who knows your history. The wedding will need to be postponed regardless—just until the mission is complete—but I'm sure Sebastian will understand."

"Commander—"

Damani holds up a finger, her eyes unfocusing as she receives a message. She glances again at James before saying, "Affirmative."

There's a heartbeat of silence, a muted *boom*—

A fiery explosion rattles the screens, the blast lifting James in the air before flinging him like a rag doll against a neighboring tree, from which a quiver of birds scatter like shrapnel. Angry shrieks of wildlife score the haze of fire and smoke, nearly drowning out James's agonized cry as he slams violently into every branch on his way down the trunk, finally hitting the forest floor with a dull thud several feet from where he once stood.

He doesn't move.

A spike of panic compels me to scream and I kill the instinct mercilessly, shuttering so far inward I begin to feel numb, alien in my own body.

I remind myself that I am dead inside.

*I've been dead inside for years.*

I watch in cold silence as striations of blood fracture the snowy ground beneath him. When I speak, my voice feels faraway. Flat.

"How did you do that?" I ask.

Damani laughs, eyeing me then with something like appreciation before studying a bloody, sooty James on-screen.

"You really are one of our best executioners," she says. "Soledad always talked about how unflappable you were. He said you once ate an entire sandwich after decapitating a prisoner."

*That's a lie,* I don't say to her.

James begins to stir, a strangled cry ripping from his throat. The bend of his limbs, I note, are unnatural; shards of bone have pushed through his pant leg, his shirtsleeve.

My chest caves in only a little.

Softly, I say, "I have no memory of being offered a sandwich."

Damani laughs again, louder this time. "Right. Anyway, we remote-detonated the stock of artillery he stole." She nods at James, now convulsing with pain. "The subject doesn't seem to understand that everything he learned from his brother was first taught to him by his father—who was trained, from the beginning, by *us*."

"Idiot," I whisper, watching him struggle.

James groans, lifting a shaking hand to his chest, then his broken arm, his broken leg. He unleashes a stream of expletives before slackening, gasping for air.

"Obviously we don't want him to die, not yet," says Damani, "but this incapacitation gives us the time we need to prepare for the next phase. Klaus predicts that, in addition to breaking major bones, the severity of the blast will cause the subject to sustain a partial tear of a mid-cervical vertebrae and a hemorrhage of the brain. The subject's powers are expected to be strong enough to revive him overnight, granting us a recess of roughly six to eight hours in the program." She turns to me, opening her mouth to say more, then hesitates.

"It's a relief," she says finally, "that no one here carries the mutative gene anymore. Isn't it?"

I say nothing at first, trying to decide whether this is a test. But then, with The Reestablishment, most things are a test.

All of us on the island were administered the mutative vaccine, the gene-editing therapy that reversed the effects of an experimental program designed by The Reestablishment in its early years. All supernormal transmutations—like James's healing powers—were erased from the population overnight. Everyone, as a result, became much easier to govern.

Everyone, except me.

"Isn't it?" she asks again.

I nod.

"The experiment," Damani says, "brilliant though it was for its time, proved an enormous headache back on the mainland." She smiles now, looking strange. "People running around with unregulated, untested powers. They turned all our hard work against us in the end. Didn't they?"

This is the circulating theory, the disturbing hypothesis about Rosabelle Wolff, daughter of the disgraced, high-ranking official who sold himself to the rebels for a song. People believe I can't connect to the Nexus because I retained the mutative gene; that I somehow possess a power strong enough to resist the advances of technology. Some people think my father had something to do with it. That I'm a plant, a double agent. The fact that they can't read my mind makes it impossible to be certain—but how this might be true, I can't even fathom.

I haven't spoken to my father in over a decade.

"Didn't they?" she asks again.

"Yes," I say. "They did."

There's a brutal *crunch,* then a piercing scream, and I turn sharply to the screens, where James is attempting to put his leg back together. His hands are slick with blood, his face contorted in pain. For a moment I think I can't imagine his agony, and then I remember that I can.

"We're learning from our mistakes, Rosabelle. We've learned we need to control every aspect of the experiment ad infinitum. Forever." Damani places a hand on my shoulder, and I resist the impulse to snap her neck. "Without constant control, we can't guarantee results, can we?"

"No," I say. "We can't."

She holds my eyes for a beat. "Your meeting with Soledad was originally scheduled for tomorrow. In advance of your imminent deployment, you'll complete your interrogation today. Once you've been cleared, Lieutenant Rivers will walk you through the next movements of the mission."

I feel the rise of panic. "Commander, with all due respect,

I need to speak with my sister—"

"Later," she says, before nodding toward the exit.

There's the gasp of glass unsealing, a rush of air—and I turn, as if through time, toward the opening door.

# ROSABELLE

## CHAPTER 10

I sag in the steel chair, my head drooping sideways.

Familiar electric pulses flash behind my eyes, ache inside my teeth, spasm down my throat. I can't seem to command my limbs. I can no longer feel my skin. For three hours I've resisted the impulse to gag against the metallic taste in my mouth. Acid roils in my empty stomach. Hunger and delirium blot out coherent thought.

I jerk upward, registering that my eyes were closed only when they unhinge open, tearing in the glare of overbright light. A high-pitched frequency of static fills my head, the murmur of voices faraway and disjointed.

"Brain capacity has dropped another percentage," someone says. "She's deteriorating now at an exponential rate. We'll have to move on to yes or no questions."

"Rosa," says a voice, the familiar tenor grating. "Rosa, there are only a few minutes left. Then you get a break."

I try to look at him, but my pupils are unnaturally dilated, details blearing in the harsh illumination of the exam room. Squinting painfully, I avert my eyes, realizing as I look down that he's taken my hand, holding it tenderly between his blurry palms. Revulsion overpowers me.

I vomit.

The involuntary action is automatic, but my empty gut conjures little but humiliation.

Someone wipes my mouth.

"Rosa," he says kindly. "Focus for me, okay? Just yes or no questions now. Do you ever consider doing harm to the people of Ark Island?"

My chest is still heaving.

"Negative," says a faraway voice.

"Do you ever find yourself sympathizing with the leaders of The New Republic?"

I lift my head, color and light smearing where his face should be.

"Negative," says a faraway voice.

"Do you ever doubt—"

The jarring alarm of a distress signal goes off, a voice straining above the clangor to say, "Brain capacity is at a critical low— Thirty seconds—"

"Rosa," he says quickly, "Do you ever doubt the actions of The Reestablishment?"

"Affirmative," says a faraway voice.

There's a tense pause.

"Twenty seconds before permanent brain damage—"

"Rosa."

My lips feel strange. Rubbery. The steady shriek of the alarm still echoes through the room.

"Fifteen seconds—"

"Rosa, do your doubts ever overwhelm your loyalty to The Reestablishment?"

My head lolls backward.

"Negative," says the voice, shouting over the din.

I jerk forward without warning, gasping as hundreds of laser prongs retract from my body, releasing me from a simulated paralysis.

The alarm goes silent.

I slump in my seat, the back of the chair biting painfully into my neck, my senses slowly awakening. Cold seeps into my skin, bruises blossoming along my inner arms and elsewhere—everywhere. I can already feel them blooming, as they always do, along my torso, wrapping around my back.

My heart rate is still too slow; my lungs still compressed. I strain for breath, my limbs trembling. I can feel the pressure of his hands now, the familiar shape and weight. I attempt to pull away but his grip only tightens.

I look up, searching, as if through water.

My pupils contract, restoring my vision by degrees, the room slowly focusing. In the clearing blur my mind conjures his face from memory, portraits old and new layering like double exposures before resolving into the present moment. Up close he's tenser; sharper; but his hair is the same as it ever was: pitch-black to match his eyes. I stare at him vacantly, even as gales of sensation wash over me: the clasp of childhood; the press of sunlight; a breathless dash through summer rain.

Sebastian smiles, but the effort is strained with genuine concern. I look away, my tired eyes falling upon the expanse of his upper body, the subject of my endless fascination. So many hours of my life I spent wondering how I might carve his heart out of his chest.

"Rosa," he says softly, a finger slipping under my chin, lifting my face. He grazes my cheek with his thumb and I'm too tired to flinch. "Congratulations. Your authorizations have been approved for another month."

I say nothing to this.

I always say nothing.

My monthly interrogations have always been managed by Lieutenant Soledad but executed by Lieutenant Rivers. Now that Soledad is dead, I suppose Sebastian—*Lieutenant Rivers*—will assume both roles. I never did get used to his promotions over the years; I never acclimated to calling him anything other than Sebastian. He and I grew up together. Our mothers were best friends.

For so many years, he was everything to me.

"I'm always grateful to be the one to do this for you," he says, squeezing my hands. "When we're married, I can take even better care of you. My personal reports will be far more exhaustive, which means I can petition for longer periods between interrogations."

I swallow, the movement painful. My throat is desiccated. "Sebastian."

"Yes?"

Again, I swallow. "May I have some water?"

He shakes his head, retreating, his eyes pinching in distress. "Your meal vouchers haven't renewed yet. As soon as they come through, I'll let you know."

Once more, I swallow.

My rations diminish from week to week, leaving nearly nothing by the end of the month; this supply replenishes only after I've cleared my interrogations. The problem is that I receive hardly enough food even for one person. Clara isn't counted in the distributions. The Reestablishment doesn't believe in wasting resources on the weak.

"Why do you have to give her so much?" he asks. "What's the use? When you know how it's going to end?"

I pull away from him inelegantly, stumbling as I fight to stand. Sebastian reaches for me automatically, and in my haste to escape him I slam into a wall of steel cabinets, awakening a cascade of sound. The lingering disorientation is almost worse than the interrogation itself.

I don't like to lose control.

"I need to see Clara," I say, trying to steady myself. "I need to tell her I'm leaving. I've never left the island before and I'll need to make plans for her. I need to wash the windows. I didn't wash the windows today and if I don't wash the windows every day soot stains the glass and she can't see outside and she needs"—I stumble, the room tilts—"she needs to be able to look outside or she, she— I should speak with Zadie. One of her boys just lost his rations for the week, and if I give her some of my meal vouchers maybe she'll help care for Clara while I'm gone—"

"Rosa—"

"I'd like to go home." I cut him off, touching my fingers

to my mouth in alarm. It occurs to me that I might be talking too much, and the realization scares me. "I'm tired," I say, my hand falling away. "I'd like to go home now."

Sebastian takes a breath. "All right," he says. "You're allowed a brief interlude before deployment tomorrow. I suppose you can take it now."

"Thank you."

"I'll fly you back, and we can run through tomorrow's itinerary one more time. Remember," he says, and I finally meet his eyes. "Klaus was only able to map out a program of action for twenty-four hours. By sunrise we'll have just under three hours of script left. After that, the subject's behavior is no longer certain. You'll be on your own to manage him."

I nod blindly. "I understand."

"Give me a minute to grab some things before we go," Sebastian says, flashing me a smile. "Now that we're engaged, I can stay with you overnight."

My head sharpens in an instant. "Overnight?"

His color heightens; he shakes his head. "I only mean that I can help take care of you."

I turn away in response, staring into the middle distance as my heart pounds. In less than twenty-four hours my life has been so rearranged as to be unrecognizable. Soledad is dead: a cause for celebration. And yet I've been freed from one aggressor only to be shackled to another.

Never again can I hold Sebastian at bay, enduring him one month at a time. I can't even reject his proposal without being accused of insanity—or worse, disloyalty. Who but a traitor would reject an opportunity to leave the pit? To marry into wealth and prestige? To never know hunger?

And then there's Clara.

*If you married Sebastian, things would be better. They'd lift the sanctions. You wouldn't have to pretend we have food in our cupboards every morning.*

I nearly startle when Sebastian reaches for my hand again, his eyes softening when he says, "You don't have to give Zadie your meal vouchers, by the way. Clara will be fine. She knows you've been given a new assignment, she knows you'll be off the island for a while, and she knows she's being transferred in the morning."

"What?" A cold wave crashes through my body, dulling my brain, slowing my pounding heart. "Transferred where?"

"I'm having her moved to my mother's house. She'll have a dedicated nurse and around-the-clock care while you're gone." He grins. "I've already gotten approval."

A fossilized fear inside me slackens, threatens to buckle. It feels almost like relief, which seems like a trap. I study the soft lines of Sebastian's face; the subtle stubble that tells me it's getting late. His eyes are earnest.

"But you've never cared for Clara," I say.

"Can you blame me?" Sebastian's smile is self-deprecating, as if he's said something charming. "The simple fact of her existence is killing you. She's parasitic."

The instinct to shut down is reflexive.

I feel it happening almost without my permission, senses

powering off until my very body feels foreign to me. My hair feels like someone else's hair; my skin feels like someone else's skin. I hear myself say, from faraway, "Then why would you care now?"

Sebastian steps forward, and I've withdrawn so deep inside my mind I hardly feel it when he pulls me close, rests his forehead against mine.

"I've always loved you, Rosa. After everything that happened with your family"—he shakes his head—"I've only ever wanted to take care of you. Even if that means taking care of your sister." His voice deepens, softens. "I feel like we've been waiting our whole lives for this. I still can't believe it's happening. After all these years, we're really going to be together."

Sebastian pulls a ring out of his pocket, and a carousel of memory sweeps through me, pushing me deeper into the abyss: the taste of blood I vomited while he looked on; the sound of his saccharine voice, echoing; *You've disappointed us, Rosa, you've disappointed all of us*; the blinding pain in my right arm; the disjointed sounds of my own screams; *You've disappointed us, Rosa*; the scrape of stone under my knees; the gasp of ragged breath; *You've disappointed all of us*; the quiet violence of the gold band he slips onto my dead finger.

I study it, glimmering against my skin.

By inches, I lift my head to look at Sebastian. A glaze of blue light winks across his dark eyes, and I realize I don't know how many people are watching.

*Only criminals need privacy, Rosa.*

"I know you can't wear it while you're gone," he whispers. "And I know we're not married yet. But I want you to take it with you, so you'll remember what we're fighting for."

He smiles at me with genuine, unbridled affection, and I am stunned, not for the first time, by Sebastian's ability to live in a dreamscape forged entirely of delusion.

He wasn't always like this.

Over the years I watched him give his mind away in pieces, devoting himself to the cult of the collective opinion—offering up blind faith in exchange for fraternity. Sometimes, when I drift safely under the veil of near sleep, I find I can be generous with my thoughts. In the twilight of consciousness my heart expands enough to remember Sebastian as he once was, enough to pity the man he is now. The feeling never lasts long enough to provide comfort.

If I fail this mission, I'll be out of options.

Sebastian will loom over me always, killing me softly for the rest of my life.

# JAMES

## CHAPTER 11

I wake up the way I passed out: pissed off.

Heart thudding, head sluggish; I open my eyes to a blur of color, squinting through a glare of light. There's blood in my mouth, in my ears, caked in my hair, crusted across my skin. Pain radiates in my joints. I blink, my vision still clearing. The blues and greens of the forest come into sharper focus, the blaze of morning sun fracturing through a screen of branches. I let my eyes fall closed, already exhausted, and run an unsteady hand down my body, feeling for broken bones. Only when I confirm that my limbs are fully intact do I exhale with relief.

*Motherfuckers.*

The ground is cold and wet under me; my clothes stiff, matted with blood. The dregs of a fever still cling to my overheated, clammy skin, and I shiver involuntarily, pressing the heels of my bloodied hands against my eyes.

This headache is award-worthy.

This headache is so bad they should study it. Someone should sell tickets to this nightmare. People should line up for the opportunity to try on my skull in order to appreciate the way my brain has melted between my ears.

I don't usually pass out unless things get really bad—life-threateningly bad—because even though sleep generally accelerates the healing process, the trade-off is rarely worth the risk. I've learned the hard way over the years that it's pretty easy for someone to finish murdering me, for example, when I'm too unconscious to fight back.

In this case, I don't remember having a choice.

I squint my eyes open again, studying the slant of sun. It's early morning, which means I've been unconscious, exposed, and completely vulnerable for at least several hours. The fact that these shitheads let me live to see daylight tells me our fun together hasn't even started. Last night was just an appetizer of all that's yet to come.

Yay.

I drag myself into a seated position, grimacing. The pain is abating, but slowly, which tells me this was a more brutal assault than normal. I heave myself against the nearest tree trunk, closing my eyes again on a sigh. Hell, I'd just finished washing off all the blood from the first round of attempted murdering.

Like I said: *motherfuckers.*

This situation isn't funny anymore. To be clear, it was never funny—but now I'm really, actually mad. *Super mad.* Like that time someone nearly killed Juliette during a public appearance and she was so messed up she had to learn to walk again. Or when we were forced to move out of our homes into a heavily fortified compound because of security concerns. Or even that time Kenji ate the sandwich I'd been saving for dinner and didn't apologize.

I look up, distracted by sudden movement, only to discover a squirrel staring at me upside down. A rare pulse of rage awakens my adrenaline, and I snatch the furry monster in one go, staring briefly into its flashing blue eyes before snapping its neck. I search the forest floor for a shard of something sharp, then use it to rip the creature open, exposing its glowing innards. My eyes narrow.

There's no electric wiring running alongside its veins, no organs enhanced with machinery. There's nothing at all to denote a change in state except a subtle blue gleam that glistens all throughout its otherwise ordinary anatomy. I prize apart the rest of its body, my fingers dripping with blood, until I discover the nearly undetectable chip buried inside its brain. I yank the small piece free, my large hands fumbling, then hold it up to the morning light, examining the strange, fingerprint-like texture of the blue metal.

I experience a grim moment of triumph.

Forget the guns. If I can get *this* back home, we might have a chance of understanding exactly what we're up against.

Fever broken, energy returning to my body, I decide to test my strength, using the tree trunk for support as I haul myself upright. Carefully, I put weight on my legs, exhaling in relief when all seems to be in working order. I toss the alien squirrel carcass into the woods, tuck the chip inside my pocket, then turn to look at the wildlife, the many eyes of which stare down at me.

"Judge all you like," I mutter. "I'm not taking another bath."

I scrabble up the base of the trunk, launch myself onto the lowest branch, and heave myself up, straightening on the bough only to knock my head on the tree limb just above me. I rub the back of my head, scowling, and when I turn to glower at the offending branch, I walk face-first into an enormous spiderweb, scream like a little girl, lose my balance, and nearly fall out of the tree.

I can almost hear the animals laughing at me.

"All right, okay, show's over," I say, meeting the many eyes watching me through the canopy. "And if the hot serial killer is watching this right now, I'd just like to state, for the record, that I'm recovering from what I'm pretty sure was a recent brain injury." I slap threads of spider silk from my face, then spit remnants of sticky web in the direction of indignant birds. "Also? Spiderwebs make my insides feel weird. Spiderwebs make *everyone's* insides feel weird. Don't pretend you're better than me."

A sparrow lands on my shoulder just then, and I startle as its wings flap and settle next to my face. The bird and I turn to stare at each other at the same time, holding a moment of weird and intense eye contact, and even though I know it's a demon robot-bird, I can't help but reach out and pet its smooth little head. It trills softly under my touch.

"I'm living Kenji's dream right now," I whisper, still petting the bird's head. "Except for all the blood, I'm basically a fairy-tale prince. All I need is a musical number and a fairy godmother. Now get the fuck out of here."

I backhand the robot-bird off my shoulder and return my narrowed eyes to the canopy.

At a glance, I'd clocked the evergreens in this remote region to be at least a hundred feet tall—some even taller. This will do.

Taking a breath, I jump for the next branch.

Carefully, I climb the tree as quickly as possible. My movements are still a little sluggish, but my energy levels are improving by the minute, and by the time I've scaled the top—breathing only a little harder than usual—I'm not disappointed.

I've got a decent aerial view of most of the island.

It's no surprise we've never been able to get satellites in the Ark's airspace, but the fact that we have no images of this place from above has dealt us some serious blows. We have no idea what kind of military infrastructure they've got out here; no idea of the scale of their weaponry; no idea what crazy new tech they might be building. But it's clear even from a cursory glance that this place was planned with precision. The bustling epicenter is crowned by tall, important-looking buildings while neat squares of residential communities ring the outskirts. It's easy to spot the schools, the bridges, the airports, the farmland. I exhale slowly, taking it in.

Somehow, it's even worse than I thought.

Warner said he'd always suspected The Reestablishment was building a sanctuary somewhere; that, in fact, it wouldn't make sense if they didn't have a backup plan. But in the weeks following the collapse of The Reestablishment, we didn't have the resources to stop the regime's elite from fleeing the mainland. Our people nearly died bringing down the system; Juliette in particular was in such bad shape that by the time they got her to safety no one was even sure she'd survive. There was no bandwidth to think about anything but the immediate fires in front of us.

But we never imagined the problem could be this huge.

Now, as I look out over the highly developed landscape, it's all making sense. The Reestablishment was never going to go down without a fight.

The problem was, we could never figure out how they'd recovered quickly enough to launch a covert war. How had they amassed a new arsenal of weapons? Established new surveillance tech? Rebuilt a spy network? How were they conducting research? What about farmland? A self-sustained system of agriculture? Airports? Medical facilities, research facilities, manufacturing capabilities?

The first cyberattack struck us only a few months after we took power. The first assassinations—of key scientists and engineers—happened a few months after that.

The hits never stopped coming.

It took us years to figure out that their plans for the island had predated their rise to power. The Reestablishment began building the Ark before they even launched the regime. Most of the founding members—my father included—had ties to the military industrial complex, having amassed their wealth as defense contractors. It turns out they used shell companies and private investment firms to buy up property on the island over many years, finally driving out the few remaining residents until the water-locked land was entirely under their control. They began to lay the groundwork for *this*—their hideout—a few years before they'd even begun campaigning for power.

That's how sure they were of their plans.

My jaw tenses as I survey the scene a few more times. Anything I can share with the team will be worth a lot, and I commit as much as I can to memory. Only on my final scan of the island do I notice something strange: one of these things is not like the others.

I screen my eyes, squinting against the glare of morning sun to get a better look. There's a cluster of small, nondescript buildings dotting a remote, abandoned valley in the far distance. The structures are so insignificant I nearly missed them, not only because they don't draw attention to themselves, but because they're planted in a region choked by wild forest on one side—and a steep cliff on the other. Their construction seems simple; from here, they appear to be made of wood, and they look almost like storage sheds. My first thought is that they might comprise a discreet weapons depot—except there appear to be curls of smoke lifting off the roofs, as if the rickety buildings might have smokestacks. Maybe they're pseudo-industrial spaces? Surveillance headquarters? Secret warehouses for a collection of creepy baby dolls?

It's hard to be sure. A pair of binoculars would be really helpful right now. Hell, the backpack they stole off my body would be really helpful right now. I had at least five protein bars in there.

All I can say for sure is that there's an entire stretch of land isolated from the main political, business, and residential zones. A deep ravine physically segregates the properties from the heart of Ark Island, almost as if the area is intentionally difficult to access. No roads in or out. Very little supporting infrastructure nearby. They *must* be hiding something.

Consider my interest piqued.

# JAMES

## CHAPTER 12

"This is nice, isn't it?" I ask, peering out the windshield. "Peaceful."

Outside, the scenes blur only a little as we soar under the clouds. The land here is beautiful: jagged mountains biting into sky, lakes shining under the morning sun. The hum of the electric chopper isn't too bad, either; I don't have to strain my voice much when I say, "I've never been on one of these things before."

My seatmate seems unimpressed, but he's been dead for at least twenty minutes now, so no surprise there.

Right now we're on our way to one of the warehouse-looking buildings that I chose at random on the map. According to the helpful screen displaying our current flight information, we should be landing in fifteen minutes.

Here I was, thinking I had to steal a jet, or a boat, or even rappel into the canals of hell on foot—and the world offered me up some kind of flying tricycle instead. I don't know how else to describe it. No doors; two-seater; single cup holder; peppy motor; leatherish interior; minimal recline; built-in navigation; and, bonus: it'll fly itself. Super bonus: it was just waiting for me. I made it back to the outskirts of civilization and the uniformed owner of this fine vehicle picked a fight with me immediately, and all because I asked to borrow his nifty little air-trike.

"Hey, how long do you think it'll take before they realize you're not the one flying this thing?" I ask, looking again at my seatmate. According to the ID I fished out of the cup holder, his name is Jeff Jefferson. Different Jeff with a side of Jeff. I can't make this shit up. "Or do you think they already know you're dead?"

Jeff says nothing, but I can tell what he's thinking.

"Yeah," I say, nodding as I return my eyes to the windshield. "They definitely know you're dead." Earlier I found a roll of mints, some kind of diet milkshake, and two chocolate bars taped together with a note that read *You're better than this* in the glove box. I jam the remaining half of a chocolate bar in my mouth now, chewing thoughtfully.

I glance at Jeff.

"You were too hard on yourself, man. You didn't eat the chocolate and now look at you—you're dead." I rip open the second chocolate bar, take a huge bite, then inspect the label on the diet milkshake. "What is this shit, Jeff? Why were you drinking this garbage?" The trike beeps angrily in response, demanding another round of biometric verification.

Shaking my head, I flatten Jeff's limp hand to the corresponding screen. A moment later, it flashes green. It's been demanding verification every other minute—probably because it's pretty sure the pilot is dead. I wouldn't be surprised if this thing tracked heart rates and bowel movements and impure thoughts, too. It started freaking out the moment I hopped on board. As if it could tell—before I'd even snapped the guy's neck—that I was going to snap the guy's neck. And then I did something to really piss off the machine: instead of going straight to the warehouses, I took a gamble and tried to fly home.

I knew it was a risk.

Not only are these things loaded with trackers and cameras, but they probably have enough data on Jeff to know his normal flight patterns. A random trip to The New Republic would definitely send an alert into the system.

Still, I figured I had to try.

But the minute I fed the navigation unauthorized coordinates, it put me on probation. Apparently people on Ark Island aren't allowed to leave this place without high-level security clearance. Apparently anyone who tries to make a run for it is immediately reported to the authorities.

Now, in addition to emphasizing the target on my back, the trike has entered a limited-usage mode, which basically means I can't take control of the steering wheel, the seat belts don't work, the lights won't stop flashing, and the aircraft won't fly too high or too fast until the alert is cleared by official personnel.

I take an angry bite of the chocolate bar.

I've barely started chewing when the trike screeches at me again, and I force Jeff's hand onto the scanner for the hundredth time. It was a little awkward in the beginning, pushing Jeff out of the trike only to drag him back on board after I realized I needed him to operate the thing. It was also upsetting for all the people who watched me do it. I know this, because they never stopped trying to kill me.

Apparently everyone on this island is armed.

Jeff was armed, too, which was lucky for me. Before I raided the glove box for snacks, I made sure to check him for weapons. Now I sit back and stretch, dried blood flaking off my body like confetti. When the sun shifts, offering me a fleeting reflection in the windshield, I'm so surprised by the sight of my own face I have to do a double take. I can practically hear the sound of Kenji's voice, holding back laughter—

*You look like someone took a bloody, chunky, runny shit on your face. Do you understand what I'm saying? The word I'm looking for is* diarrhea. *Do you know what diarrhea is? It's you.*

The thought almost makes me smile, and then it almost kills me. Suddenly I miss home so badly the feeling nearly penetrates. *Fear* nearly penetrates.

I take a tight breath. Less than ten minutes left. The forest grows thicker and denser as we get farther from the populated region of the island, shrouding our destination in mystery.

My knee bounces.

There's a reason Warner never led a mission into the Ark. His theory was that our only chance at winning a fight against The Reestablishment 2.0 would involve luring them back to the mainland. He has all kinds of ideas about the dark shit they might be developing out here and doesn't think we're ready to match them on their home turf.

I thought he was losing his touch. Going soft.

Now I realize I should've listened.

This is a suicide mission. I was worse than stupid for thinking I knew better than Warner, and stupider than that for thinking I could do this on my own. The moment this tricycle touches land I'll be surrounded. I still have no idea how I'm going to get out of here. I don't know what they're planning for me or why they've kept me alive so long. I'm mostly just making it up as I go, hoping things will work out. And right now the sting of real emotion is burning a hole in my heart and I have to beat it down. I can't let these assholes see me sweat.

I force myself to look at Jeff. "So. Jeff. Who made you think you had to lose ten pounds to be loved?"

"Beginning initial descent," says a smooth female voice. "Touching ground in five minutes."

"Five minutes?" I straighten in my seat so fast Jeff jolts beside me, falling into my arms. I shove him back into his chair and peer out the open door.

We're descending over the sea, the water shimmering in the rising light, and as the trike makes a steep turn toward land, I catch my first glimpse of the warehouses in the distance—just as Jeff slumps into my lap again. Irritated, I shove him back into his seat.

I return my eyes to the scene, and my irritation is quickly replaced by confusion. From this vantage point it's absolutely clear: these are not warehouses.

They're *homes*.

Shitty cottages clustered together in one of the most bleak, postapocalyptic scenes I've seen in a long time. People mill about, parents and children looking grim and malnourished. The fresh snowfall of yesterday is already soot-stained and dirty, rays of sunlight struggling through a thin layer of smog. The scene comes together all at once, with little time to reflect before we touch down—

"Input verification."

The biometric scanner shrieks once more in angry warning. Annoyed, I turn to grab Jeff's hand.

Except, suddenly, Jeff's seat is empty.

"Oh. Shit."

I scramble, craning my neck out the other open door as if I might catch him still tumbling to his second death—but of course the effort is useless. I've lost Jeff, and now the air-trike is pissed.

"Warning," says the voice. "Input verification." It won't stop yelling now. *"Warning. Input verification. Warning. Input verification—"*

I consider placing my own hand on the screen, but then I think it's probably a lose-lose situation to straight up verify that I've stolen Jeff's vehicle, so, instead, I decide to panic. I'm only about fifteen feet off the ground but the thing is refusing to land, and I don't know what's worse: the fact that I'm drawing attention to myself, or the fact that I was right about being mobbed by The Reestablishment. As predicted, there's a swarm of armed soldiers waiting in the distance, where larger, more impressive versions of my air-trike litter the landscape like toys. I'm guessing those will be much harder to steal.

"System shut down in five, four, three, two—"

The motor cuts out and suddenly I'm free-falling, everything happening so fast I never get to decide whether to jump. The steel frame strikes the ground with thunderous force, juddering to a chaotic stop as waves of pain rocket through my battered body.

I blink, and it seems to take forever.

My ears are ringing. I touch the side of my face and my hand comes away wet. Red. I suck in a breath as the pain spirals, pinching a shard of glass out of my arm just as I hear a young girl scream.

I stiffen at the sound.

My heartbeat picks up swiftly, scaring me. I react badly to the sound of children screaming. It's the most broken thing about me; the part of me I'm always trying to manage. I grew up listening to children screaming. Fell asleep listening to children screaming. Children dying. Children disappearing. Children being tortured, starved, abused. I was one of the lucky ones in the orphanage; I had a big brother who came back sometimes. Who sent food sometimes. Who eventually saved up enough money to get me out. But I was raised with the kids whose parents were slaughtered trying to fight The Reestablishment. There were so many children left behind we'd flood the streets like schools of fish. There were never enough beds. There was never enough food.

We were always, always unprotected.

I force myself to look around, light streaking across my vision as I survey the chaos: dented metal; smears of blood; flashing lights; *input verification*; crushed glass; *input verification*. My eyes home in on the gleaming edge of an automatic rifle. *Input verification.*

I tumble out the open door, hitting the cold ground with a thud, struggling to clear my vision.

Again, the girl screams.

The sound is like a strike to the face. I take a breath, grit my teeth. For years I couldn't even be around Adam's kids for too long. When Gigi or Roman cried too much I'd lose it; I'd lash out even though I knew, intellectually, that sometimes kids cried even when they were safe. I could see the horror in Adam's eyes when I'd lose control. I could see how it killed him to realize I was so messed up.

*Still* messed up.

Eventually I learned how to fake it for his sake—timing my visits, dissociating from the moments I couldn't escape—but I've tried for years to shake it off for real and never could. There's a rage that lives inside me I've never been able to kill. A rage that lives buried, like magma, miles beneath still waters. The rage of a child still too young to fight the monsters when they came calling.

When I hear the girl scream for the third time, I stand.

My head is pounding; my heart is pounding; sweat beads along my brow. I squint at the crush of soldiers in the distance, my anxiety ticking up a notch, and in my haze it takes me a moment to realize they're not facing me.

Hell, they're not here for me at all.

They've surrounded one of the cottages, its front door flung open to reveal a child so thin she looks skeletal. I blink rapidly, my head steadying, and as my sight sharpens I realize she looks strangely familiar. White-blond hair, super pale skin. Two soldiers are forcing her out the door, handling her so roughly I'm worried she'll snap in half. Her cheeks are hollow, her body shaking—but she's looking at something with focused desperation, and when I follow her line of sight I nearly rock back on my heels. There's a young woman on her knees in the dirt, thrashing violently against the soldiers pinning her arms behind her back. A broad, dark-haired man looms over her, his face in shadow. He's half-bent, hands planted on her shoulders. And that's when I remember—

*Please*

*Tell them to be gentle with her*

*She's just a child*

*When I die, they'll throw her in the asylum*

The soldiers aren't pointing their guns at me, they're pointing their guns at Rosabelle, and I should be thrilled. This is the perfect diversion. I don't need to be here. I don't need to listen to this. This is not my problem. I could run for it. I *should* run for it. Steal a vehicle, base jump into the ocean—

"You promised me," she says, and her voice is unnaturally calm, on the verge of breaking. "You *promised—*"

"Rosa, enough—"

She spits in the man's face.

A soldier slams the butt of his gun into her eye so hard I hear the crack of bone, and when her sister screams for the fourth time, it practically rewrites my DNA.

"All right, fuck it," I mutter, grabbing Jeff's gun from the overturned trike. "Let's do something stupid."

# ROSABELLE

## CHAPTER 13

The impact takes my breath away.

Like a small explosion, light streaks across my vision. I can almost see the sparks as the gun strikes my head, a blinding pain spearing my right eye. The sound of Clara's scream slows and stretches, warping in the slowing frame rate of the moment. I lift my head and everything blurs.

I regret nothing about spitting in Sebastian's face.

At the same time, I regret it deeply.

Never have I displayed anything but careful respect for Sebastian, and now I've shown my hand. Worse: Clara will suffer for the small, fleeting satisfaction of the moment.

A pyrrhic victory.

A trickle of blood has carved its way into my eye, and I blink painfully, diverting its path to my mouth. The morning air is bracing, the damp ground painting patches at my knees. My arms are still wrenched behind my back, nearly pulled from their sockets. I hear the flap of wings, a distant *caw,* crows beginning to circle. The events of the morning return to me in agonizing flashes: the asylum order nailed to the front door; the guilty look on the face of the man I'm meant to marry; the violence of the unannounced entry moments later.

Clara.

*What is it, Rosa? What's wrong? Why are they here? Rosa— Wait, why are they taking you— Why are you taking her? ROSA—NO—*

Someone touches me and I recoil, prizing my eyes apart to find Sebastian tenderly wiping the blood from my face. Inspiration arrives unbidden:

*A rusted shovel.*

I'll cut off his head with a rusted shovel. Dull, impractical. It'll take forever. He'll scream endlessly.

"Sometimes we don't know what's best for us," Sebastian is saying, his fingers grazing the bruise forming along my temple. "And I only want the best for you, Rosa. You'll see."

For so long, I accepted this life like a debt deferred: my parents had refused to pay the price, so I would. My father was a traitor; I was not. My mother had chosen death; I would not.

When nothing made sense, logic sustained me.

The Reestablishment had always protected me; it was my father who'd betrayed me. It was my mother who'd left me. It was my parents who'd failed us.

If I could be all that they weren't, I could fix everything. I could be stronger. I could be better.

I could be patient.

I gave the past ten years of my life to this system, trusting that as long as I kept my head down and worked hard, I'd be rewarded for my loyalty. I trusted that, ultimately, an apparatus of justice underpinned my daily suffering.

But now—

I turn my head, searching past the smear of Sebastian's face. Now I can't see Clara anymore.

They must've dragged her away, out of my sight line, still screaming. I feel the stutter of my nervous system again; a glitch in my heart; the telltale tremble of my right arm.

Hope, like breath, leaves my body.

I can see it: the bruises their hands will leave on her skin; the cruelty with which they'll strap her down; the frozen abyss of her rotting cell; the putrid scraps they'll toss her; the unclean water she'll be forced to drink; the endlessness of solitude—and worse, and worse—

I'm no better than my parents.

I've failed us, too.

A cold paralysis seizes my body. I lose feeling in my legs. My chest locks down, compressing my lungs. My vision fades in and out. Clara, three years old, covered in my mother's blood. Clara, four years old, clinging to me constantly. Clara, five years old, wanting to know what it feels like to be full—

*Do you remember, Rosa? Can you describe it?*

A feverish sweat breaks across my skin, chilling me to the bone. Clara, six years old, vomiting uncontrollably. Clara, seven years old, handing me a note—

*I'm sorry for upsetting you when I'm sick I don't mean to upset you I promise I'll try to be better*

My eyes flutter and I feel it: I'm going to faint.

No.

No, you've been dead inside for years, I tell myself.

You've been dead inside for so long—

Die, I tell myself.

*Die.*

"What on earth?" Sebastian looks up sharply, over my shoulder. "He's not supposed to be here yet. He's not even supposed to be on his feet for another five minutes—"

Shock pierces straight through my deadened skin, penetrating my heart like a blade. Suddenly, I can hear myself breathing, feel myself shaking. Suddenly, I'm freezing.

I know, somehow, it's him.

*James.*

Warped memories of the past twenty-four hours rise, like bile, to the surface of my mind, reminding me of all that I'm meant to do, the mission I'm meant to complete.

I can't remember how to care.

I want to know what they've done with Clara.

A murmur moves through the crowd, heads turning all together toward something out of view. One of the soldiers loosens his grip on my arm just enough that I'm able to crane my neck to see—

A dented mini chopper is careening toward us.

The windshield is cracked, obscuring James's face from view, but he's only half inside the cockpit; his boots are visible through the open door, footfalls hitting the ground in faster and faster strides. The small, damaged aircraft is hurtling up a slight hill, wobbling on three wheels at a dangerous speed, and when he gains enough momentum he jumps back inside and drives directly into the crowd.

# ROSABELLE

## CHAPTER 14

Everyone rears back.

A detachment of soldiers charge forward, forming a barricade in front of the oncoming aircraft. They lift their weapons, an electric thrum zipping through the air just as Sebastian bolts ahead, aiming his gun at the broken chopper barreling toward us.

"Stand down," he shouts, his voice booming. "Stop the vehicle immediately."

James pops his bloodied head out the open door. "What'd you say?"

"I said *stop*—"

James leans farther out the door, revealing a sophisticated automatic rifle. "I was just kidding, dumbass," he calls back. "I heard what you said."

James opens fire.

The crowd screams.

Sebastian dives out of the way; the soldiers don't hesitate. They shoot over and over at the trike, glass shattering everywhere.

"Steady your fire!" Sebastian bellows, clambering to his feet. "Don't alter course! We have fifteen minutes left in the script—"

James steers the broken chopper directly into the fray, people diving for cover as he unloads round after round. Occasionally he runs alongside the battered aircraft to give its slowing momentum a boost, risking his life in the process. I watch him get shot three times; twice in the legs and once in the shoulder, each assault punctuated by a colorful epithet. It's clear they're not trying to kill James, and I wonder if he can tell.

I can't take my eyes off him.

I have no idea what his intentions are. I don't know whether he's here for revenge, intent on killing me along with everyone else for what we did to him. I can't find the energy to concern myself with his motives, not now that Clara's been taken from me. I've never cared less to live. Without Clara, I have no worth as a person.

Without Clara, I am a killer, nothing more.

I watch the impossible scene melt around me from a cold distance, disappearing further and further inside myself with each passing second. It's not until two shots explode right next to my head—one for each of the soldiers restraining me—that I'm jolted back into my body. Only then do I realize what's happening.

James came here with a plan.

"Get in," he shouts, steering the dilapidated vehicle in my direction.

I don't hesitate.

My arms ache, screaming now that they've been released from their tortured positions, but the torment feels distant: a photocopy of a photocopy.

"You okay?" says James, sparing me a glance.

For a moment I only stare at him.

I slit this man's throat. I literally killed him, and now he's asking me if I'm okay. I think there might be something wrong with him. Gunfire rains down upon us, battering the bullet-resistant body of the trike. Smoke curls in the sky like loose calligraphy. I sit back in my bloodied seat as we bump and judder over rough terrain and fallen bodies. James looks like a creature of the night, so covered in matted blood and baked-on dirt he's the very definition of grotesque.

I wonder how he found my cottage.

"There are pedals," I say, amazed by the steady sound of my own voice. "In the wheel well."

He freezes; then looks down; then looks at me; then looks down again. "Are you fucking kidding me right now?"

I don't answer this; I am suddenly enervated. Energy leaves my body in a stunning defeat, so all-encompassing I seem to lose my bones. I wonder then whether I should even bother with this mission—whether I owe any loyalty to The Reestablishment after what they've done—before I remember, with a start, who I'm dealing with. The Reestablishment would never be so stupid as to *kill* Clara.

I go solid.

Gone is my boneless fatigue; fear grows roots and branches inside of me, animating me against my will.

Killing Clara would be stupid. Killing her would mean forfeiting their power over me. Torturing Clara, on the other hand, would be far more effective, as I only have one weakness.

I've only ever had one weakness.

I watch, through a haze of renewed horror, as James kicks away a panel in the floor, the blood from his boots smearing the white paint to reveal a set of traditional foot pedals, which he jumps on without delay. Three bullet wounds and still, his eyes light up. He grins at me like this is the best thing that's ever happened to him, and he starts pumping his legs like a kid learning to ride a bike for the first time.

"Yes!" he says, slapping the dashboard with his hand. "Hell yes!" Almost immediately, we pick up speed. He turns to look at me. "All right. Okay. Where'd they take your sister? The asylum, right? But, like, how do we get there?"

These words blow open a hole in my chest.

The pain is so unexpected that I make an involuntary sound, lifting a hand to my sternum only to discover I'm still intact.

*How do we get there*

*How do we get there*

I am unwell, my heart hammering as I study him. The words left his lips without guile, as if he meant what he said. More anomalies. I can't make sense of him.

No one in the pit helps each other—certainly not without the promise of compensation. People have too many problems of their own. Those who reek of neediness are pariahs; there's no faster path to isolation than to ask for help.

I asked for help once, when I was ten years old.

My mother had just killed herself, her remains still spattered against the wall. Clara had scooped up a bit of Mama's brain and couldn't stop staring at it. I was worried she was going to put it in her mouth so I pried it out of her grubby fingers and Clara cried for two days straight. I had no idea how to care for a three-year-old. I could hardly care for myself. I ran from cottage to cottage, hysterical and half out of my mind. The only neighbor who answered her door slapped me in the face so hard I fell silent. She looked me up and down a long time.

*Just you two girls alone in there now?* she asked.

*Yes, ma'am. Clara hasn't eaten in days—*

*You're going to need this,* she said, and handed me a shotgun.

"Hey," James says sharply, glancing away from the road.

I look up.

"You okay?"

James blurs as I stare beyond him, my mind fracturing. Even if we could get to Clara, how could I help her? Where would I take her? How would I care for her? They took Clara from me to torture her. They're going to bring her to the point of death only to destroy her over and over and over—

*"Hey,"* he barks.

I look up again. I hadn't realized I'd looked down.

"Your name is Rosabelle, right? Or is it Rosa? I heard someone call you Rosa just now."

*No one but my family ever calls me Rosa,* I answer in my head. Sebastian lost the right years ago.

"Look, I realize you're in a bad place right now, but if

we're going to save your sister we really—"

"There is no saving her," I say quietly.

"What? What do you mean?"

"This is a small island with highly developed surveillance technology. If I try to save her, I'll be easily caught and executed for treason. When I'm executed Clara will die."

James slackens, his feet slowing on the pedals for the first time. "Oh," he says, deflated. "Damn."

I nod, taking the moment to dissolve inside myself. Feel nothing, taste nothing, be nothing.

*Die.*

I glance out the open door.

James's efforts have earned us a slight lead, but a swarm of aircraft is gathering in the sky above us, soldiers' footfalls thundering toward us. James tries to shoot back but the effort is short-lived; the magazine is empty. He shakes his head before rifling through the glove compartment, chucking something angrily out the door as he mutters, "Seriously, Jeff? A fucking diet milkshake but no ammo?" and I choose not to ask him what he means.

Sebastian didn't share the details of the program with me; as with my first encounter with James, Klaus felt it necessary that I participate in the mission as organically as possible. All I know for certain is that I'm not supposed to kill James; in fact, I haven't been instructed to kill anyone yet. My job is to remain close enough to James to get the two of us off the island and into the heart of enemy territory in order to initiate a broader offensive. I'll receive communications about the next steps of the operation only after I've touched down in The New Republic, where an undercover agent will find me.

This is phase one of six.

Each phase must be completed within a prescribed time period. Right now, for example, I have as long as it takes to get out of here before someone kills me.

If I fail at any phases of the operation, I'll be executed.

I glance at the cracked screen in the dashboard, the flashing demand for biometric verification. Soon, we'll be surrounded. Soon, I'll be on my own to manage all aspects of this situation, which means, for Clara's sake, I need to do my job and get us off this island as soon as possible. The trike appears to be working, at least a little, which—

"All right." James sighs, giving up the ammo search. "Get out."

I go suddenly still. "Excuse me?"

"I said get out." He nods toward the door. Circles a finger above his head, gesturing to the helicopters above us. "I have shit to do."

"I don't understand." I hesitate. "I thought you were trying to save me."

Now he looks annoyed. "You really thought I was trying to save the serial killer who murdered me? Honestly, I'm offended. Get out before I push you out. You can fucking save yourself."

A feathery sensation moves inside me at that, something akin to joy. "You wanted to save Clara," I say softly. "You *only* wanted to save Clara. You don't care about me at all."

"Look, are you okay? Like, I get that you've had a bad day, so it's cool if you haven't noticed the ten pounds of blood all over my body, but I'm kind of having a bad day, too, and I've got two new bullet wounds to deal with—"

"Three," I say, glancing at the encroaching masses. "You were shot at least three times."

"Okay smart-ass, I've asked you twice to get the hell out of this vehicle, and now you're starting to piss me off—"

"Can you swim?" I ask.

At this, he hesitates. "Yeah, but—"

"The only way off this island is *off the island*. Do you understand what that means?"

He glances away from me, toward the sea. "You're suggesting I jump off the cliff? Thanks for the brilliant insight. I already thought of that. Get out."

"*Drive* off the cliff," I clarify. "And I'm not getting out. I'm coming with you."

# ROSABELLE

## CHAPTER 15

James goes rigid. "Coming with me? Coming with me where?"

"To The New Republic."

"Hell no."

"Why not?"

"Because you're a fucking serial killer, that's why."

"I'm not a serial killer."

He raises his eyebrows. "You're telling me you haven't serially killed people? For a living?"

"I can help you," I say, ignoring this. "I can get the chopper to work. I can get you home. But you have to take me with you."

"*No.*"

"Why not?"

He throws up his hands. "Are you joking? You're clearly some kind of psycho mercenary servant of the fascists. Why would I take you with me? So you could kill everyone I care about? Imagine being invited to a potluck and bringing the plague." He points at me. "You're the plague."

My jaw tenses. "If that's true, why did you try to save my sister?"

"She's a kid," he scoffs. "That's different."

"And your arrogance is breathtaking," I counter. "You came to this island as part of some covert op and slaughtered dozens of people in the process, but you think you're better than me because you've decided your motives are worthy. Well, I think my motives are worthy, too."

He casts me a sidelong look. "Aren't you getting married next week?"

"Not anymore."

"How convenient."

"It's true."

A helicopter opens fire overhead, an earsplitting *boom* preceding the launch of three warning missiles fired in perfect formation. The explosions rock the aircraft so hard we nearly knock heads. The din is deafening; the heat stifling. I look around to discover we're trapped in a triangulated inferno.

"Jesus," says James, wincing. He presses his hands to his ears, shouting over the small firestorm. "They really don't know how to kill me, do they?"

"They're not trying to kill you," I say, coughing. "You're worth more alive than dead."

"You know," he says, squinting at me through the smoke, "beautiful girls are always saying things like that to me. It's starting to go to my head."

The careless compliment catches me off guard, nicking an exposed vein. A fragile shoot of pleasure pushes up through the fallow fields of my vanity—chased immediately by shame. It's embarrassing to discover I can still care about such things.

"All right, okay, fine." He sighs, glancing at the flames roaring just outside the open door. "Let's get out of here. But the minute you land on my soil you'll be locked up and vetted by the authorities. You know why?"

"Why?"

"Because I'm going to turn you in."

"Okay," I say. "I accept—"

"I'm not done," he says. "If you run, I will kill you."

"Fine."

"If you try to kill me again, I will definitely kill you."

I blink slowly. "Fine."

"And if I find out that any of this"—he twirls a finger to indicate the general disaster of things—"is part of some sick plan to get close to my family, I will take you apart. Do you understand?" His eyes flash with barely concealed fury. "You hurt my family," he says, leaning in, "and you will meet a very different version of me, Rosabelle. *I will take you apart*. And then I'll feed you, one piece at a time, to the vultures."

At this small speech, a part of me dissolves.

His words generate within me the opposite of fear; instead, I find my thoughts dipping into the absurd. I wonder, briefly, what it must be like to be loved by someone like him. To have someone always in your corner, someone willing to fight for you. James was ready to risk his life for a little girl he's never met; I can only guess at what he'd do for his own family. I wonder if they have any idea how lucky they are. How many of us would kill for that kind of fierce, unshakable loyalty.

"I understand," I say quietly.

He holds out a hand, ostensibly to shake on it, but for reasons I don't fully understand, the idea of touching James scares me. I steel myself before finally slipping my hand into his, neutralizing my expression as I grow uncomfortably, acutely aware of him. His skin is warm and calloused and streaked with dried blood, large and rough against mine.

I look up. We lock eyes.

He smiles a strange, amused sort of smile, and suddenly the cabin is overcrowded, the distance between us too small. He lets go of me slowly, his fingers sliding against my palm, and I experience a shocking spasm in my chest—the same terrifying spark I did the day I killed him.

"Truce," he says.

"Truce," I agree.

My skin seems to be buzzing. I ignore this unwelcome development by flattening my hand against the cracked monitor without further delay. The aircraft hums to life, and the screen unlocks, greeting me.

"Good morning, Unfinished Profile. Please update your information. Otherwise, enter destination."

I experience a modicum of relief. Only yesterday did Sebastian grant me small-aircraft authorization; Klaus must've anticipated this moment. Quickly, I zoom out on the map. Ark Island is located off the northwest coast of what used to be North America; there are a cluster of other islands nearby, many of which remain under the control of The New Republic. I make a selection at random, choosing a set of coordinates on an enemy island closest to us.

"Your destination does not exist," says the vehicle. "Override or enter new destination."

"Override," I say.

"Battery is dangerously low," says the vehicle. "Aircraft operation not recommended. Override or enter new destination."

"Shit," says James.

"Override."

"Rear-left wheel underinflated. Tire pressure dangerously low. Override or call for assistance."

"Override," I say again.

"Okay," says James, "this thing is more messed up than I thought—"

Another explosion rocks the chopper without warning, the impact nearly blowing out my eardrums. I'm thrown back in my seat, grimacing through the pain. I blink my eyes open, peering through the remains of the shattered windshield, and I can just make out the familiar lines of Sebastian's figure, fast approaching.

Panic clears my head.

"Override," I say again, tapping the screen. "Override."

"Safety belts nonfunctional," says the vehicle. "Aircraft operation not recommended. Override or call for assistance."

*"Override."*

"I thought you were supposed to be helping me," says James. "You're making things worse."

"Be quiet."

"Airbags nonfunctional. Aircraft operation not recommended. Override or call for assistance."

*"Override."*

"Maybe we should steal a different one?" says James. "A better one?"

"There's no time—"

"Camera sensors nonfunctional. Aircraft operation not recommended. Override or call for assistance."

"Oh, for the love of—"

I throw the chopper in manual, climb over James, seize control of the steering wheel, and floor the accelerator. The vehicle pitches forward violently, throwing me back against James, who unleashes a string of expletives as I land hard against his injured legs.

There's no time to apologize.

I can hardly see through my good eye, much less through the broken windshield as we bolt through flames ten feet high. I keep my foot planted on the accelerator even as the low-battery signal screeches dire warnings. We head directly toward the cliff, careening wildly on two unbalanced wheels as circling helicopters machine-gun rounds of ammunition at us, taking out the remaining wheels one by one.

Suddenly, we're sliding.

The trike spins wildly out of control, clipping trees and bushes, branches and brambles scraping painfully along the outer body. I hit the brakes, hard, and we stop spinning only to skid backward off the cliff, launching badly into the air. I hear James shout something profane and then—

And then we're free-falling, spiraling toward the sea.

# ROSABELLE

## CHAPTER 16

I don't allow myself to panic.

I shift gears, manually overriding preset controls in order to activate the rotors. When the blades finally catch, whipping the air at a satisfying clip, I push the throttle forward to full capacity, straightening the dying aircraft just inches before it kisses water. We bump and skid along the tide, water lashing the frame with the force of a knife, but before long the curve of a distant coastline comes into view.

Still, my relief is short-lived.

The helicopters aren't far behind, three of them appearing in the distance, firing more warning shots that whiz dangerously past our heads, occasionally dinging the metal body. The only thing keeping us from certain death is the fact that they want James alive; otherwise they'd take us out with ease. If I allow them to get close enough, a sniper will put a bullet through my throat before whisking James back to base—where they'll no doubt recalibrate under Klaus's guidance. Right now I'm running on adrenaline and the power of a small pilot light: the promise Klaus made me in the cradle.

*Complete this mission to satisfaction, Rosabelle, and we will set you and your sister free.*

I'm monitoring battery levels, trying to squeeze as much life out of this dented carcass as possible, but I can feel the motor giving out. We're almost out of time.

"Keep your foot on the accelerator," I tell James, shouting to be heard above the clamor. "And hold down the throttle." I climb over him again, returning to the passenger seat before overriding the user interface, typing prompts furiously into the command line.

"What are you doing?" James shouts back, taking over as instructed. "We've got maybe a few minutes left before this thing is deadweight. We need to jump."

"I know," I call out. "I'm trying to buy us more time."

I'm still desperately running commands, hoping the aircraft's computer has sufficient power to execute complex functions. Only when the chopper gives an unsettling jolt do I breathe a quick sigh of relief. Then, quickly, I unlatch the glove compartment and find what I'm looking for: a compact tool kit.

"Hey—wait—tell me what's going on—"

I stand up on the seat and get to work, dismantling parts of the fuselage in order to access the battery storage. A couple of excruciating minutes later the blades pick up speed and the chopper ascends several feet in the sky. Relieved and exhausted, I sink back into my seat, ignoring the tremble in my right arm as I snap the tool kit shut. I allow myself a second to close my eyes and breathe, relishing the relative quiet. Now that we're not clipping the water every other second, the deafening noise has settled.

"Okay, what the hell did you do?" James demands. "The choppers fell back and the flight deck shut down. No one is trying to kill us and none of the screens are working."

Reluctantly, I open my eyes. "I ran a simulation and rerouted the power source."

"Explain this to me like I'm an idiot."

I feel an urge to laugh at that, except that I haven't laughed in so long the compulsion surprises me. Bothers me.

Instead I say, "There are different kinds of choppers—civilian grade and military grade. They look different, but people don't realize that most of these aircraft have similar programming—and use the same computer chips. The civilian models just have massive security restrictions." I tilt my head at him. "So I tricked the computer into thinking it was a military chopper."

"What does that mean?"

"I unlocked stealth mode."

James's eyes widen, a flash of respect quickly displaced by suspicion. He sits back in his seat. "What about the flight deck?" he says, nodding at the dead screens. "How are we airborne right now?"

I turn away, studying a crescent of shorn metal around the windshield. "There are two battery packs. A big one for the motor and a smaller one for everything else—monitors, sensors, air-conditioning, locking mechanisms—that sort of thing. The secondary battery isn't as powerful, of course, but it wasn't damaged and appears to be near full capacity. It might be enough to get us to shore. As long as our speed remains constant, I'm hopeful we'll reach the coastline of The New Republic in about thirty minutes. We might not have to swim at all."

James says nothing for so long I finally look up.

He's staring at me. Stonily silent.

I avert my eyes again. "You can't see our flight path onscreen anymore, but I've directed the chopper to pilot itself to our destination," I add, feeling uncomfortable now. I nod at his injuries. "I thought you'd appreciate a break from operating the vehicle. Considering the state you're in."

When he continues to say nothing, I reach underneath my seat and unlatch the emergency kit, hefting it onto my lap. I tap the metal case. "There are life vests in here, in case everything fails and we need to jump. But I thought we could use the remaining flight time to deal with your wounds. Your legs seem to be healing; those injuries must've been a result of DEWs. But you still have a bullet lodged in your left tricep. I don't know whether you've noticed."

"I've noticed," he says, shifting. "What the hell is a DEW?"

"Directed-energy weapon."

He raises an eyebrow. "Try again."

"Laser guns."

James laughs, but the sound is hollow. Nerves snake through me, and I distract myself by releasing the snaps on the kit.

"Wow," he says. "First she kills me, then she cares for me. Everything about this scenario is believable. Consistent."

I tense.

I don't know why his derision bothers me. I've spent most of my life perfecting a perception of myself. I've never wanted anyone other than Clara to imagine me capable of emotion. I should be pleased he thinks I'm cold and inhuman. Instead, it makes me feel ill.

I rifle through the medical supplies, searching for scissors and antiseptic. "Do you—"

"How did you know how to do that?" he says, pointing to the ceiling. "How'd you know how to reroute the power supply? How are you capable of genius-level computer hacking? How'd you know where the emergency kit was? How'd you know there were life vests on board? How are you so familiar with the tech and mech of this aircraft? And while we're asking important questions: What, exactly, is the purpose of your mission? Because you're clearly much more than a serial killer. You're some kind of highly trained operative, and I'm going to give you one chance to prove me wrong before I punt you into the ocean."

I go uncomfortably still. This is my own fault. I should've anticipated this. I should've anticipated the pitfalls of proximity.

I underestimated him.

# ROSABELLE

## CHAPTER 17

My mistake.

I knew James wouldn't trust me right away, but I thought he'd be easier to manage. He's a stronger, more formidable fighter, but I pegged him as emotionally inferior. He struck me as ridiculous; unserious. His easygoing, playful attitude tricked me into thinking he might be lazy, less observant, unlikely to ask too many questions.

I pick out a pair of medical scissors, weighing the variables of the situation.

I've been trying to pin James's character to a pattern without success; every time I think I've found consistencies in him, he introduces deviations. So far, my only concrete discovery is that he lives by some kind of moral code. If he didn't, he wouldn't have cared to save Clara. If he didn't, he wouldn't have offered me a chance to prove him wrong. Based on many of his actions, I'd categorized him as rash and impulsive; instead, he wants to be sure he's making the right decision before he kills me. Another inconsistency.

This is interesting.

It seems clear to me now that James's conscience is the only thing keeping me safe from ejection. If I give him a solid reason to doubt my intentions, he'll likely toss me off the chopper and head home without a second thought. I can't risk underestimating his intelligence again by feeding him a thin lie. I have no choice, then, but to settle for an admission of truth.

"I used to build these things," I say.

"What does that mean?"

"It means sometimes I'm allowed to do regular work. Factory work." I gather up rolls of gauze and tape from the emergency kit, a pair of tweezers. "Some of our manufacturing isn't fully automated yet, so for a while it was my job to oversee the assembly of mini choppers. I was required to memorize not just the manual but the schematics. These," I say, glancing around the hull, "are called PEARLs. Personal electric aerial recreational lifts. Civilian grade. I'm familiar with the military iteration because Ark Island is a militarized state. I see them everywhere. I've ridden in them. I know what they're capable of." I hesitate then, adding quietly: "I'm not a genius-level hacker. But I appreciate the compliment."

For a full minute, James stares out the broken windshield, silent and hardly moving. I've never witnessed a quiet, contemplative James, and the character reversal is making me anxious. It occurs to me then that I've spoken more in the last several minutes than I have in years.

"I should cut off your sleeve," I say, leaning forward. "I think your body is trying to heal itself around the bullet—"

"If I'm worth more alive than dead," he says, moving out of reach, "why were you sent to kill me?"

"I don't know." Slowly, I sit back in my seat. "At the time, I wasn't told who you were."

He crosses his arms, wincing only slightly. "And once you found out who I was you decided to change the course of your entire life? Dumped your fiancé, abandoned your sister—"

*abandoned your sister*

"—walked away from a fulfilling career as a murderer—all for me? I'm flattered."

*abandoned your sister*

The words catch in my head, repeating on a painful loop.

*abandoned your sister*

*abandoned your sister*

The reminder nearly rearranges me. Images of Clara attempt to crowd my mind: where she might be, what they might've done to her—

*abandoned your sister*

I shutter the thoughts desperately, withdrawing further and further inward until I fear I've lost my soul.

When I finally look up, I find James watching me with a fascination I've never felt before. Soledad only ever stared at me with suspicion; Sebastian with a mixture of longing and pity. No one has ever studied me as if I might be interesting, or worse: a real, comprehensive person. The intensity of James's inspection makes me feel naked.

I don't like it.

"I should really take a look at your arm," I say, breaking the silence. "If the bullet moves—"

James stretches his neck, the action issuing cracks in the hardened blood on his face. "Thanks, but I think I'll pass," he says. "The last time you came at me with a sharp object you slit my throat."

Quietly, I say, "Are you going to hold that over my head forever?"

He raises his eyebrows. "The fact that you *killed* me? The fact that you watched me die without remorse, then sent me off to have my organs harvested? Yes, yes, I am."

A rare heat creeps into my cheeks, and James doesn't miss it. He doesn't miss anything, I'm realizing.

"But I just saved your life," I point out. "We have a truce."

"Fine." A muscle tics in his jaw. "I'm going to ask you one more question, and if you answer it honestly, maybe I'll let you take a look at my arm."

"I really don't want to answer any more questions."

"And I really don't think you're in a position to negotiate," he counters.

I stifle a sigh, bracing myself.

After all these years, I thought I'd be used to it: the surveillance, the interrogations, the constant suspicion, the endless threats against my life. And yet, somehow, being hated by James feels worse. He doesn't seem like the kind of person who hates many people, and I'm surprised to discover how much it bothers me to be the exception.

"All right," I say. "What's your question?"

"When was the last time you ate a proper meal?"

This is so unexpected it disarms me. My right hand

trembles again, and the scissors I'd been holding clatter to the floor.

My heart begins to race.

*Rosa? Rosa, my stomach hurts. Rosa—*

I freeze, my eyes unfocusing, my breaths loud in my head. There's something wrong with me. My legs are cold. My hands are tingling. Something's wrong with me and I don't—

*Rosa, what's wrong with me?*

"Hey," says James. "You okay?"

I look up and there's Clara, sitting in bed, tearing into a loaf of bread with a smile I haven't seen in weeks. I stand by the door in my boots, watching her.

*Aren't you hungry, too, Rosa?*

*No,* I lie to her.

*Are you sure?*

*When you eat, Clara, it's like I eat.*

"Rosabelle," he says forcefully.

I shake my head. I can feel the hard chair beneath me, the wisp of hair stuck to my neck, my hands holding each other. "I'm sorry, what was the question?"

"When was the last time you ate a proper meal?"

I reach for the fallen scissors and my right hand shakes so badly I have to grip it with my left, dropping the other supplies in the process. Something's wrong with me. Something's wrong with me and it's scaring me. I'm losing control of my facade and I can't seem to pull it back into place. Maybe because I don't know whether I'll ever see Clara again. Maybe because interrogations have never included questions about my welfare. Or maybe it's because there's no chip in James's body. No audience watching through his eyes. I haven't had a private conversation with anyone in years and I feel safer with this stranger than I do with my own sister and it's emotionally destabilizing.

"Why won't you answer the question?"

"Why are you asking?" I blink, trying to focus. I can't seem to return to my body. "Why are you—"

I suck in a breath.

The hunger I've been compartmentalizing for days roars suddenly back to life, spearing me with a shocking, breath-taking pain. It's a reminder to me that underneath the bursts of adrenaline my body is slowly atrophying, stripping nutrients from my bones, metabolizing itself.

"Rosabelle, are they starving you?"

I shake my head. I shake my head and it won't stop, Clara won't stop crying, won't stop screaming. There's blood on her lips, smeared across her sallow cheeks. She's three years old again, gnawing on her fingers. Four years old and I can count her bones. I curl around her every night, pressing down on her stomach so she can sleep, trapping the pain with my hands. She whimpers for hours and I can't get it out of my head. I can never get it out of my head.

I can't stop shaking my head.

*Aren't you hungry, too, Rosa?*

"No," I say out loud.

"So you're defending them? Protecting them?" James

sounds angry. "Great. That's two good reasons to throw you into the ocean right now."

I look up, no longer able to hide my alarm.

Never mind the fact that I haven't eaten in three days, I rarely sleep through the night anymore. I haven't felt warm water on my skin in years. My mind falters more these days; my body isn't as resilient as it might've been. The only clothes I've ever owned are the castoffs of my mother and father. I'm wearing yesterday's hospital scrubs and the moth-eaten sweater I once used to wipe down the kitchen counters. I haven't engaged in hand-to-hand combat in two years. The tremble in my right arm has gotten progressively worse, and it's becoming a liability. The Reestablishment knows this. The weaker I become, the more they downgrade my assignments. The weaker I become, the less I'm worth.

My last mission was to assassinate a professor in the Academies District; he'd been flagged by Klaus as a zealot with the potential for domestic terrorism. The man spent so much time with his kids that it took me two days to get a clean shot. This mission is expected to last well over a month, and I haven't even been ordered to kill James yet; I've been ordered to *use* him.

In order to use him I have to inspire him to trust me, and he's too smart to survive on a diet of lies—which means I have to be willing to part with more and more truth. But I'm only good at my job when I disconnect from my own humanity. The hunger helps keep me hollow. I survive only by freely and quietly dying, over and over, inside my head.

Dealing with James will require accessing my soul, and few things have terrified me more.

I look up, into his eyes—

# JAMES

## CHAPTER 18

"She just passed out," I say, throwing up my hands. "I've already explained this like fourteen times. I have no idea what happened."

"And you didn't do anything to her?"

"No, I didn't do anything to her!"

"All right, everyone needs to chill," Kenji says, biting into a carrot stick. He offers me the bag and I reach for a carrot, muttering thanks when he says, "Obviously James didn't do anything to this girl, because if he had any idea what he was doing he would've killed her days ago."

"Hey—"

"Look," Kenji says, crunching. "I love you, you know I love you, and props for coming home mostly in one piece, but you literally shaved years off our lives. We thought you were dead." He chews for another second, then: "Honestly, if we weren't over the moon to have you home right now, I'd beat the shit out of you."

"I second that," says Adam.

Kenji reaches for another carrot, then nods at Adam. "The snack game gets stronger every day, man. A little peanut butter, too? In its own little container?" He takes another bite. "Did you cut these carrots yourself?"

"Yeah, and I've got apple slices, too," says Adam, rifling through the backpack at his feet. "Roman decided he's only eating apples this week."

"Wasn't he only eating bananas last week?" asks Winston, intercepting the bag of apple slices.

"Yeah, but—"

"*Hey,*" I say, sitting forward. "Why'd you call for a meeting if you're not even going to talk to me?"

"I didn't call this meeting," says Kenji. "Warner did. And we're ten minutes early, so technically the meeting hasn't started yet. This is snack time."

"Yeah," says Winston around a bite of apple. "This is snack time. We work hard for snack time."

I sigh. "Do you know where he is?"

"Who? Warner?" Kenji crunches. Shrugs. "Probably thinking up the best way to kill you without J finding out."

"How's she doing, by the way?" I sink back in my seat. "I haven't seen her yet."

"She's okay. Slight improvement. She wanted to visit you in recovery, but the doctor says she shouldn't be exposed to idiots. They think it might be contagious."

I throw my carrot stick at his head. "Don't be a dick," I say. "I'm genuinely worried about her."

"If you were genuinely worried about her," says Winston, "you wouldn't have disappeared like that. We were planning your memorial."

"How many times do I have to say I'm sorry? *I'm sorry.* I'm really sorry. I've apologized a million times."

"You weren't here," says Kenji. "You don't know what it was like. Even when we got the call to come get you yesterday, people had a hard time. People were really overwhelmed. People cried."

"You cried," says Winston. "I didn't cry."

"I said *people* cried—"

"Hey, have you seen Warner yet?" Adam asks, turning to face me.

"Yeah." I tense a little at the memory. "Only for a second, though. He came to see me in recovery."

"Did he say anything?" Adam asks.

"No. He just stared at me from the doorway."

Adam and Winston share a glance.

"What?" I say.

Kenji swallows the last of his carrot, then looks into the empty bag. "Yeah, um, you should know," he says, raising an eyebrow at me. "Warner is *mad* mad. If he actually tried to kill you I wouldn't even blame him. J cried for like twelve hours straight. Inconsolable. That man damn near lost his mind— *Oh,*" he says to Adam, "hey, do you have any more of those gummy bears?"

I drag my hands down my face, exhaling through my nose.

Adam tosses a small package to Kenji, a blur of color arcing across the room. Kenji catches it easily, turning the packet over in his hands before ripping it open.

The rustling plastic and synthetic fruit scents instantly transport me to another moment. Heightened feeling snakes through my body, thrills of fear and excitement. I realize then that I'll never be able to look at gummy bears without remembering Rosabelle.

"Does anyone know if she's awake yet?" I ask.

"Who? Gigi? She's five, bro, she doesn't really nap anymore—"

"Not Gigi," I say, fighting a wave of irritation. "Rosabelle."

"Oh. Yeah." Winston nods. He's still working on his bag of apple slices. "I mean, I don't know about *awake*, exactly, but she's been stable for a few hours. Consciousness comes and goes."

"A few hours?" I stiffen. "A few hours and no one thought to tell me?"

Adam laughs. "I don't think people are going to tell you much of anything anymore. Warner's already removed a bunch of your security clearances. She's officially no longer your concern."

"Are you fucking kidding me?"

"*Hey,*" says Kenji, pointing a gummy bear at my face. "Language. You know Grandpa Winston is a delicate flower. Profanity wilts his petals."

Winston looks up sharply. "Call me grandpa one more time, asshole, I dare you—"

"Can you guys be serious for a second? Please?" I straighten, stressed out. "How the hell is this fair? I actually went to Ark Island and came back alive with intel, and I'm being *punished* for it—"

"James. Look." Kenji shakes more gummy bears into his palm, chooses two red ones, and pops them in his mouth. "I don't think you understand," he says, chewing. "This is, by far, one of the stupidest, most dangerous things you've ever done in your entire life. The fact that you went into the Ark without clearance is bad enough. But you go all the way to Fascist Town and what? You bring home a souvenir?"

"She wasn't part of the original plan—"

"I'm not sure you had an original plan," Winston mutters.

"Ouch," says Adam, laughing.

My jaw tenses. "When she offered to help me get off the island I figured I'd take advantage of her help—and get rid of her as soon as she became inconvenient. I was being smart about it."

Kenji shakes his head. "Nope. She became inconvenient the minute she slit your throat."

"Look." I lean forward, elbows on my knees. "I wasn't sure whether she was, like, legitimately running from The Reestablishment. It's not hard to believe that some people on the island are there against their will, right? They're not allowed to leave without authorization. And there was enough evidence to indicate that she might've been in actual danger. I watched a soldier bash her in the head while they carted her sister off to an asylum—"

"Did you actually see her sister carted off to an asylum?" asks Adam. "Or did she just tell you that's what happened?"

I blow out a breath, choosing not to answer this.

"The Reestablishment is tricky," says Kenji, carefully

choosing another gummy bear. "You don't know what kind of nonsense they might've orchestrated in order to make you believe this girl might be innocent. And I really hate to break it to you, but based on everything you've told us about your time there, it sounds like they laid a trap for you, and you walked right into it. You brought this girl directly into the heart of things here, and we have no idea who she is."

"I was trying to figure that out," I say, pushing my hands through my hair. "She literally collapsed. I thought she might be dying." I sigh. "I didn't heal her. I didn't help her any more than I absolutely had to. I just figured keeping her alive for interrogation might be useful. Don't I get any credit for that? What else was I supposed to do?"

"Could've pushed her into the ocean," Winston says calmly, biting into another apple slice.

Kenji nods at that, then counts on his fingers: "Could've pushed her into the ocean; could've stabbed her in the throat; could've *never accepted help from the enemy in the first place—*"

"I didn't have enough evidence to kill her," I nearly shout. "She wasn't armed; she'd clearly suffered abuse; she might've had a legitimate case for seeking asylum. Besides, what kind of assassin faints in the middle of a mission?"

"A smart one," says Kenji, grabbing the backpack. He starts searching through it. "Why are there so many wet wipes in here? Where are those little crackers that look like fish?"

"At least he came home," Adam says, coming to my

defense. ("Check the side pocket," he says to Kenji.) "No one's ever gone into the Ark and come home, right? That's worth something."

"Objection," says Kenji. "That's like if a kid sets the house on fire for fun, burns it to the ground for fun, but manages to get out alive. We're happy the child is alive but we're still angry with the child."

"I am *not* a child," I say darkly.

Kenji turns to look at me. "You are a child. You proved that you were a child when you went on an unauthorized recon mission and came home seeking medical attention for the mercenary who killed you. Seriously. James. *I love you.* I'd die for you. I'd cut off my arm for you right now if you needed it. But what the fuck is wrong with you?"

"Listen, I know I messed up—I realize now that I shouldn't have brought her back here—it's just—I don't know, there's something different about her. I really think there's something different about her and if you give me some time to figure it out, I think she could be a really important resource for us—"

Kenji rolls his eyes so hard it's practically a sentence.

"What?" I demand. "Why is that so hard to believe?"

"No, you're right," says Winston, snaking the bag out of Kenji's hands. "We've all seen the girl, and there's definitely something different about her." He meets my eyes. "She's beautiful. Really beautiful. Ethereal, looks-like-a-painting kind of beautiful—"

"That's not what I meant."

"Oh shit," says Winston, reaching into the bag. He beams at Adam. "You got the good juice boxes this time."

"Are there bad juice boxes?" Kenji grabs the bag back from Winston. "I love all juice boxes equally."

"Look—that's not what I meant—"

"Alia did a grocery run yesterday," says Adam, ignoring me. "I told her you like the fruit punch flavor—"

"*Hey,*" I say, frustrated. No one is looking at me. No one is listening to me. God, this is exactly the kind of garbage that pushed me off the edge to begin with.

No one takes me seriously.

"Yes, okay, she's beautiful," I say, admitting this on an exhale. "She's really beautiful. But that's not why I brought her back here. I'm not that stupid—"

"Bro." Kenji pops the straw into his juice box. "Literally no one believes that."

"It's true!"

Kenji shrugs. "Whatever you say, little man." He's smiling now, his eyes alive with barely suppressed laughter. "Either way, Warner is going to *fuck* you up."

"But I didn't—"

Adam glances at his watch. "Hey, I've gotta pick up Roman soon. Do you think he's running late?"

"Warner's never late," the rest of us say together.

Just then, the door opens.

# JAMES

## CHAPTER 19

"What are you three doing here?" Warner takes one step into the room before coming to an abrupt stop.

The sight of him is so familiar it startles me; I haven't really seen him in days, and sometimes I forget how much we look alike. It's like staring into the wrong mirror. Our eyes are different colors and his hair is pure gold where mine is more of a bronzed mess, but there's no mistaking our DNA. When I look at him, I see home.

Currently, the feeling is not mutual.

"What do you mean?" Kenji says to Warner, taking a pull on his straw. "It's snack time. We always use this room for snack time."

"Um, I thought we were *supposed* to be here," says Winston. "Aren't we supposed to be here?"

Warner's exhale is slow and controlled. "No."

"Oh."

"Hey," I say, nodding up at him.

Warner turns to look at me with a cool, inscrutable expression, and suddenly he's not my oldest brother, my mentor, my role model, the guy I've been living with for ten years. Right now Warner embodies every inch of his reputation, and I swear my life flashes before my eyes.

Aaron Warner Anderson is a living legend.

Sometimes I forget how terrifying he can be. His eyes are a surreal pale shade of green, so piercing it's sometimes difficult even to hold eye contact with him.

"Get up," he says quietly.

My eyes widen. "Uh—what?"

"Now," he says. "We're leaving."

"Leaving?" I look around. "But—"

"Yeah, I'm gonna get out of here," says Adam, zipping up the backpack. "See you guys tomorrow?"

Kenji stands to give Adam a hug, clapping him on the back as he pulls away. "Hey, can you bring those fruit rolls tomorrow? The chewy ones with the jokes printed inside the wrapper?"

Adam grins. "Yeah."

Winston shakes his empty juice box. "Kiss the kids for us. I'll swing by around noon tomorrow. Tell Roman we're building robots this weekend."

"Will do," says Adam, still smiling. "He'll be thrilled." He nods at Warner, then tosses him something. "As promised."

Warner catches the offering, then looks up. "Thank you," he says quietly.

"Hey, I didn't know you liked jelly beans," Kenji says, peering over his shoulder. "You've been holding out on us. You should join us for snack time—"

"They're for my wife," Warner says sharply.

"What? You have a *wife*?" Kenji throws his arm around Warner and squeezes. "You're *married*? Congrats, man. I had no idea. You literally never mention it."

"Shut up." Warner shoves away from Kenji, who only looks delighted to have pissed him off. Then, out of nowhere, Kenji chucks his empty juice box at my head.

"Ow, what the hell—"

*Get up,* he mouths.

I look up to see Warner watching this exchange, studying me impassively as he pockets the candy. He tugs up his shirtsleeves, then crosses his arms.

He's wearing lavender.

He's the only guy I know who can wear a lavender crewneck and still be terrifying.

"So, we'll see you guys for dinner next week?" Adam glances at Warner as he heads toward the door. "Alia was hoping to check in on Juliette."

Warner nods. "She'd love that. James is cooking."

"What?" I go rigid. "I didn't agree to cook."

*"Oh."* Adam snaps his fingers, turning his attention to me. "You should know," he says, "Roman isn't eating broccoli or rice or melted cheese anymore. He'll eat pasta, though."

"Then he's going to starve," I say. "All I know how to cook are chicken breasts and protein shakes. Eggs. Maybe a hamburger."

"You don't cook protein shakes," Winston says.

I nod at him. "Thank you for proving my point."

"I'll make him pasta," Warner offers. "He likes it with red sauce, doesn't he?"

Adam shakes his head, hefting the backpack over his

shoulder. "Not anymore. Only cheese sauce."

Warner frowns. "I thought he wasn't eating melted cheese."

"On bread or vegetables. He's okay with cheese in pasta," Adam explains. "But only if it's white cheese. He won't touch it if it's yellow."

"What is happening to your kids, man?" Kenji says, stunned. "When I was growing up it was a choice between food or no food. And I always chose food."

"Gigi will eat anything," he says, shrugging. "Roman gets in his head about it."

Warner's frown deepens. "I think I need to have a talk with Roman. But first I need to have a talk with a different child." To me, he says, "Get up."

*"I'm not a child,"* I practically shout.

"You're right. Most children learn to stand by the age of one. How old are you?"

Reluctantly, I get to my feet. "All right, fine, I'm up." I hold out my arms. "Where are we going?"

"Jesus, the balls on this kid," mutters Winston. "I'd have pissed my pants by now."

Warner holds my eyes a beat longer, exhales audibly, then leaves the room.

*Just leaves the room.*

"Hey," I call after him. "Where are we going?"

The door snicks shut.

"You better chase him down," Kenji says, gathering up his snack wrappers.

"What the hell is going on?" I demand, looking around. "Where is he trying to take me?"

"Somewhere they won't find the body," says Winston.

Adam laughs.

"C'mon, how can you think this is funny?"

"I don't know," says Adam, glancing at his watch. "I kind of hope he does kick your ass. You have no idea what you put us through these last few days."

Sighing, I squeeze my eyes shut.

I thought the gentle mocking and constant babying was bad before I left for the Ark. I thought, at minimum, coming home alive would inspire some respect, if not outright admiration for surviving the unsurvivable. Instead, it looks like I've made things worse.

They're never going to let me live this down.

When I finally catch up to Warner in the hall, he doesn't stop moving. He doesn't even slow down.

He only glances at me and says, "Idiot."

"I'm sorry— Look—"

"You will apologize."

"I did apologize," I say, matching his stride. "I am apologizing. I've apologized to everyone—"

"You will apologize to Juliette. You will do it today. You will sit with her for as long as she likes, and you will *not* tell her stories about being exploded out of a tree or having your organs harvested. You will never do this to her again." He stops suddenly, turns to face me. "Do you understand me? You will never, ever do something this stupid again or I swear to you, James, you will live to regret it."

I turn my eyes to my boots, the polished concrete floors underfoot. In that moment, I feel more guilt than fear. I know what his anger is really about. I know how much he loves me even if he's only admitted it once, by omission, when Juliette was trying to mediate an argument between us and said, *All right, that's enough—you two love each other,* and Warner didn't correct her.

The man practically raised me.

I love Adam to death, but when we overthrew The Reestablishment and he decided he wanted to live a quiet, normal life—I went directly to Warner. At the time he was the brother I barely knew, the one I'd just met.

I asked him to take me in.

At eleven years old I didn't even understand the breadth of what I was asking; I just knew I didn't want a quiet, normal life. I'd only just discovered I had healing powers; I'd only just discovered my family heritage; and there was more I wanted to learn, more I wanted to become. I knew I couldn't achieve my goals with Adam, because even then I understood the difference between my brothers.

Adam wanted peace. Warner wanted justice.

But I'd realized at a young age that you can't have peace without securing justice; and when you're living under tyranny you can't secure justice without violence. I didn't want to live a passive life. Besides, I wasn't blind. I saw the way the world looked at Warner: with the kind of awe and fear and respect I'd always dreamed of. He'd worked hard for that kind of power, living a terrifying and propulsive life that made me think he was invincible.

I wanted to *be* him.

Warner and Juliette took me into their home without hesitation. They were newlyweds deep in the chaos of a post-revolution era, trying to reshape a disfigured world, but they never made me feel like a burden. Growing up, Adam was too busy fighting for our lives to be around for my childhood; I spent most of my time alone, fending for myself, living a semi-orphaned existence. By contrast, Warner rarely let me out of his sight. He tucked me under his wing, teaching me and training me. Rebuilding me. And by virtue of living in his home I've seen glimpses of him most people wouldn't believe possible. Softer versions of him; laughing versions of him. Loving versions of him.

Right now, all of that is gone. Right now, he's an invulnerable shield. A wall of ice.

*He's upset.*

"So, uh, how's she doing?" I ask the floor. "Are the doctors still worried?"

I hear him sigh. He shifts, his boots turning away from me. "She's better," he says quietly. "Now that you're home."

"I'll go to her now," I say, looking up. "I'll head to the house right now—"

"You'll go," he says darkly, "when I'm done with you."

I open my mouth. Close it. Try again. "What does that mean?"

He starts walking. "It means we still have a lot to do before the day is over."

"Wait—what's happening?" I chase after him, my footsteps echoing down the polished concrete corridor. "Where are we going?"

"Take a wild guess," he says dryly.

"Why won't you just answer my question?"

"Why do you ask so many questions?" he counters.

"For *clarity*," I say. "Why else would I ask questions?"

"Your entitlement is exhausting."

"Entitled? You think I'm entitled for wanting to know what we're doing before we're doing it?"

"Yes."

"That's crazy—"

"Juliette spoiled you."

"*You* spoiled me," I shoot back.

"Shut up."

Now I'm smiling, falling into easy step beside him. I glance at Warner out of the corner of my eye, wondering whether he'll berate me any more than this, but he doesn't. Weird. One time, as a kid, I dropped a rack of weights on my arm, snapping it in two places, and his angry (panicked) tirade lasted an hour. This speech lasted only a few minutes.

And then it hits me:

"You're not even that mad, are you?" I say, my spirits lifting. "You're actually a little bit impressed with me, aren't you?"

Warner doesn't look at me.

"You are, aren't you?" Now I'm excited. Tension loosens my shoulders. My smile widens. "You think I'm amazing. You think I'm a genius for making it back alive—"

"I think you're an idiot," he says sharply. He comes to a stop behind a closed door, flashing me a warning look. "You think coming back alive is something to be proud of? You think death is the worst thing that can happen to you? Dying is easy. Enduring your own pain is a mercy. Hell is when you're forced to stay alive, looking on as your enemies take away someone you love—*torture* someone you love—while you're helpless to save them. Sometimes we pray for death, James. Sometimes making it out alive is worse than death."

This kills the smile on my face immediately.

"But this," Warner says, subdued as he reaches into his pocket, "is perhaps an interesting result of your time spent on the island."

He holds up the little blue chip I ripped out of the squirrel. No longer bloody. He's clearly been examining it.

I manage a tentative smile. "So . . . I did okay?"

"You hand-delivered a mercenary of The Reestablishment directly into the epicenter of the resistance, granting her access to every high-profile leader of the opposition. You brought her here without forethought, without even checking her for concealed weapons—"

"I did, actually," I say in a rush. "I did search her—"

"Did you search inside her *head*?" he asks, cutting me off. "Did you peel back her skin to scan for surveillance tech, trackers, subtle explosives—"

"Shit. No." I take a tight breath. "No. I didn't do that."

Warner touches a hand to the door and it scans his data, unsealing a moment later with a sigh. He pulls it open, and I follow him inside the dark room, lights pinging on as we enter the narrow hall. I've never been in here before. An interior vestibule opens up to a larger room, sparsely furnished, its only distinguishing characteristic the massive window taking up one wall. I do a double take.

On the other side is Rosabelle, lying in a hospital bed.

The sight of her stops me in my tracks.

# JAMES

## CHAPTER 20

I haven't seen Rosabelle in thirty-six hours.

When she collapsed on the chopper I caught her on impulse, pulling her into my arms so she wouldn't tumble out the open door. The seat belts—and a bunch of other features—had malfunctioned after I stole the trike from Jeff, which meant I had to hold Rosabelle against my chest for the remainder of the thirty-minute flight. She was so small and distressingly lightweight that it was almost too easy to gather her in my arms, her cheek pressed against my neck. I checked the wound above her eye, and her skin was like silk, so soft.

For half an hour I'd held her tight with my good arm, navigating the aircraft with my bad arm. When I finally managed to land the chopper, I had to carry her through dense forest and steep terrain. By the time I reached the nearest town, I was so wiped I nearly fell to my knees, holding Rosabelle up like an offering.

Even now, remembering this, my heart begins an unsteady beat. Holding her had felt natural and easy, as if I'd done it a hundred times. I couldn't understand my reaction to her then, and I don't understand my reaction to her now. All I know is that the instinct to protect her comes so naturally to me that I have to actively work to shut it off.

Hell, I couldn't even help reaching for her when she was about to kill me.

I swallow, staring at her through the window.

This is bad. This is really bad. Blood is actively rushing to my head now, making me stupider. I can still feel her under my hands. The scent of her still lives in my head.

"Are you done?" Warner asks grimly, plucking a glowing tablet off the wall. "Or do you need more time alone with your delusions?"

This clears my thoughts in an instant.

I look at him, mortification radiating a slow heat up my neck. Warner has the supernatural ability to sense people's emotions. This translates in more powerful ways, too—he can steal other people's powers—but most of the time his superstrength is just making life really embarrassing for the rest of us.

"I'm good," I say, forcing a smile.

Warner scans the tablet as he speaks. "As you know, the patient was unconscious upon arrival. She'd sustained a closed head injury resulting in a linear skull fracture and mild orbital swelling, but overall limited damage to the eye itself. She was dehydrated and dangerously malnourished. She had an elevated heart rate despite being unconscious—very unusual—and bruises covering most of her body. The bruises, 247 in total, were the exact same size and shape, leading us to assume they were born simultaneously and caused by the same weapon. No theories yet as to what kind of weapon might've caused them, though the consistency of the injuries points to some kind of standardized torture. Otherwise, we've done several scans for subtle tech and she's come up clean."

He looks at me. I feel him look at me.

But I'm staring at Rosabelle again. *Linear skull fracture. Dehydrated and dangerously malnourished. Bruises covering most of her body. Standardized torture.* I'm having a really bad reaction to this news.

I can feel it: the spike in my pulse, the anger collecting inside of me. I clench and unclench my fists, trying to shake the feeling loose. I don't know this girl. I have no reason to feel anything but hatred for this girl. But I keep hearing her broken, desperate voice in my head—

*Please*

*Tell them to be gentle with her*

*She's just a child*

I know how vicious The Reestablishment can be. I know what they'll do to people, how they'll drive them into the ground, out of their minds.

What the hell did they do to her? *Why?*

With her eyes closed Rosabelle looks unreal, fragile. Her white-blond hair is longer than I expected, released from its practical knot, fanned out beneath her head. Her hands are clasped atop the sheet folded neatly at her waist. Her injuries have been healed, the blood wiped clean from her face. She looks fake, like a porcelain doll. It's hard to believe this is the same girl who murdered me and countless others.

Warner clears his throat, annoyed.

"Obviously, The Reestablishment would've anticipated such scans," he's saying. "They wouldn't have sent her here with evidence of her intentions woven into her DNA. In fact, it's possible they chose her for this mission precisely because she bears no proof of their tech in her body—which I have cause to believe is highly rare among the Ark population. There is, however, a distinct, poorly healed scar on the inside of her right forearm. Considering the medical advancements pioneered by The Reestablishment, this is highly unusual, and perhaps the most interesting thing about her. Either they can't remove this scar for some unfathomable reason, or they *want* her to bear this scar as punishment. Or a reminder."

"A reminder of what?" I ask, tearing my eyes away from Rosabelle. "A punishment for what?"

"That remains to be seen."

My anger only intensifies. "What about the bruises? The malnutrition? You said they were torturing her."

Warner's irritation at this is obvious.

"Very well," he says, slotting the tablet back into its holder. "I suppose we'll do this now." He takes a careful breath before meeting my eyes. "Extinguish your hopes and dreams. There exists no scenario in which her intentions are honorable. Don't be fooled by her appearance. The Reestablishment loves to destroy faces of innocence; they find it perversely satisfying to forge murderers out of the most unassuming figures, especially young women who exhibit both physical and mental promise as children. In fact, it's to their great advantage that she presents as small and delicate," he says, meeting my eyes. "They did the same thing with Juliette."

"But—"

"I'd guess she's about your age, more or less"—Warner glances at her through the window—"which means her formative years were shaped under the imperial era of The Reestablishment. I'd be shocked if she hadn't been trained for this from a tender age. So put it out of your head," he says. "She's no fragile innocent. Neither does she consider you her hero. You did not save her life. She is not running from her captors, and she didn't help you escape the island in hopes of finding a better life—"

"Then why were they starving her? Why did they hurt her sister?"

"James. You already know this."

"Yeah," I say, crossing my arms. Then, quoting Warner, "'With few exceptions, The Reestablishment can generally be relied upon to control people through coercion, blackmail, or torture. Sometimes all three.' But doesn't that just prove my point? She's being tortured. Probably blackmailed."

"Her situation is not uncommon and does nothing to prove she's sympathetic to you or our cause," Warner says. "In fact, if the girl loves her sister, as you seem to believe, that only makes the situation worse."

I raise my eyebrows. "How does that make it worse?"

"She has more to lose," he says, walking up to the

window. "And she's already proven she's willing to kill you to achieve her own ends."

I exhale, surprised by the weight of this blow. I hadn't even realized how high my hopes were until they came crashing down. It's honestly a little embarrassing.

"Yeah," I say quietly. "You're right. Of course you're right. I don't know what I was—"

Something clicks for me then.

My eyes widen in something close to horror. "Holy shit," I breathe. "Did you bring me in here to kill her?"

Warner looks instantly disgusted. "Ten years of living with me—learning from me—and you still resort to profanity. I blame Kent. He raised you to think it was okay to speak like a criminal."

"And Kenji," I point out. "Kenji inspires me on the daily."

Warner's jaw tightens. "You don't have to kill her today," he says, answering my question. "Today, I want you to go in there and talk to her. I'd like to observe your interactions."

"Um." I laugh, but it comes out strangled. "Why?"

"They're using you, James," he says, turning fully to face me. "They've already used you. She's already manipulated you so seamlessly you can't see the strings. You were naive enough to bring her here, and now we have to manage the situation. Rewrite the rules in our favor."

"You really think it's that bad?"

"Yes."

I blow out a breath. "Okay. So you don't want me to interrogate her? You just want me to *talk* to her?"

"She's expecting an interrogation," says Warner. "She's expecting to be handled like a criminal, to be on the defensive." He begins to pace slowly. "If she's a mercenary of The Reestablishment, her threshold for suffering will be high. She's likely been subjected to unspeakable cruelties, the likes of which we'd never implement in our own procedures. Whatever hardship she faces in our custody will be nothing to her. Easy, even.

"What she's not expecting," he says, absently spinning his wedding ring around his finger, "is to be treated with any kind of kindness. She's not expecting anyone to look after her well-being. She's not expecting to be treated with humanity."

"Humanity?" I say with a smile. "You sound like Juliette right now."

He stops to look through the window. "I know you meant that as an insult, so consider yourself lucky I like you enough not to murder you for disrespecting my wife."

This makes me laugh out loud.

Warner holds my gaze a beat, his eyes light with muted humor. Sometimes I think Warner secretly loves having me around, because even though I probably annoy the shit out of him, I'm the only one who isn't afraid of him. No matter what he says, I know he'd never hurt me. He's my big brother, and I genuinely love the guy.

Warner's face changes as I have this thought, emotion flickering across his features before he turns away.

"I often try to think the way Juliette does," he says quietly. "She has a more thoughtful, holistic perspective on the world than I do. And right now, I'm weighing my options. We cannot proceed without a clearly defined plan. And before I decide on the best course of action, I'd like to know what kind of leverage you have over her."

"What makes you think I have any leverage over her?"

"Because she's been saying your name in her dreams."

A shock of pleasure moves through me. Automatic endorphin rush. "What? Really?"

"No."

"Wow, okay, fuck you."

Warner actually smiles.

It's one of his rare grins, dimples appearing and disappearing just to mess with your head. He goes from murderer to boy next door to murderer in two seconds flat. "Look how disappointed you are," he says softly. "How delighted you were when you thought a minion of The Reestablishment, sent here to kill you and your entire family, was having inappropriate dreams about you."

"You know," I say, crossing my arms, "I really, *really* hate that you can sense other people's emotions."

"Don't feel too sorry for yourself." Warner's expression cools. "Imagine managing the unceasing psychic deluge of every person I encounter. You have no idea the emotional excrement I have to sift through every day. Sometimes I can't hear myself think." He turns away. "Living with you while you were going through puberty, for example, was a unique kind of hell. Sometimes I think you're still going through puberty."

I scowl. "I don't like hearing you say the word *puberty*. In fact, I don't think I need to hear you say that word ever again—"

Warner holds up a hand to silence me just as Rosabelle's eyelids flutter.

Her hands twitch.

She blinks her eyes open slowly, studying the room in a squint. I watch as she sorts through disorientation, nearly sitting up in a sudden flare of panic. She appears to sort things out in phases, eventually coming back to herself, settling into her new surroundings. Then she turns her head, still blinking softly, and looks directly at me.

I stiffen.

No, not directly at me. She's looking in this direction, her glazed eyes pulling together, tracking the sweep of window. Trying to solve a riddle. Even now, I realize, she knows she's being watched.

"Don't be fooled," Warner says quietly. "Go in there with your guard up."

"Yeah." I take a breath. "Yeah, okay." I hesitate as something occurs to me. "Hey, has she been given anything to eat yet?"

Warner shifts his weight. "Fluids have been administered intravenously, but she's not eaten anything solid yet, no. Why?"

"I have an idea."

# ROSABELLE

## CHAPTER 21

I might be dreaming.

The problem is, my eyes are open. The problem is, the glare of overhead lighting is unromantic. The problem is that the steady beep of medical monitors winds a tension in me that coils only tighter even though my hair is loose, freed from its knot. The problem is that I am not safe even though my body feels stronger, better in a way I can't qualify. I close my eyes, forcing myself to take a deep, steady breath, but the hallucination intensifies, my senses attacked by the mouthwatering scent of flame-broiled meat; my stomach contracting at the promise of food. The honeyed aromas of sautéed onions and garlic fill my head. I smell mint and basil. Lemon. Pepper. Cheese.

*Delirious.*

I open my eyes.

I can hear my heart beating in my chest; its movements echoed out loud by the kind of machine I haven't seen in years. The equipment in this room is old, except that it looks new. It hadn't occurred to me to consider that they might not possess the same technological advancements here. I frown. Where?

*Not a dream.*

I tell myself that I have arrived in The New Republic.

Phase one complete.

I'd breathe a sigh of relief except that I can't remember landing here. The details recounting my entry into enemy territory do not exist; where there should be memories there is only blankness. I have been at the mercy of the rebels in a state of unconsciousness, and I have no idea how I might've exposed myself or what they might've done to me. I implore my mind to use reason: remain calm. Stay the course. An agent of The Reestablishment has been assigned to contact me within forty-eight hours of my arrival.

I have no idea how long I've been here.

My immediate priority is to find a way out.

"Hey," he says, holding out the glass. "Seriously, it's just water."

I go very still.

James is sitting next to my hospital bed, magically whole. I'd noticed him earlier, but as I hadn't decided yet whether I was dreaming, I hadn't known how to account for him. His presence is so vivid he feels dreamlike, his energy taking up most of the room. There's a weight to him that I like. He seems solid. Unshakable. But without a thick layer of blood and grime obscuring his face, he's much harder to look at, and I struggle to meet his probing stare. He's studying me with a flat, slightly curious expression. He is otherwise unreadable.

*Not a dream.*

He walked in a few minutes ago with only a glance in my

direction, wheeling in a table piled with plates of food the likes of which I haven't seen in years.

He's still holding out the water glass, waiting for me to take it. His eyes are a kaleidoscope of blues; like the sea, at turns tranquil and turbulent. Right now he's unhurried and easy in his body. I have a strange thought: I wish I could gather up his calm and pull it over me, sleep beneath it as if it were a blanket.

"Rosabelle," he says. For the first time, he cracks a smile. "C'mon. I swear it's not poison."

"I don't understand," I whisper.

"Can you sit up a little more?"

"Why?"

"You need to eat," he says. "I brought you food."

"No." I say it like a question.

"Yes," he says emphatically. "Come on. Sit up a little, but don't move too fast."

"I don't understand," I say again.

"What don't you understand?"

"Why are you being kind to me?"

He places the water glass on the tray in front of me, then sits back in his seat, the smile gone. In fact, his face shuts off altogether, and this bothers me more than the offer of food. I sit up without thinking, as if the action will return the smile to his face.

The smile does not return.

"I'm not being kind to you," he says. "This is called being a regular person. I'm not going to let you starve."

I swallow, surprised to find that my throat isn't dry. Pain radiates all throughout my body, hunger clawing at my insides. I stare at the table of food, allowing myself to believe, for the first time, that this might really be happening. I shake my head. I wouldn't even know where to begin.

"You never answered my question, by the way," James says. I look up at the sudden shift in his tone. His shoulders seem tighter, his eyes tenser. "How long has it been since you ate a proper meal?"

My heart thunders in my chest at that question, and when the monitor mirrors this change James looks up at the machine and I panic. I force myself down into nothingness, disconnecting my body from my mind, crushing what's left of me into dust. I need to pull myself together and remain that way. I can't afford any more missteps.

When my heart rate slows I look at him and say, "Three days."

"Three days," he repeats.

I nod, as if this is normal. "I haven't eaten in three days."

His face has gone cold. His voice is hard. "And what did you eat three days ago?"

*Mushrooms.* "I don't understand why this is relevant."

"Look, will you please just drink the water?" he snaps, his composure breaking.

His anger surprises me.

I look at him, then around the room, my eyes flicking over everything in the bright, sterile space. I consider the situation. This is clearly a holding cell refitted with a hospital bed. There's a massive, generic painting of a summer field taking up most of one wall, behind which is likely some kind of observational deck. I have no doubt that I'm being watched by any number of people right now. I don't know how long I've been here, but James's physical recovery points to a lapse in time long enough to accommodate recuperation and cooperation. He's had hours to shower, to eat, to sleep, to restore the healthy glow in his skin. This means he's had time to reconvene with his officials, which means they know what he knows. He hasn't come to visit me without authorization; he came in here with a plan.

This food is not a mercy, I realize with some relief.

It's a test.

I tell myself: A normal, hungry person with no ulterior motives would not be afraid of eating freely offered food.

I reach for the water glass with an unsteady hand, spilling it slightly as I lift it to my lips. I take a sip and close my eyes, savoring it. The water is room temperature, easy to drink, gentle on my throat, but it takes me by surprise to realize that I'm not actually thirsty. I look up at the ancient IV bags and the answer is obvious: they've been giving me intravenous fluids. That's why I feel better. Clearer. Lighter.

I put the glass down.

James pushes a plate of chicken in front of me, the meat already cut into bite-sized pieces, as if I were a child. The sight of it does something to me, threatens to drown me.

"It's probably cold now," he says, apologetic.

As if I would care. I look up at him, trying to keep my

heart rate steady. "You're just going to watch me eat?"

"Yes."

This is a kind of torture I did not anticipate. Everything about this moment feels charged and strange, and fear clenches in my gut. My hunger is something I can only control when I'm starving. Sometimes the starvation is a mercy, stripping out my insides so completely it's easier for me to shut down, remain empty. I have only faded memories of being full. I don't know what my body will do when I feed it, and this unknown scares me.

I pick up the fork with trepidation, aware of the many eyes that must be watching this moment. My hand trembles a little, and I hide this by spearing the meat more forcefully than I'd like, then lifting it to my lips with hesitation. My mouth waters automatically, the savory scents of fat and salt making me ill with longing and guilt.

*Rosa, what does meat taste like?*

My eyes flutter. My chest clenches.

*Rosa, we're having a banquet. You sit there, and I'll sit here, and we'll pretend my bedsheet is the tablecloth, okay?*

*Okay,* I said, taking my seat. *What's on the menu?*

*The chef has prepared us a roast chicken! Do you like chicken, Rosa? I saw a picture of it in a book—*

My stomach churns with self-hatred. Roiling with need and disgust. My hand trembles again.

*Rosa, that's private,* she'd said, frowning as I uncrumpled a piece of scrap paper. I'd found it while stripping her sheets. It was a list, and I'd read the title and the first two line items before handing it back to her, my heart racing.

*Things I Will Eat One Day,* it read.

*chikin*

*candy*

I force myself to stare at the speared chicken on my fork, force myself to part my lips. I inhale through my mouth and worry I'm going to be sick. I feel my stomach pitch and I fight the compulsion, my chest heaving slightly.

"Rosabelle?" he says.

I look up, horrified to realize my eyes are swimming.

*No.*

I am dead inside. I've been dead inside for years.

"Hey—"

*Die,* I tell myself.

*Die.*

I force the piece of chicken into my mouth, force myself to chew it, force myself to taste it.

*What's it like, Rosa? Is it very delicious?*

I hear the monitors from far away, the machines screaming as if through layers of fog. The meat feels strange in my mouth. Foreign. Soft. This is real chicken, I realize. Real meat from an animal, not lab-grown. It has a texture I haven't experienced since childhood. My teeth seem brand-new to me, sharp. The flavors are too bright, too much. I heave, clap a hand over my mouth. Force it down. Spear another piece.

"Hey," he says again, a note of panic in his voice now, "you don't have to eat it—I just thought—"

*Do you think we'll ever get to eat real meat, Rosa?*

*I like the bread they give us and I don't mind the porridge, really, but remember they gave us eggs once, and those came from a chicken, and one time they gave us milk, and that comes from a cow, so maybe—*

I push the next piece into my mouth, knuckling through the nausea. My jaw is tired already, the repetitive motion robotic. My skin is heating and cooling, my hands clammy. A light sweat has broken out across my forehead. Pain wrenches my gut as I swallow.

I spear another piece of chicken.

"*Stop*," he says, prying the fork out of my hand. He sounds different now. Scared. "You don't have to eat it. I'm sorry—"

"I'll eat it," I say. My eyes are hot. Wet. I reach for the chicken with my bare hands, forcing another piece into my mouth. "I'll eat it."

"Rosabelle, stop—"

He grabs my dirty hands, forces me to look at him. Resolve trembles inside of me, shuddering up my throat. My face is damp. My heart is beating outside of my chest.

"I'm sorry," he says desperately. His eyes are wild. "I'm sorry. You don't have to eat it if you don't want to—"

I feel it, the way my body seizes in the silence, and I try, I really do, but I can't control it.

I throw up all over him.

# ROSABELLE

## CHAPTER 22

I turn my hands over, staring at my wrinkled fingers. I've been sitting under the hot water for so long my skin has begun to itch and still I can't bring myself to get out. This is luxury: the thundering white noise, the steam beading along my limbs, the peaceful quiet.

*The peaceful quiet.*

I'd forgotten what it was like to be alone. I'd forgotten what it was like to experience privacy. I keep forgetting that the people here aren't connected to the Nexus. That it's not standard to surveil people everywhere, all the time.

I close my eyes, let the water pelt my face.

My hospital room was swarmed not long after my humiliation, nurses storming inside, barking hazmat protocol at James. They carted him away from me even as he protested. No doubt they'll be checking him for trace amounts of poison or explosives, sending my vomit to a lab just to be sure I didn't do it on purpose.

The thought nearly prompts a bleak smile. The rebels aren't stupid, though they appear to have overestimated me in this case. In the aftermath they handled me as I expected them to, shuffling me into the shower in quick, rough motions, stripping off my hospital gown with cold efficiency.

It's time to pull myself together.

Clara is not dead.

*Clara is not dead.*

I know this with absolute certainty; they wouldn't have killed her when they could use her to manipulate me. The problem is that I keep losing control of my imagination. I keep allowing my thoughts to wander, to wonder how they might be torturing her. But losing my head means making mistakes, which is no doubt the surest way to guarantee her death.

I will compartmentalize.

I will hermetically seal Clara into my heart. I will accept the paradox that in order to save her life I must ignore her suffering. Clara, I will manage.

It's James I don't know how to control.

I don't understand what's wrong with him. I'm tired of trying to make sense of him. He confuses me at every turn, rewarding me with patience and kindness when he should be assigning me a prison cell and a violent inquisition. I'm not practiced in this kind of subtle warfare. He's manipulating me with sophisticated mental disruptions, and the consequences are disturbing. I'm beginning to make positive associations with his name, with the sight of his face. When I think of him, I don't feel fear at all.

It's making me angry.

I realize I've clenched my fists only when they begin to hurt. I look down at my hands, exhaling as I release them. I'm breathing too hard. Emotions are building inside me unbidden; my quietest thoughts are beginning to unspool. I feel it growing, this desperate desire to finally occupy more than a small corner of my own mind. For years I choked myself into silence, and spirals of thought are now unraveling from around my throat, the danger of forbidden words and feelings rising up inside me like a scream—

*I've always hated The Reestablishment.*

I stiffen even as I think it, bracing for the familiar stutter of my heart, the compression of my chest. I press my hands to the hard floors, searching, instinctively, for something. Paranoia swells and retreats within me, fed by fear, starved by logic. They would not risk watching me here, I tell myself. Never before has The Reestablishment successfully delivered a mercenary from the Ark into the nucleus of The New Republic; they would not risk my exposure during this unprecedented mission. My gaze pings around the simple, industrial shower, searching through steam for the familiar strobe of blue light. I remind myself that I'm far from home; that I am alone.

My heart does not slow down.

I remind myself that I hate the rebels, too—and this more acceptable direction of my thoughts calms me.

I take a deep, steadying breath, tasting water.

The truth is, I hate everyone equally.

The founders of The New Republic are responsible for thousands of deaths and indescribable violence, yet they're always quick to condemn The Reestablishment, claiming moral superiority. They promise fantasies of unsustainable freedoms to a populace even while exposing them to the ills of famine, anarchy, ignorance, conflict, and bloodshed—and a climate beyond repair. They challenge the breakthroughs of science and modern technology. They insist that self-governed chaos is preferable to regulated world order.

The Reestablishment is an iron-fisted, immoral authoritarian enterprise, but The New Republic is worse than naive, and for this reason alone they will never prevail.

It still astonishes me that my father pledged his allegiance to a revolution doomed to fail, and in so doing, sentenced the rest of his family to a fate worse than death. I always wanted revenge against the rebels responsible for the destruction of my life and the upheaval of the world—even as I found the actions of my own regime to be worse than despicable. I aligned myself with what I believed to be the lesser of two evils, trusting that no government could be trusted.

And yet—

I draw a finger down the condensation of the tiled wall, marveling that I've just had terrible, treasonous thoughts about The Reestablishment, and no one will be interrogating me next month to find out.

A sound leaves my body, something like a laugh.

I test the muscles in my face, run my tongue along my teeth, touch the pad of my finger to the soft give of my lips. Water runs in rivulets down my heated skin, skimming the dips and curves of my body.

While I'm here, at least, I belong to myself.

"I'm cutting off the water now," calls the nurse. She's been waiting just beyond the shower door all this time. "I'll be here with a towel."

Too soon, it's over. The thunder, the steam.

The quiet.

The heat has turned me bright red, and I stare down at myself in the proceeding moments, a steady *drip drip* battering the tile underfoot. I pull myself up off the floor, my skin embossed by the windowpane design of the tile work. My head is steaming. My stomach, screaming.

The nurse, as promised, is waiting for me.

She does not avert her eyes; in fact, she looks me up and down as if to ascertain that I'm unarmed. I grab the towel and wrap it around myself, and when I finally exit the shower into the cold, concrete bathroom of the holding cell, my hot feet seem to shrink against the icy floors. A chill moves through my body, and I wrap the towel more tightly, hair dripping. I look at the nurse.

She's tall and middle-aged; dark skin, dark eyes; her face angular and interesting. I remind myself that people in The New Republic still have preternatural powers. Even an unassuming nurse might possess a secret strength, capable of killing me with a single motion.

As if sensing my appraisal, she raises an eyebrow. Then she looks intently away from me, and I follow her gaze to a corner, where a neat pile of folded clothing is set atop a small, unmarked box.

"Those are for you," she says, watching me again. "Get

dressed. You're being transferred in ten minutes."

"Transferred?" This information animates me.

Concerns me.

I spent part of my time in the shower trying to sketch out escape options; I knew they'd eventually move me into a proper, high-security prison cell, but I was hoping for time to scan the premises, make a map in my mind. "Transferred where?"

"To a rehabilitation facility."

I'm reaching for the stack of clothing when she says this, and I freeze. I turn slowly to look at the nurse, my instincts sharpening in warning. *Rehabilitation facility* is always code for something worse: asylum; laboratory; a place for experiments and dissections.

"I see," I say, unfreezing as I gather the clothes into my arms. The material is soft against my skin, and I can't help but run my hand along the fabric, my eyes unfocusing as the gears shift in my head.

My incident with James must've been worse than I feared. Escaping a laboratory—or an asylum—will require an entirely different plan. Especially if they intend to drug me.

Still, in some ways, this is a relief.

Torture is not ideal, but at least it's familiar. I can deal with pain. Besides, the rebels are weak-willed; they don't even believe in certain methods of punishment. My mind is working quickly now, running scenarios as I dress myself. I hardly notice that the garments are well-made until they're pressed against my body: a soft blue sweater and a pair of jeans that almost fit.

These aren't prisoner's clothes.

I glance at the nurse, who offers no explanation. She only crosses her arms as I walk over to the vanity. I brush my teeth with the supplies provided, then brush my hair, tying it back, wet, in an unflattering knot. I study my reflection in the small mirror over the sink. I don't like to look at myself. When I look at myself, I see my mother. *Death.* My sister. *Suffering.* My father. *Betrayal.*

My face has cooled from red to pink. My hair almost has color when it's wet. My eyes, I realize, are bright and frightening, feverish.

James called me beautiful.

The memory triggers a dormant feeling inside of me, something elemental I've never encouraged. I watch as a slow blush flares along my skin, melting into the heat receding in my body. I used to be beautiful, I think. Sebastian used to say things like that to me.

My skin goes cold at the reminder.

I did not take his wedding ring with me. I threw it at his face when he came for Clara, the consequences of which I will no doubt face upon returning home.

I kill the thought as I reach for the unmarked box.

Inside I find a small messenger bag; a pair of sturdy tennis shoes; socks; a small bag of mixed nuts; a bottle of water; and a bar of chocolate. The chocolate bar surprises me.

I haven't had chocolate since I was a child.

I decide right then to save it for Clara. When I make it home I will have proven my worth and my loyalty to The Reestablishment, and Clara will have chocolate for the first time. Klaus promised us freedom in exchange for my efforts—and Klaus is not human enough to lie.

Neutralizing my expression, I take an even breath. A plan is forming in my mind, a surge of hope giving me focus.

I gather up the sundry items and place them inside the messenger bag. I sit down on a small bench to put on the socks and shoes, but I struggle a little with the left shoe. The sizing is fine, but there's something like a pebble caught inside the sneaker, just under the insole. I reach inside, pull up the removable sole, and my finger nicks a small, flat disc. It's about the size and weight of a coin.

I stiffen at once.

I sneak a look at the nurse, who's still watching me. An uncanny feeling courses down my spine.

"Hurry up," she says. "I have to escort you out."

I turn back to the shoes, my hands mercifully steady. I peel the metal disc away from the sole. It's smooth and unmarked, polished silver. The nurse is still watching me.

All that time in the shower I thought I was far from the watchful eye of The Reestablishment.

*Mistake.*

"I wonder what time it is," I say, repeating the words I was instructed to speak.

She shifts, considering me, then holds out her hand, where a flare of blue light pulses just inside her forearm.

"It's late," she says. "You nearly missed the window."

This fills me with alarm.

I quickly pinch the bit between my thumb and forefinger and it offers immediate haptic feedback, responding to my fingerprints.

With a final buzz, it unlocks.

The disc spirals open, producing a hologram. It's a perfectly rendered image of a glass vial. The object is about the size of my hand, the liquid inside of it pitch-black. I commit the image to memory just before it disintegrates, the coin vaporizing without warning—so hot it scalds my skin.

Finally, I look up at the agent.

She's studying her arm. The blue light is flashing faster now, counting down. It occurs to me that she was just as anxious as I was to complete this task. If she hadn't delivered the holo-coin within forty-eight hours of my arrival, she'd likely be punished, too.

When the light finally crescendos and dies, she visibly exhales. "Phase two," she says, "is now complete."

I sit with this reveal for a moment, and then, slowly, I begin lacing my sneakers, mentally filing and sorting new information. If phase one was to escape the island with James, and phase two involved receiving the holo-coin, I've just been launched into phase three: acquire the vial.

When she meets my eyes, I shake my head.

"Where do I find it?" I ask.

"I don't answer questions," she says. "The next one will. You have two weeks."

"Two weeks?" I say, stunned. "I don't even know where to begin."

"Pay attention. If you're smart enough, you'll see it coming."

"But—"

"I don't answer questions," she says again, eyes flashing. "The next one will."

She holds the door open for me, and I get to my feet with a cold twist in my gut. This is going to be much harder than I thought, and I never thought it would be easy.

*Pay attention,* she'd said.

I should be worried I won't be able to figure this out in time—that I'll mess things up and ruin my chances of saving Clara—but despite the vagaries, I feel strangely calm. If there's one thing I'm good at, it's paying attention.

Instead, as I sling the messenger bag over my shoulder, I can't help but think of James, who was willing to sacrifice his life to save my sister. Foolish enough to give me a chance to prove him wrong. Naive enough to concern himself with my hunger. I'm relieved to think that I'll probably never see him again. But I wonder whether the rebels have any idea how easily they've been infiltrated.

This fantasy world they've built won't last much longer.

# JAMES

## CHAPTER 23

"I think it's a great idea," says Juliette, smiling at Warner the way she always does. Like he can do no wrong.

"I think it's a stupid idea," I argue. "It's messy and dangerous—"

"You've lost the right to vote," Warner cuts me off. "We're in this situation because of you. The girl has clear vulnerabilities, and we should be utilizing every advantage we have over her. While we're in the discovery phase this is possibly our best course of action for gathering intel—"

"I'm not doing it," I say angrily.

"Why not?" he shoots back.

"Because," I say, pushing my hands through my hair. "Because it's weird. It feels weird."

Kenji laughs. He's eating popcorn. "Bro," he says, shooting me a look. He makes air quotes with one hand. "*It's weird* is not the counterargument you think it is. We've all had to do uncomfortable shit over the years in order to survive. Take Jello over here," he says, throwing a piece of popcorn at Juliette's face.

She swats it away.

"You want to talk about weird? This girl was once mind-controlled by your own dad. She was forced to become his super-soldier—"

"Oh God, don't remind me," I groan. "I hate this story."

"—and she nearly killed all of us just because Daddy Anderson asked her to."

"Jesus." I drag my hands down my face. "Don't call him Daddy."

My brother, I notice, has gone sheet white.

Nothing sends Warner spiraling faster than a reminder of how much Juliette suffered at the hands of our father. As if he's somehow complicit in the sins of the man who tortured him every day of his life. Maybe because I was a kid when it all happened, I can make this distinction.

Warner can't.

Kenji goes on, undeterred. "And if Warner hadn't been able to save J through the power of love"—he mimes a firework with one hand—"we'd all be mind-controlled puppets of The Reestablishment right now."

"Let's not relive all the details," Juliette says, squeezing Kenji's arm. She's looking worryingly at Warner, who's now staring into the abyss of middle distance.

"That was a long time ago," she says gently, "and, actually, it was lucky that I underwent—and survived—the experiment, because otherwise we wouldn't have known the extent of the program. We had no idea they'd already begun connecting civilians to a neural network, and we didn't realize that destroying Operation Synthesis would sever the nervous system of the program." She glances again at my brother. "Warner thinks they've rolled out a new version of the network on the Ark. His theory is that they never abandoned the project."

Then, beaming at me, she adds brightly: "That's why he's so excited about the chip you brought home. He's really proud of you, James. It's a big deal, what you did, despite the way it made us feel. He talks about it all the time."

This last bit is a stroke of genius, and achieves what I realize is her desired effect: Warner is instantly snapped out of his gloom.

"I wouldn't use the word *excited*," he says, shooting me a warning look. "Or *proud*. Or *big deal*. Or *all the time*."

Still, I feel a little like I've been shot with sunshine.

"Wow," I say to him, fighting a smile. "Look at you. You can't even help it. You love me so much it disgusts you. You're disgusted with yourself."

Juliette laughs.

"I'd like to get back to the original topic," Warner says stiffly. "Stop trying to change the subject. We have important things to discuss—"

Kenji ignores this, adding, "Warner loves me, too," around a bite of popcorn. "Sometimes it's a little too much, you know? It's always *Oh my God, Kenji, you're amazing, you're my best friend, don't tell Juliette but I love you the most*—"

"How is it that every time you speak," Warner cuts him off, "you have food in your mouth?"

"Don't exaggerate because you're jealous," says Kenji. "If

you want popcorn, all you have to do is ask."

"I shouldn't have to ask," Warner counters icily. "You're supposed to offer."

"All right, you know what? I can't even take you guys seriously right now," I say. "This isn't a real meeting. This is some kind of sabotaged slumber party—"

"It is by no means a slumber party," Warner says, alarmed.

"And it's not sabotaged," Juliette adds, stifling a yawn. "Kenji and I are going to stay up late and watch old movies. You can join us if you like." She shifts to sit cross-legged on the bed, her long brown hair cascading down her shoulders. She's cradling her enormous baby bump with Kenji propped up beside her, his long legs sprawled out in front of him. They're absolutely surrounded by junk food.

"The hell he can," Kenji mutters. "He talks through all the good parts. And anyway, he needs to go, like, shave and shit. Shower a couple of times. Run around the block and release those pheromones. Get ready for romance."

Warner raises an eyebrow at him. "If that's what you do to get ready for romance, I can see why you're single."

Kenji pauses mid-chew, cocking his head at Warner. "You know what? Not all of us can have some kind of happily ever after the way you did, okay? The rest of us live in the real world, where the loves of our lives don't quite love us enough, and it has nothing to do with how many times we shower. Or maybe it does. She wasn't really clear on that point."

"Kenji," Juliette says softly. "You know it was more complicated than that—"

"I don't want to talk about it," he says. "But, for the record, we, the people, do not appreciate having the past thrown in our faces. Especially not on movie night."

"I didn't mean it like that," Warner says, his voice clipped.

Kenji shrugs. "I've made peace with it. Besides, I'm not alone in my misery." He pops another piece of popcorn in his mouth. "Winston and I both got dumped years ago, and we've been happy being bitter ever since. In fact, we've decided to make ugly collages and use them to decorate our place. He's going to gather up anything with Brendan's handwriting on it and use it to papier-mâché a bunch of toilet rolls. I'm going to bang my head against the wall until it leaves an impression. We figure it's finally time to put up some art in the living room." He crunches some more. "Winston calls it *depressing chic*."

"Is this a joke?" Warner looks at Juliette, then Kenji. "I put up that drywall myself. We repainted those walls just last month—"

"Nazeera didn't dump you," I point out, pulled into this discussion against my will. "You know that. She just couldn't stay here. She has to live on the other side of the world. Her people are there—"

"I know," Kenji says, holding up a hand. "And look, I'm not bitter about it. We had a good run, but we're rebuilding our world. I get it; we all have work to do. She needs to be in

West Asia, and long distance is super hard. But she wanted to reconnect with her roots, her culture, her people. *For an indefinite period of time.* That's called being dumped. That's called *I'm probably going to marry some hot Arab dude and lose your number.* Anyway, I don't want to talk about it anymore."

"Kenji—"

"I said I don't want to talk about it." He says this with finality, and the room falls silent. Then Kenji points at me and says, "Anyway, for what it's worth, I also think Warner's idea is solid. This Rosabelle girl is"—he blows out a breath—"yeah, she's, wow. You should absolutely pretend to best friend the girl who (a) murdered you, and (b) threw up all over you. The results will be adorable."

I'm about to respond to this when Juliette cries out without warning, doubling over as she sucks in a sharp breath. Warner shoots upright, his eyes flaring with panic.

*Shit.*

# JAMES

## CHAPTER 24

"I'm fine," says Juliette, breathing out. Her eyes close as the pain recedes and she waves Warner down, still grimacing. "It's fine. Really. I swear."

There's a collective tension in the room as we all watch her and wait. I study my older brother, the severe lines of his face. He's been terrified for months.

Juliette, like me and Warner, was born into the arms of The Reestablishment; I didn't know who my father was for a long time—Warner and I have different moms—but we're all children of supreme commanders. The major difference was that Juliette's parents were scientists, whereas my dad was strictly military. Juliette's mom was the one who launched the experiment responsible for rewriting human DNA, generating preternatural powers for use as weapons by the regime. My dad was a unique monster, but Juliette's parents were sadistic on a whole different level. They had kids for the sole purpose of experimentation, using their offspring as guinea pigs, building and breaking them down over and over in increasingly inhumane ways. The consequences eventually killed Juliette's sister.

Juliette herself was never meant to bear children.

I fall back into my chair with a sigh. I look up at Warner,

who's standing, unmoving, by the matching chair beside me.

"Are you sure you're okay, love?" he says to his wife, thawing as he approaches her. He sits on the side of the bed, takes her hands. He presses his forehead to her temple, then whispers something in her ear.

Quietly, I hear her say, "The bleeding stopped a few hours ago," and I turn away, not wanting to eavesdrop.

They weren't expecting to get pregnant.

After ten years of marriage and endless tests, they'd accepted that it was practically impossible to reverse the near-sterilization her parents forced on her. The baby was an enormous shock. The entire pregnancy has been fraught. She nearly miscarried three times. At one point we couldn't hear the heartbeat. There've been a lot of dark days.

Juliette calls the whole thing a miracle.

Warner calls it a "fucking nightmare," and he never uses explicit language. Once, when we thought she'd lost the baby, I heard him having a panic attack in the bathroom. Kenji had been with him then, calming him down.

The memory strikes me in the chest.

We like to give each other shit around here, but at the end of the day we'd all die for each other, no questions asked.

"Really, I'm fine," I hear Juliette say, and I glance up to catch her forcing a smile, her hand still caught under her belly. "I just hate that I can't get out of bed."

"Just a few more weeks," Kenji says, his own eyes sobered. "You got this, J."

"We can have as many meetings in here as you like,"

I add a little eagerly. "And I'll make sure to come by more often."

"Really?" Her eyes brighten. "I'd like to hear all the Rosabelle stories—"

"No," Warner says sharply. "Nothing upsetting."

She only looks at him, her smile blossoming into something so openly adoring I have to look away. "I'll be all right," she says softly. "You don't have to worry so much."

"That's like telling water not to be wet," Kenji mutters, crunching popcorn again. "This man lives to worry about you. It's his favorite thing to do. Between worrying about you and talking about you and frolicking through fields aggressively shouting your name at wildlife, I'm surprised the man has any time left to fuck with the world."

"Hey, don't make fun of my husband," Juliette says playfully, and pinches him. "He works hard."

Kenji yelps. Popcorn forgotten, he turns to look at her with wide eyes. "Did you just, like, zap me with your killing power?"

She laughs. "Only a little bit."

"Only a little bit?" His eyes go wider. "J, you can literally murder people with *only a little bit*—"

"She can murder whoever she wants," Warner says flatly. "Don't stifle her."

Kenji's jaw drops open. "You two are disgusting. This whole situation is disgusting. I hate everyone in this room."

"Except for me," I point out.

"Except for you," he says, nodding. He hesitates, then

frowns. "Wait, no, I'm still mad at you."

"I thought we forgave him," says Juliette.

"No, we haven't," says Warner, crossing his arms. He turns fully to face me. "And we're not done with this discussion."

I sigh, slumping deeper into my chair.

"At first I thought cutting you off from the girl was the right course of action," says Warner, "but it's clear to me now that you need to finish what you started. She's exhibited enough vulnerability—enough instability—in her interactions with you to prove she's human, and that makes her weak."

"Write that down," Kenji says. "Remember this moment. Hell, make it the title of your memoir: *Being Human Makes You Weak*, by Aaron Warner Anderson."

Juliette fights a smile, but Warner ignores this. He's still looking at me when he says, "If the girl has one weakness, she has others. It's your job to find them."

"She's not going to do it!" I shout, throwing up my hands. "Rosabelle the serial killer is not going to participate in a therapy program. Can you imagine her opening up? Talking about how The Reestablishment hurt her feelings? The steps she's taking to be a more mindful individual?"

Warner's mouth is a grim line. "No one is expecting her to actually participate. This is nothing more than an opportunity for you to have regular access to her in a controlled environment. If we want her to believe that we've accepted her bid for asylum, we need to establish an equally believable transition into our world. It's what we do with all theoretically reformed members of The Reestablishment. By the end of the program, we've compiled a thorough dossier on each member, all of which informs next steps."

"How long?" I ask. "How long would I have to do this?"

"The rehabilitation program takes about eight weeks altogether. As her sponsor, you would spend most days with her, and you would oversee all her progress, convening with her doctors and so on. You'll report everything, of course, directly to me."

"It might be useless," I say. "We might not get anything out of her."

"It's a risk," Warner acknowledges. "Regardless, it's a psychological move to buy us time. We want to wear her down. Give her the illusion of freedom. Allow The Reestablishment to believe we're stupid enough to have taken the bait, and that she's still on course to complete the mission she's been assigned. While you're with her, you'll have the opportunity to coax information out of her with plausible deniability; she'll find herself forced to play along in order to placate you, which means she'll have to give up some truths in order to survive. Glean what you can about who she is. Right now, you don't even know her last name."

I make a sound of disbelief. "How am I supposed to know her last name?"

"You claim to have possessed her alleged wedding invitation—"

"Oh."

"—and instead of keeping it as evidence, or, at minimum, memorizing its details, you decided to toss it into a fire."

"Okay, wait a second, that's not fair—"

Kenji lets out a low whistle, shaking his head at me in something like amazement. "You're really lowering the bar for the rest of us, man. I appreciate it." He glances surreptitiously at Warner. "Now maybe someone will finally cut me some slack for failing to file a report on time."

"You filed the report *incorrectly,*" Warner says, turning sharply to Kenji. "And the oversight cost us three months of chaos—"

"Come on," Kenji groans. "You've got to let this go. That was two years ago—"

"Look," I say desperately. "I didn't think Rosabelle would end up being so important. I didn't think I'd ever see her again, and at the time I was a little distracted by what I thought were much bigger issues—"

"I don't care." Warner returns his eyes to me. "You're going to make up for it. I want to know her family history. I want to know what she's capable of. I want to know about those bruises on her body and the scar inside her wrist. I want to know more about her sister. And obviously I want to know what she's really doing here. We're trying to slow down their plans, James. What we need is time. Time, and enough information to prepare a counterattack."

"Fine," I sigh, crossing my arms. "I hate it, but fine. When do I have to start?"

"Tomorrow," Kenji says, throwing a piece of popcorn at my head. "Obviously."

Warner nods. "Ten a.m."

"Fine," I say again.

"One last thing, James."

I glare at the ceiling. "What?"

"You are not to put a hand on her unless it's to kill her. Do you understand?"

My head snaps forward. "Excuse me?"

"You heard what I said. Don't touch her. Ever. Not unless it's absolutely necessary."

Juliette and Kenji are looking at me with renewed interest, exchanging glances.

"Oh shit, *twist*," Kenji whispers loudly.

He rips open a familiar bag of jelly beans, offers the bag to Juliette, and then dumps a fistful of beans into his own mouth. Chewing, he says, "This might be better than movie night."

My jaw clenches. "What makes you think I'm going to touch her?"

"I don't think you have plans to," Warner says. "I'm only advising you not to do it when, inevitably, you want to."

"I just gasped," says Kenji, not gasping.

"Me too," says Juliette, also not gasping.

"This is genuinely insulting," I say to Warner. "You think I don't know how to handle myself? I'm twenty-one years old. You were two years younger than me when you led a fucking revolution—"

"Language!" Kenji says gleefully, grinning as he rips open a bag of potato chips.

"—and everyone around here still treats me like I'm a child. I'm *not* a child. Maybe you didn't notice, but I grew up a long time ago. Maybe it's time you stopped treating me like I don't know how to wipe my own ass—"

"You didn't grow up the way we did," Warner says, deathly calm. "Your generation has been coddled. Untested. You didn't have to grow up as fast as we did—"

"Shouldn't have said that," Kenji says under his breath.

"Are you joking?" I'm on my feet now. Livid. "I was six years old when I watched my friends get dragged into back alleys to have their organs ripped out. You know what'll fuck you up? Watching adults terrorize children over and over again. You think I didn't grow up as fast as you did? Who do you think buried the bodies? You think anyone cared to organize funerals for street kids? I was seven the first time I fired a gun. *Seven* the first time I killed someone. You have no idea what kind of shit I've seen—"

"Aaaand he shouldn't have said that," Kenji mutters.

"Would you like an award for your troubles?" Warner says, rounding on me. "You think you're the only one who had to watch people die? You think you're the only one tainted by misery? What you've suffered is tragic, but it doesn't come close to the levels of darkness we've had to endure—"

"Sweetheart," Juliette says softly, and Warner immediately stills, his body tensing. "This isn't the kind of competition any of us wants to win."

Warner lowers his head, steadies his breath. "You're going to be on your own," he says, turning to face the wall. "You'll be alone with her for long stretches of time. Only occasional surveillance, as promised. I need to be able to trust you."

"Of course you can trust me," I say angrily. "What kind of a bullshit thing is that to say?"

"James," he says, a warning in his voice. "Don't insult my intelligence."

"She's, like, *really, really* beautiful," Kenji explains to Juliette in an undertone. He shoves some chips into his mouth. "James is very into her"—he crunches—"even though she killed him, and later threw up on him."

Now Juliette does gasp. "Do I get to meet her?"

*"No,"* everyone shouts at the same time.

Juliette shrinks back, surprised.

"I'm sorry," Warner says instantly. He blanches. "Forgive me, love. I didn't mean to shout at you."

She softens, beaming at him like he's some kind of baby animal. Sometimes I think she sees Warner in a way literally no one else does. She seems to think he has no thorns at all.

"Okay, for real, though." Kenji turns to look at her. "Why would we introduce you to the mercenary who definitely wants to kill you? None of us are going to meet her. She gets no access to any of us. That's part of the reason why we decided Genius over here"—he nods at me—"needs to be the one to handle this mess."

I exhale angrily. "Can we wrap this up, please? And for clarity, I am not *into* her, and I am fully capable of doing my job. Just because I think she might be a complex human being doesn't mean I'm into her."

Warner shoots me a look.

"What?" I say. "I'm not."

"Good," he says darkly. "Then this won't be a problem for you at all."

# JAMES

## CHAPTER 25

I'm breathing hard when I hit the button for the elevator, sweat slick down my chest, my shirt sticking to skin. I take a pull on my water bottle and mop my face with a towel. I'm still catching my breath. The gym is never quieter than it is before dawn—though you never can tell when you're down here. Our HQ was constructed entirely underground.

The idea was heavily inspired by Omega Point, obviously. Point was the first underground headquarters, and Castle, the now-retired leader of the original resistance group, helped us transform his vision into a modern masterpiece. It took several years to meticulously build it out, but as far as I'm concerned, this is Winston and Alia's greatest accomplishment. It's like a small city down here, heavily fortified, extremely secure. Bonus: it has state-of-the-art fitness facilities, and they're almost always empty. No one seems as excited about hitting the gym as me and Warner.

I tap the button again, sweat snaking down my collarbone.

Warner started training me not long after I moved in with him, and I loved it immediately. Something about the constant dopamine hits changed my brain chemistry. Usually he's here to make me feel bad about my reps, but he wasn't around this morning. It makes me wonder if everything is okay with Juliette.

The elevator finally dings, and I step inside.

I have to place my hand on the scanner in order to access my floor, but otherwise I make an effort not to lean on anything as the carriage ascends, containing my sweaty self until I can get in the shower. I glance at my watch, reminded in yet another small moment, of my brief stint on the Ark. They took all my things—including the watch off my wrist—and that one cost me a lot. The one I'm wearing now is less suitable for the gym and much simpler overall: traditional hour and minute hands, single complication, no tech. Not even a battery. You have to wear it so that it winds itself, otherwise the clock stops.

I like it. I like not being tethered, constantly, to the mainframe.

I watch the floors tick by on the monitor.

The Reestablishment was so obsessed with the future—so obsessed with constantly advancing technology in terrifying ways—that I think it gave our generation a complex. After the revolution, we established and subsidized programs to encourage people to learn practical trades. It was Warner's idea. He argued that we had to relearn self-sufficiency as a nation; bring back manufacturing and innovation so that we'd never be so reliant on technology that we'd abandon the building blocks of life. A lot of the kids I used to know are real, bona fide farmers now.

We're still pretty high tech, though.

The elevator stops at a lower floor, the open doors illuminating a gleaming, sparking laboratory just beyond, where people in technical coats are already bustling across the floor. An older man gets on the elevator, his long black dreads reminding me of a younger Castle. I've seen this guy several times around here, especially during my early morning gym sessions. His name tag reads: *Jeff.*

I shake my head, fighting a private laugh as I say good morning. There's an overabundance of Jeffs in my life.

Jeff gets off on yet another floor—the engineering lab.

Once he's gone the elevator slows down, requiring fresh verification. I place my sweaty hand on the biometric scanner again, and then, as we climb even higher, my retinas are scanned before I've cleared security altogether. After that we ascend quickly; so fast, in fact, that I'm a little nauseous by the time we come to a halt at the top floor.

The doors ping, opening directly into our living room.

"Hey," I say, lifting a hand. I step out of the sleek, modern elevator and onto the hardwood floor of our modest, old-world home. Shafts of morning light reach through the windows, illuminating the rooms in the rising dawn. Golden rays gild the edges of fixtures and furniture. A squirrel swishes its tail from the branch of the huge live oak tree in the front yard, beyond which the sounds of life awaken in the street. There's the distant murmur of voices; the whoosh of a passing car. The birds are loud.

Warner, of course, is quiet.

He's fully dressed at seven in the morning, sitting at the

breakfast table in black slacks and a gray knit sweater, composed even at rest. I thought he was impressive at twenty; at thirty years old he radiates the kind of quiet, effortless power I find aspirational. Even now he looks anointed, his golden hair suffused with fresh sunlight. I know without a doubt that he's been up since five. Maybe earlier. I see him straight across our small, open-plan house, drinking a cup of coffee. I can smell it from here: black, very black. No cream, no sugar.

Just battery acid.

I kick off my sneakers, placing them on the designated shoe rack before padding toward the kitchen in my socks.

Warner puts down his cup, then the tablet he'd been reading. As I approach, I catch sight of the massive stack of files beside him.

"You should shower," he says by way of hello.

"No shit," I say, dropping my gym bag on the kitchen floor. I place my water bottle by the sink and start prepping a protein shake. "Why weren't you in the gym this morning?"

"Juliette needed me."

I freeze, my hand on the cabinet door. "She okay?"

"She's okay," he says quietly, picking up his coffee cup.

"You want to talk about it?"

He hesitates, the mug inches from his mouth, and just looks at me.

"No, that's cool," I say, grinning as I mix the shake. "You want to write it all down in your diary later. I get it."

He puts down the mug. "Rosabelle was asking questions about you yesterday."

This hits me, *pow,* right in the sternum. I actually need a minute. Finally, I say, "Asking about me how?"

"She asked the girls if you had the same powers. She wanted to know whether you could heal other people in addition to yourself."

I consider this a moment, then narrow my eyes when I say, "Did she really ask about me? Or are you just messing with me again?"

"Not this time," he says, sitting back in his chair.

*The girls* is an affectionate shorthand for Sonya and Sara, the twin healers who oversee our HQ's medical facilities. These days they spend most of their time researching and developing curative technologies, but they started out with Castle years and years ago at Omega Point. I studied under their guidance for a long time; they're the ones who taught me exactly how to use my power.

"What was she doing with the girls?" I ask, leaning against the kitchen counter.

"They always oversee the physicals for high-profile transfers." He says this with a hint of impatience, like I should already know this. "Especially those who've entered with injuries."

"Right," I say, remembering that I did know this. I turn to stare out the window. A finch jumps up onto the sill and studies me, and I'm reminded of robot-birds. "I'm assuming the girls didn't answer her questions."

Warner takes a sip of his coffee, watching me. My heart, traitorous asshole, kicks into high gear. The back of my neck prickles. Damn. It's a good thing I'm already sweaty.

Honestly, I've been trying not to think about Rosabelle.

Every time I look at my watch I'm trying not to think about Rosabelle. I've been trying not to replay the horrors of yesterday's fiasco on a loop, trying not to remember how I managed to make a serial killer cry by feeding her lunch. I broke her, and I don't even know how I did it. It makes me sick to my stomach.

I know she's technically a horrible person. I know this. I've got the scar on my neck to prove it. But no one breaks down crying trying to eat a piece of chicken unless they're carrying serious pain. And the fact that I'm going to be alone with her day after day, forced to mine her for information—to break her again—in pursuit of her deepest, darkest secrets, makes me feel even shittier. And then, of course, I feel shitty for feeling shitty, because at the end of the day it doesn't matter how much she cries. I'm going to do what's best for my family, for my people.

Fuck The Reestablishment.

"Good," says Warner, picking up his coffee cup again. "Just checking."

"*Hey,*" I say, stunned. "Don't eavesdrop on my feelings."

"You smell," he says, tapping his tablet back to life.

I ignore this and peer over his shoulder. I catch a glimpse of a header that reads *Sector 52, A Brief History* before he turns the tablet face down.

"So what's all this?" I ask, nodding to the stack of files beside him. "What are you researching?"

He doesn't even lift his head when he says, "You haven't earned the right to know."

"What's that supposed to mean?" I frown. "Wait—are you doing Rosabelle recon?"

"Obviously." He takes another sip of his coffee.

"And you're not going to loop me in?"

"You don't have the necessary security clearance. Now leave me alone."

"Are you joking?" I go slack. "This is a joke, right? You put me back on her case—I'm supposed to head over to the rehab facility in a few hours—and you're not even going to prep me?"

Now he looks up, confused. "I left two binders on your desk last night."

"Oh," I say, hesitating. "I thought that was, like, optional reading."

Warner closes his eyes on a controlled sigh, and when he opens his eyes again he looks mutinous. "You didn't read any of it?"

This is my cue to leave.

I can feel a lecture brewing the way some people can smell rain in the air. "I'm, um— Actually, I was going to go read it right now."

He shakes his head at me, jaw tensing, then picks up his tablet. "You want me to stop treating you like a child?" he says. "Stop acting like a child."

"Thanks, big bro," I say, backing out of the room. "I appreciate the advice. I love you, too."

"Pick up your gym bag. You're not an animal."

I swipe the bag off the ground as I leave the kitchen, pointing my protein shake at him. "I'm so glad we had this heart-to-heart. I'm feeling good about today, too. Loving life. Pumped."

"Don't forget to shave," he says, eyes fixed on the screen. "And do a clean job this time. Use the straight razor like I showed you."

"Do you have nothing positive to say to me?" I ask, heading for the hall. "Maybe a little encouragement? Maybe something about how great I am, how talented I am, how I'm such a pleasure to have in class—"

"Don't mess this up today."

"What's that?" I cup my hand to my ear. "You think I'm more handsome than you? Smarter than you? Taller than you?"

Warner sits up in his chair, his eyes flashing.

"You're right," I say, darting up the stairs. "I crossed a line. Won't happen again—"

# ROSABELLE

## CHAPTER 26

"No," I say.

"Okay. Well, we're about to conclude our morning session, and so far you've shared only your first name with the group. What about your full name? Do you feel ready to share your full name? First, middle, last?"

"No."

"What about your age? Would you feel comfortable helping us understand how long you've been struggling?"

"No."

"I see. Rosabelle, do you have any *I statements* you'd like to share before we wrap up? How about an *I feel*? Can you complete that sentence? How are you feeling today?"

Heat coils inside my chest, brazing my lungs together, unfurling up my throat. This is worse than a high-security prison cell. Worse than physical torture. I'd prefer solitary confinement to this—this—therapy circle—

"That's all right, you don't have to share anything today if you're not ready," says the group leader, a wiry man who introduced himself to me as "Ian Sanchez, I don't perform miracles, we've got a lot of work to do."

I close my eyes, unclench my fists, exhale steadily.

"It took me a long time to open up, too," he's saying now.

“We’re in no hurry to force healing.” He keeps saying that. *We’re in no hurry to force healing.*

Inside, I scream for a full three seconds.

I imagine exploding out of my body, running straight for the wall and then straight through it. I haven’t decided yet whether this is an elaborate set piece, whether I’m a pawn being moved across a chessboard. If the rebels have done this to me on purpose, I have no choice but to acknowledge their skill. If, however—

A hand goes up in the group.

Ian nods at the large man in the small chair. “Jing. Yes. Did you have something you wanted to share this morning?”

“The Reestablishment killed my family.”

A murmur goes through the group, people nodding. Ian nods, too, as if this is brand-new information. “You’ve shared that with us before, Jing. Are you ready to talk about what happened?”

Jing shakes his head.

Jing is a liar. Jing claimed he was a soldier serving under the chief commander and regent of Sector 18. He’s claimed twice now that The Reestablishment murdered his entire family, and he further claims to have killed his CCR in an act of insurrection, in the interest of revenge and justice. He claims to have been reformed ever since.

I happen to know that the ex-CCR of 18 is comfortably situated on the Ark, alive and well. Jing thinks this is a joke. I saw him snickering with Aya, the two of them whispering in the hall outside this infernal session.

In my head, I'm making my own lists.

It's possible that someone here, in this circle, might be the very operative I'm looking for. There might be eyes on me right now, watching my every move. It's also possible that these idiots are entirely useless. It further occurs to me that there are other, more valuable opportunities in this ring of hell. The Reestablishment would potentially reward information on traitors—those who might be selling secrets to the enemy. I could buy clout back home, exchanging information for security. But when I remember how their family members will pay the price for their treason, the instinct in me goes cold.

Ian clears his throat.

Another hand goes up.

"Yes, Elias," he says to an older, bearded man. "Do you have something you want to share?"

"I do," he says with a thick accent. "There is a fungus on my foot. All of my foot is fungus, nails falling off."

"I see. And is there a reason you wanted to share that with the group?"

"Yes," he says, and points angrily at Jing. "I hope Jing gets a fungus on his foot, then his legs, then his whole body. I hope his skin rots and falls off his body!"

"I hope *you* get fungus!" Jing shouts at him.

"I already have fungus!"

"Elias," says Ian, exhibiting remarkable restraint. "You still seem to be harboring frustration toward Jing after last week's incident. Let's solve to resolve this."

Jing begins to protest, but Ian holds up a hand. "Jing, you'll have an opportunity to respond in a moment. Elias, go on."

"He stole my slippers and still denies it!" Elias says, standing. "I have a fungus on my foot! All of my foot is fungus! I hope he gets my foot fungus and dies of fungus!"

Ian nods. "Okay. These kinds of elaborate visualizations can be useful, helping us process anger in the safety of our imaginations. I hope saying it out loud helped exorcise some of that emotion so that we can begin to move past this. Jing," says Ian, turning. "How does that make you feel?"

"The Reestablishment killed my family!" Jing cries, lunging for Elias.

I sit back in my chair, looking around the room.

*If you're smart enough,* the agent had said to me, *you'll see it coming.*

The group does not react to Jing's absurd outburst, making me think it happens with some frequency. As if on cue, Jing's sponsor appears, conjuring a band of electric light with her hands. She uses this light to lasso Jing, who's still shouting at Elias, and drags him away on a veritable leash, muttering an apology to Ian. Ian looks tired.

"Anyone else?"

He waits another minute, making eye contact with each of us before finally concluding the interminable session.

There's a slight lift in mood as the sounds of movement

susurrate through the room. Ian is loudly encouraging everyone to journal, talking over the din of dismissal. "Tomorrow we'll be discussing survivor's guilt," he says. "Think about what you want to bring to the group, okay? I'm sure we'll all have a lot to discuss."

I drag myself upright, my patience for this spectacle already thinning. I can't believe I'll be forced to endure this over and over again. I can't believe I might, at some point, be forced to participate.

It almost makes me miss my time with Soledad.

In the proceeding moments we gather up our journals and head to our respective sponsors, like children being returned to their parents. The sponsors follow us around everywhere, hovering nearby at all times. Listening. Watching.

I haven't been assigned a permanent sponsor yet. So far I've been shuttled around by an interim attendant named Agatha, a petite woman with a neat Afro and an affinity for turquoise, who sat me down last night and told me that true courage was saying yes to life when it offered you a hug, but if I tried anything with her she'd melt my mouth off with her hands. With a sigh, I scan the room for her, coming up short at the sight of a familiar face.

At once, my body flushes with heat.

It's automatic, instinctive, and unprecedented. I'm not this kind of person. I have never physically *reacted* to another human being before, and right now I feel as if someone has flipped a switch inside of me, flooding my veins with light. It's so foreign a sensation I have the sudden desire to examine it, to search inside myself for the cause and kill it.

James is standing by the exit.

# ROSABELLE

## CHAPTER 27

He's leaning against the doorframe in a black T-shirt and technical pants and that's all it takes for my heart to start racing. It's the shock, I realize, of his physical presence; there's something staggering about his beauty. The wry smile on his face makes me irrationally angry. His arms are casually crossed, drawing attention to his muscular build, his strong forearms. His hair is a little wet—darker than usual—as if he might've recently taken a shower. His blue eyes are cold, closed off. He doesn't seem happy to see me, and this disappoints me even as I can't conjure a single reason why the sight of me should please him. After yesterday, I didn't think I'd ever see his face again. I thought I was finally done with him.

I've been trying not to think about him.

I've been trying not to remember the panic in his eyes. The way he'd grabbed my wrists and apologized, over and over, for trying to feed me. I'm suddenly terrified that I'll never be rid of him; that his voice, like Clara's, will live on in a loop in my mind forever.

*Where'd they take your sister? The asylum, right?*

*But, like, how do we get there?*

"Hey," he says, tilting his head. "You coming?"

*But, like, how do we get there?*

I hesitate a moment more, willing my body to cool. The effects of his initial, disorienting impact are beginning to recede, and I'm now becoming painfully aware that seeing him again might be the precursor to something darker. I thought that James, having served his purpose of delivering me to the rebels, was no longer useful. I thought my focus had shifted exclusively to the procurement of the vial.

*If you're smart enough, you'll see it coming.*

Maybe James is more important than I thought. Maybe he's the one in possession of the vial. And maybe it will soon be my job to kill him—again.

It's enough to reanimate my limbs.

I cross the room and he steps back as I approach, gesturing for me to precede him down the hall. "Lead the way," he says.

I come to an abrupt stop.

I stare up at him, something like fear raising goose bumps along my arms. "Lead the way where?"

"To your room," he says. "Which one is yours?"

Warning bells sound throughout my body.

In response I turn slowly forward, guiding him to my room in silence. The rebels continue to surprise me. Outwit me. I have no idea why he's here.

To be fair, I've been trapped in this facility for less than twenty-four hours, and I'm not sure why I'm here, either. I suppose it's plausible to assume that after my behavior yesterday they decided I was truly in need of rehabilitation. It's an unlikely theory, but I can't rule it out altogether. If the rebels actually think gathering ex-members of The Reestablishment in a room together is a good idea, then I'm dealing with levels of stupidity so astronomical as to astonish. In some ways a stupid adversary is more dangerous than an evil one. I can't map stupidity. I can't extrapolate theories from stupidity. I can't solve for patterns in stupidity.

Then again, maybe that's the point.

I hear James exhale behind me, the steady *hush hush* of his pants as he moves. I'm too aware of how close he is to me, how he seems to take up all the allotted space. The dark, musky scent of him is flooding my head with dizzying thoughts I've never had before. *Never* have I felt the absurd compulsion to press my face to a man's chest and breathe him in.

I certainly won't start now.

This place feels like a small college, with different wings for classrooms and dormitories. It also appears to be sealed entirely underground, or else the cinder blocks are impressively dense. There are windows out of reach, too high to access, and I need more time to study the light to be certain of its origin. It might be synthetic, or I might simply lack a baseline for this geographical region. Ark Island is located in what would've been the Pacific Northwest of The New Republic; but because I was unconscious for the duration of my arrival here, I have no idea where we are relative to my home. I'm still assessing. Mapping. This is without a doubt some kind of prison masquerading as a sanctuary.

Finally, we come to a stop.

"Hiiiiiii, Rosabelle No-last-name," says Leon, poking his head out of his room. "Hiiiiiii, my beautiful Rosabelle, Rosabelle. I was waiting for you."

Leon is my neighbor.

Right now he's grinning at me the way he did yesterday when I arrived, with a fervor that might frighten someone else. He's tall with golden hair and golden skin and vivid green eyes that rarely blink. He's handsome and unhinged.

"Rosabelle means *beautiful rose*," says Leon, his head still hanging out the door like a dog in a window. "Rosabelle, Rosabelle, Rosabelle, Rosabelle—"

I glance at James, indicating with a nod that we've arrived at my bedroom door, and I'm surprised to find that he seems angrier now than he did upon arrival. His expression is stormy as he watches me, and I fumble a little under his silent fury as I search my pockets.

Finally, I procure the ancient brass key.

I enjoy the tactile, classic feeling of a key, but I don't understand the logic. Why not lock us in our rooms using modern security mechanisms, opening and closing them remotely, regulating our freedom? Why give us the illusion of power?

"Rosabelle," says Leon, tittering. "My beautiful rose. I can hear you at night. I listened to you all night, Rosabelle, I'll give you a little earth, Rosabelle, let me look inside you, Rosabelle, Rosabelle, Rosabelle—"

James reaches forward, palms Leon's face, and physically launches him backward into his room. There's a strangled cry, a violent crash, and then James pulls Leon's door shut with a slam.

He turns to look at me, and I'm frozen in shock, my key still stuck in the lock.

"This piece of shit lives next door to you?" he says.

"Yes."

James turns away and says nothing more. I study the column of his neck, his throat as it bobs.

My right hand shakes slightly as I turn the key, and then we're entering my room and he's closing the door behind us, and this simple action cuts the air supply in half.

I back myself up against my dresser as he steps into the small space, heat braising my head. I'm suddenly, irrationally terrified by the idea that he might touch me.

He does not.

He doesn't touch anything. In fact, James doesn't even come near me. He keeps the length of the room between us as he inspects it, and I see the small space the way he might: bare white walls, a twin bed with a matching nightstand. There's an adjoining bathroom with a full-length mirror affixed to the back of the door. He doesn't move from his spot, but his eyes are trained on my bed.

"Wow," is the first thing he says. "You make your bed like a soldier. Impressive."

I look at it: the tight, crisp sheets; the perfect corners; the smooth blanket. The pillows are uncrushed, plump like a pair of eggs.

I stiffen with alarm.

I'd not been expecting an inspection, and perhaps I should have. I didn't sleep in my bed last night. Instead, I sat with my back against the door, staring into my messenger bag at the bottle of water and the small bag of nuts.

I ate all of them, every single one.

And then I licked the salt off the plastic and drank all the water from the bottle and stared into the dark and fought to breathe. I listened to the quiet, straining my ears for signs of life. I scoured every inch of the bathroom, fished my arm down the toilet, touched my fingers to the mirrors, unscrewed the stopper from the sink. I pulled every drawer out of the dresser and ran my hands down the walls and pressed my ears to the carpet, listening.

Nothing.

Nothing.

Each time, nothing.

It began to drive me wild. The idea that they might allow me to lock myself in my room without a shred of surveillance was driving me wild. I needed to find something, needed to know whether The Reestablishment had found a way to watch me here, and if not, why my enemy hadn't, either. I finally collapsed in the middle of the room, my heart beating so hard my vision had begun to blur. I never made it to the bed, the sheets of which I'd yet to strip. I lay there, starfished on the floor, my eyesight blearing with fatigue, wondering how I'd ended up there, in that moment. I remembered something my mother used to say to me. When I'd whine for something she couldn't give me, or when I was frustrated with a problem she couldn't solve, she'd say—

*Rosabelle, when there's something you want but can't have, you can either be patient or be creative. Choose a path.*

When the bullet in my mother's gun went off, the path was chosen for me. Nothing could slow the force of a shot that expelled her from her world and me from mine.

In an instant, I stopped being a child.

I had one dark skill for which I'd been trained in the most rudimentary of ways, and it was all I had to barter. Suddenly at ten years old I was a parent, a provider, a student, an idiot—and then, without ceremony, a murderer.

"It's been two minutes."

I look up, blinking.

"I counted," James says, leaning against the wall. He looks at his watch. The straps are made of leather, the style out of place: an anachronism, noted. "It's been two minutes and thirty-seven seconds since I made a comment about your bed, and instead of responding, you left. It's like you just walked out of your head."

I feel it again: heat, threatening to consume me. It flares up my chest, my throat. I don't like the way he watches me. I don't like the way he seems to pay attention.

I don't like it.

*I don't like it.*

*I don't't—*

"Where did you go?" he says.

"Nowhere," I say quietly. "I'm right here."

He flashes me a look that borders on amusement. "I'll be right back," he says, and leaves the room.

I'm standing in exactly the same position, my head held at exactly the same angle when he reenters the room a few minutes later, this time carrying a chair.

The door slams shut behind him, and I flinch.

He sees this but says nothing. Instead, he pushes the chair up against the far wall and takes a seat, giving me as much space as the room will allow. He nods to the bed.

"Have a seat, Rosabelle."

"Why? What are you going to do to me?"

His eyes seem to die out, like a guttering flame. "I'm going to talk to you."

I exhale, but slowly, keeping my body still. This is a relief. Finally, something that makes sense. Something I know how to manage. "You've come to interrogate me."

"No," he says, leaning forward, arms on his knees. "I'm just going to talk to you."

My heart rate spikes again. I blink away the sudden rush to my head, backing up against the bed in confusion, my calves knocking against the frame. I draw upon an inner reserve to calm myself, crush myself.

*Die.*

You've been dead inside for years, I remind myself.

You've been dead inside for *years*—

Then, with a force that takes my breath away, I finally understand. In a moment of pure, undiluted panic, I finally understand. This is why I keep making mistakes around him— This is what's wrong with me— This is why I can't seem to die and stay dead, why my skin keeps burning, my heart keeps racing, my head keeps spinning—

*He* is what's wrong with me.

After so many years being dead inside, James makes me feel alive.

# JAMES

## CHAPTER 28

She's so fucking beautiful.

I'd never seen her in normal clothes, and now I wish I never had. She looks even more ethereal in these soft colors and fabrics. Her platinum hair is in a long, messy braid, and she keeps batting loose strands away from her face. Her cheeks are pinker. Her skin and eyes are brighter, more alive. She's sitting in bed in white socks, knees pulled up to her chin, and she's both effortlessly stunning and deeply unaware of the havoc she's wreaking on my nervous system. She doesn't look capable of hurting a dust mote.

God, this is a nightmare. An actual nightmare.

We've been doing this—I check my watch—for two hours now, and I'm already losing my cool. Warner was right. I have several more hours of this to sit through, and I don't know how I'm going to make it. I wasn't trained for sitting in rooms and talking about nothing. I'm drowning. If she keeps this up I might just have to leave.

I drop my head, push my hands through my hair.

She's got these soft, grayish eyes I don't know how to describe. It's not even about her eyes, really. It's not the color or the shape. It's more about the way she looks at me, like I'm brand-new, like each time she sees me it's the first time, like it blows her mind. I feel it when we make eye contact: the way she sort of stills, like she's been stunned. She doesn't look at me a lot, but when she does it's like driving a hot knife through my chest. Most of the time I feel like she's trying *not* to look at me.

Like right now.

I sit up. She's staring at the wall.

"Rosabelle," I say. "Please answer the question."

She turns toward me, locks eyes with me and *boom*, again. Like a slingshot, strikes me in the heart. I try not to breathe too hard as her eyes widen, searching me like she's never seen me before, and then she goes soft: her eyes gleam, dreamlike, her lashes lowering, lips parting as she lingers on my face.

It's doing things to my head.

I want to go for a run. Jump in a lake. Drive a thumbtack into my forehead.

Warner might actually murder me if I bail.

"What was the question?" she asks, and she's staring at the wall again.

"These are really easy questions," I say, trying not to notice the elegant line of her neck. Her sweater is a little big for her, and it keeps gaping at the collar, torturing me with glimpses of skin I shouldn't be glimpsing. I press the heels of my hands to my eyes, speaking toward the ground when I say, "I asked you what your favorite season is."

"Why?" she says, and it's the first time in hours I've

heard some heat from her. "What's the point of knowing my favorite season?"

I sit up, and she looks at me again, and—

Fuck it, I have to get out of here. Cool my head. Tackle a bear. There's too much adrenaline running through my veins right now, and I'm going to start climbing these walls soon.

"You know what," I say, getting to my feet. "I think, uh, I'm going to get something to eat. You want anything?"

She unfurls slowly, arms unwrapping from her legs, unclenching from her chest. She turns, sits on the edge of the bed, her socked feet not touching the floor.

I'm staring at this, studying the distance between her feet and the ground when she says, carefully, "What do you mean?"

"I'm going to the dining hall." I gesture toward the door. "Do you want me to bring you something?"

"Dining hall?" Now she's standing. "What does that mean?"

"It's"—I frown—"it's a dining hall. It's where you eat. Did no one give you a tour?"

She shakes her head. Her cheeks are suddenly pinker. "Agatha said that my sponsor would show me around today. I don't have a sponsor yet."

I laugh out loud, then seriously consider throwing myself off a building. "*I'm* your sponsor," I say to her. "Did I not mention that?"

Apparently, this is the worst news she's received all day.

The color drains from Rosabelle's face. She becomes a statue before my eyes. When she does this I feel so powerless I want to put my head through a wall. It takes everything I've got not to do something as elemental as comfort her.

This is not a level playing field.

It doesn't come naturally to me to orchestrate the downfall of vulnerable women. I liked it better when she was actively trying to murder me. I liked it better before I made her cry. Hell, I could've sworn she used to talk more. And she never used to look at me like this, like a cat when it's comfortable. Softly blinking, sleepy eyes. I don't like it. It's freaking me out. I need her to try to stab me or something, and soon. Really soon.

Wait, why *isn't* she trying to stab me?

"No," she says finally. "You didn't mention that."

"Well, yeah, I am." Clearly, I've never been a sponsor before. Now I understand why Warner left those binders on my desk last night. I did not, in fact, do more than glance at them this morning.

"Oh," she says. Then, again, a whisper: "*Oh.*"

"I guess, uh, I can give you that tour. If you like."

# JAMES

## CHAPTER 29

When we finally sit down to eat, we sit across from each other, and it occurs to me that I've only made the situation worse. Suddenly we're only a couple feet apart. I can see shades of blue in her gray eyes. The gentle slope of her nose, the satin finish of her skin. Suddenly I'm staring at her mouth.

Mentally, I punch myself in the face.

"I can come here whenever I want?" she asks, eyes on her tray. There's a single plate in front of her, and on it, a single apple.

Practically nothing, but it still feels like a win.

She stood in front of the sandwiches for so long it nearly killed me. She'd reach out, then retract her hand. Reach out, then retract her hand.

Like she was afraid of something.

"Yeah," I say, trying to remember what she'd asked me. I spear a small tomato in my salad. I don't even know what's in this salad. I just grabbed it so I'd have something to do. "Yeah, uh, you can come here whenever you want. Well, I mean, during dining hours, but yeah." I nod at a sign on a nearby wall with the hours listed. "You can't take food back to your room, though. That's the only thing. Sometimes people hoard stuff, and then things go bad, and then"—I shrug, popping the tomato in my mouth—"it gets gross."

She picks up her apple, and I notice, not for the first time, that her right hand trembles a little. I remember what Warner said about the scar inside her forearm, but she's wearing long sleeves, so I can't—

She bites into the apple.

She bites into the apple and her eyes close, and then she makes a tiny sound of pleasure in the back of her throat that messes me up so badly I have to put down my fork.

No. Never mind. I should definitely keep the fork, keep myself busy. I need to not be thinking about the look on her face or this deeply inappropriate, primal feeling of satisfaction in my chest. She'd seemed so overwhelmed going through the buffet line that I figured it was a bad idea to pressure her to eat more than she was ready to eat—especially after yesterday. I'm just so happy she's eating something. I'm so happy she's comfortable enough to eat something in front of *me*. These are weird thoughts to be having about a serial killer.

"So, uh, things you should know," I say, spearing another tomato. "The people who come through here have already served prison sentences. They've been judged and vetted and cleared for this program. This is the last phase of calibration before they're allowed to reenter society. What else? Um, you have to attend all the meetings—"

"You give free food to people who went to prison?"

I look up, surprised at her sharp tone, my fork halfway

to my mouth. I set down the fork. "Yeah," I say. "I mean, we feed people in prison, too, obviously."

"Oh."

She puts down the apple and looks away from me, her eyes darting around. She clasps her hands, her thumb rubbing circles into the opposite palm as she searches the room. I wonder whether she realizes she's self-soothing right in front of me.

"Why does that upset you?" I ask.

She jerks back to me, her eyes bright, stunned, *pow,* ow. "I didn't say it upset me."

"You didn't have to," I point out. "It makes you sad that we feed people in prison. You've got sad feelings about it."

"How would you know that?"

"I mean." I gesture at her face with my fork. "It's obvious."

"It's not obvious. Why are you saying it's obvious?"

"Okay," I say, laughing a little. I spear my tomato again. "Now you're mad."

"No, I'm not."

"Definitely mad."

"*Stop saying that.*"

I'm picking through my salad, searching for another tomato when I say, "Now you're scared."

"Stop it," she says, loudly this time. "Stop it right now."

"Stop what?"

"*I said stop,*" she cries.

I look up, food half-chewed, and freeze. I've literally never heard her raise her voice before. Rosabelle looks genuinely terrified, and now I'm confused.

"Do you— Are you—" She's flushed, still searching the room in sharp, erratic motions. "Are you—"

"Am I what?"

"Can you"—she swallows, stares at me—"can you see into my head?"

"What?" I laugh, relaxing. Stab a piece of lettuce. "What are you talking about?"

"Are you connected, too?" she says, and she sounds angry. "Are they watching me right now?"

Okay, fork goes down again.

"Rosabelle, I realize The Reestablishment has seriously messed with your mind, but I swear I'm not seeing into your head. I mean"—I shrug—"look, okay, I guess in some ways you can call it *seeing* into someone's head, but it's not—"

"So it's true." She physically backs away from me, her chair screeching as she pushes away from the table. "They aren't in my room because they're in *you*."

"Who?" I shoot back. "What are you talking about? Why are you freaking out right now?"

"I'm not freaking out," she says sharply.

"Clearly." I roll my eyes.

"If you're not seeing into my head," she says, "how can you know what I'm feeling?"

"Because I'm a human being?"

"No."

I raise my eyebrows. I can't fight my smile. "You're just"—I wave a hand—"rejecting my answer?"

"Why are you laughing at me?"

"I'm not laughing at you," I say to her. "But I think it's interesting that this is sending you into such a panic."

"I'm not panicking," she says, color rising in her face.

I blow out a breath. Really struggle to fight back that smile. Nope, I can't help it. The laugh just leaves my body.

This *really* pisses her off.

Happy cat is long gone.

"Um. Yeah, look," I say. "Just because you say something, doesn't make it true. You know that, right?" I gesticulate with my fork. "You can't just say, look, I'm invisible, and suddenly it's true." Well, except for Kenji.

"I don't like it when you laugh at me."

"I know," I say. "It makes you mad. You think I'm not taking you seriously."

Her eyes widen. Stunned. *Pow.* Happy cat is back.

"Except, I do take you seriously," I say to her. "You just think it requires, like, magic or something in order to see into someone's head—"

"Not magic." She cuts me off. "It's extremely advanced science. Cutting-edge technology."

"What is?"

"The Nexus."

"Right, obviously," I say, super calm, even though inside I've just burst a blood vessel, had a heart attack, and died.

*What the hell is the Nexus?*

Oh my God, Warner is going to flip. Right? Or wait, does he already know what the Nexus is? Shit, he probably already knows what the Nexus is.

Maybe this was not a big reveal.

I keep going: "But there are other ways to connect with people."

"What do you mean?"

"You know," I say, popping a piece of lettuce into my mouth. "Like, just paying attention. I pay attention to you."

She turns pink. Almost all of her turns pink. It's fucking adorable. I want to die.

"I pay attention to you, too," she says quietly.

I sit straight up at that, my brain cells in a panic, all of them running around shouting *what the hell does that mean* at the same time.

A poorly edited version of this question leaves my mouth: "What?"

She seems calmer now, her eyes narrowing. "I don't need technology to understand you, either."

"Whoa, wait." I hold up a hand. "Look, I wasn't threatening you. I was just trying to explain—"

"You think you're so mysterious—"

"No, I don't—"

"Well, you're not," she says sharply. "You're not mysterious. Your methods are obvious. You rely on veils of distraction, using humor and charm to cast yourself as a hapless, incapable opponent, only to then slaughter your enemies as if it costs you nothing. You pretend to be reckless when you're not. You pretend to be weak when you're not. You pretend to be stupid when you're not. You live by some impenetrable moral code, deciding at your own discretion whether something is worth dying for, and then act as if your sacrifice means nothing. You feign boredom even when you're paying attention. You smile even when you're angry—especially when you're angry." She leans in. "You're a liar. Deep down, you don't think this world is funny. Deep down, you're simmering with rage. You think I can't see straight through you? You live your life as if nothing can hurt you even though your body is covered in scars."

These words detonate inside me.

The result is a mess: my heart is beating out of my chest; my head is surging with heat. I want to go back to the person I was five minutes ago. It's like my rib cage has been split open, like a magician just pulled the organs out of my body and is now tossing them into a jeering crowd.

Jesus. I can't stop staring at her.

Rosabelle is sitting back in her seat, looking at me with those slow, sleepy eyes, and I'm so arrested in the moment I can hardly make out anything beyond her head. I'm not even mad that she just tore me to pieces. No woman has ever stripped me bare like that. Hell, no woman has ever studied me with this level of intensity, and the longer our eyes hold the harder my heart beats.

I want to know what else she thinks of me.

I want to know what she's thinking right now. I want to know what other things she's hiding behind those strange eyes; she's clearly keeping all kinds of secrets. And I don't even realize I'm staring at her like a prepubescent teenager until I drop my fork and the metal clatters, startling me.

I swallow. Sit back in my seat.

*Fuck*. This is bad.

It takes me a second, but I finally reset my head, find my voice. I clear my throat and say, "That was, um, really mean."

"What?" She recoils in surprise. "No, it wasn't."

"It was," I say, picking up my fallen fork. "You hurt my feelings. I think you should apologize."

Her eyes widen. She actually seems to consider this, and the split second she spends weighing her options tells me everything I need to know about this girl.

When she sees me fighting a laugh, she goes rigid with outrage.

"You just did it again," she says. "You're such a liar—"

"Listen," I say, shaking my head. "I'm going to take a wild guess here and assume you don't have a clue how to have a normal, polite conversation. I'm guessing the serial killer life didn't teach you how to be casual. It probably wasn't the relaxing stress reliever you thought it would be when you first signed up for the job—"

"I didn't sign up for it," she says, cutting me off.

"Okay."

"I was born into it."

Now it's my turn to go very still. The Nexus thing was maybe not a big deal, but this feels important. I keep my eyes on my food, reintroducing motion a little at a time. I pick at the lettuce slowly, keep my shoulders loose. Wait for her to fill the silence.

"I wouldn't have chosen this life," she says. "It was what my parents wanted for me."

Yes. Okay. This is good.

*Horrible.* Objectively *horrible,* but good intel.

Finally, we're getting somewhere. Warner will know what to do with this information, but I understand enough about the classist hierarchy of The Reestablishment to know that, if Rosabelle's parents chose this path for her, she must've come from a rich family. When the parents choose the profession, they pay for it, and they start the kids young. Which means Warner was right. She's been trained in this since childhood. Rosabelle is probably some kind of super-high-class mercenary. That would explain the fancy wedding invitation to the fancy douchebag. Except—

What about her sister? Why was she in that weird, shitty cottage? Why have they been *starving* her?

Wait a second. Where the hell are her parents?

There's a lot to think about here, but I intentionally ignore the bombshell so as not to draw attention to it. "Right," I say, "so, you're proving my point—"

"Hiiiii, Rosabelle No-last-name! Rosabelle, Rosabelle, Rosabelle!"

I hear him before I see him, looking up just as the next-door shithead slams his tray down on our table.

My first instinct is to be angry, but when I get a good look at his face I realize there's something wrong with him.

He looks—drunk?

That can't be right. Alcohol isn't allowed here.

"My beautiful rose, I've been looking for you. I wanted to see you," he says, slurring a little. "You're a rose, my rosy rose." He drops himself into the chair next to Rosabelle, then lunges at her so quickly I only have enough time to jump out of my chair before I hear his bloodcurdling scream.

Rosabelle pulls her fork out of his neck, carefully wipes it on a napkin, and picks up her apple.

Shithead is gurgling blood. He's grasping at his neck, pawing at the wound, and I can see that she didn't just stab him with the fork, she ripped his throat open a little, too.

"What do we do with our trays?" she asks, pushing away from the table. She's giving me that look again.

Happy cat, sleepy eyes.

# JAMES

## CHAPTER 30

"So, what have we learned?" says Kenji, tugging a pair of sunglasses out of his pocket. He flips them open with one hand, balancing a to-go mug in the other.

"Nothing," says Winston, looking more irritable than usual, dragging his feet down the sidewalk. "We've learned nothing."

"That's not true," says Kenji, pausing to nod good morning to someone he knows, then promising to stop by a bakery later. He glances at Winston as we walk. "We've learned that you shouldn't be allowed to meet new people on your own."

"We already knew that," I point out. "We've known that for years. Why did you let him go out last night?"

"*Let* him go out?" Kenji whips off his sunglasses, immediately regrets it, then shoves them back on. "The man is a hundred and fifty years old—"

"Forty-one," Winston says miserably. "I'm forty-one."

"Like I said, he's a thousand years old, nose practically crumbling off his face, and it's *my* job to keep him from going out at night?"

"I don't like people," says Winston. "I know this about myself. It's just that I forget I don't like people until I actually meet people, and then I remember why I never meet people. It's because I don't like them." He rubs at his eyes from underneath his glasses, the action setting them off-kilter on his face.

"God," he says, groaning. "I'm too old for this. Brendan told me to my face I was too old for this."

"He did not say that."

"He implied it."

"He wanted to see the world!" Kenji says, forcing enthusiasm. "He didn't want to settle down—he wanted to do young-people shit, find his inner star, swim in the radiation-infested waters of life—"

"I'm going to die alone," says Winston.

Kenji claps him on the back. "C'mon, man. Grandpa Winston has at least five good years left in him before the arthritis takes him out."

"Fuck you."

I smile into my own travel mug. It's a perfect winter day and we're heading to our favorite breakfast spot, so all things considered, I'm pretty happy. Here, a few miles inland from the ocean, the sun doesn't disappear in the winter. It just cools off. I take a breath and savor it. I love the soft light, the crisp breeze. We used to live in a part of the continent where winter meant months and months of oppressively gray skies and dirty snow, and I hated it. I was made to live near water. Mountains. Open land. When I was kid, I used to pretend to be a kite. I'd jump off chairs and tables and eventually dumpsters and squat buildings, hoping to catch the wind.

It usually ended with a scream.

Anyway, I already know I won't be getting outside as much these next few weeks, so I'm trying to appreciate the time I've got with the sky.

We move down the sidewalk, nodding to familiar faces as we pass, Winston and Kenji exchanging barbs. Our neighborhood is located directly above the underground HQ, so, with the exception of the rehab facility—which is a couple miles out—our daily commutes are easy. The elevator in my living room goes straight down, twenty floors. I love it. I love that our headquarters are sleek, state-of-the art facilities but our houses are old. We live in pre-Reestablishment-era residential builds with patched roofs and groaning floorboards. We have spotty yards. Rusting mailboxes. Occasionally, termites. We've been renovating slowly over the years, but what matters most is that we all live right next to each other. The first homes we lived in post-revolution were small, refurbished houses, and we liked the style so much we kept the tradition alive even after we moved.

We had no choice but to move.

Things had gotten bad. We were living off the kindness of Castle's daughter, Nouria, who'd built a sanctuary for her own minor resistance group. She and her wife, Sam, allowed us to shelter there for a while, but our presence was causing them problems, exposing them to danger—and after the fifth terrifying attempt on Juliette's life, Warner was done. He decided it was time to finally fulfill one of his wife's biggest dreams: to design a dedicated, fortified mini city purpose-built for our needs; a place where we'd be able to live with the pretense of freedom. After a rough winter, we decided collectively to plant our flag in a more temperate area.

It started out as a single street, then two, and now our humble neighborhood has since expanded into a sprawling campus that includes hospitals and parks and small businesses. The residential zone exists on a more heavily fortified plane of security and access, but everyone who steps foot in this city-within-a-city has to go through a screening process. From the janitors to the baristas to the scientists and engineers. No one comes here unless they work here, and no one *lives* here but us.

It's informally called The Waffle.

We call it The Waffle because that's what Roman called it the first time he saw the grid map. He then asked for waffles with extra syrup and said, *Uncle James, I have a booger.*

"Look," Kenji is saying to Winston. "It could be worse, right? Take James, for example."

"What?" My head snaps up in alarm. "What about me?"

Winston looks over at me, cataracts of gloom clearing from his eyes. "Yeah," he says, nodding. "Okay."

"Right?" Kenji is nodding, too. "Young, handsome, well-connected. Girls literally throw themselves at him—"

"That happened once," I protest.

"At least ten times," Winston says with disgust.

"*Literally* throw themselves at him, camp out in the streets waiting for him to walk by—"

"Wait, how is that my fault? People think I'm Warner.

That's why I don't like leaving The Waffle—"

"—and look at him. Just look at him."

Winston does as he's told, and looks at me.

"This ungrateful son of a bitch has been single for years," Kenji is saying. "At least we've been in relationships, right? At least we know how to love."

"Hey, I know how to love—"

"Yeah," Winston says again, this time with more conviction. His shoulders straighten. He considers the horizon. "Yeah, okay, that's true. What else?"

We've come to a stop, hovering on the sidewalk just steps from The Waffle's Waffles. I can already smell the syrup. Powdered sugar. Over-brewed coffee.

"Can we go inside?" I ask, looking around. "I'm hungry, and this conversation isn't even supposed to be about me—"

Kenji counts off on his fingers. "He still lives at home; he still has night terrors; he still sucks at his job—"

"I don't suck at my job," I protest.

"Are you joking?" Winston says, his mood visibly improved. "Your track record is shit lately."

"The audacity," says Kenji.

"The stupidity—"

"The girl literally *murdered* a man on your watch."

"He's still alive!" I counter. "I healed him almost immediately! We sanitized the dining hall. No permanent damage was done."

"Whatever," says Kenji, peering into his empty coffee cup. "You're lucky you have healing powers, or else that could've gotten really messy, really fast." He hesitates, then pulls off his sunglasses, black eyes narrowing. "Hey, why aren't you with the mercenary right now? Aren't you supposed to be there every day?"

"Yeah." I nod, ignoring the way my chest reacts to the idea of seeing Rosabelle again. "Yeah, but she's being disciplined. She has to spend a few hours alone in the Emotional Garden this morning. I'm supposed to meet up with her in an hour."

"What the hell is an emotional— Oh, *shit*—"

Kenji goes invisible, reappearing a second later in the entryway of The Waffle's Waffles, flickering in and out of sight. "Shit, shit, shit—"

"*What?*" Winston and I say at the same time.

We crowd him in the entry, on high alert. "What's going on?" I say. "Did you see something?"

"Okay, I might be out of my mind," he says, pulling back his invisibility, "but I could've sworn I just saw Nazeera walking down the street."

Winston and I exchange a loaded glance, and a beat later Kenji slaps us both, hard, upside the head.

"Ow," we shout at the same time.

"What the hell?" Kenji cries angrily.

The owner of the restaurant, a bearded redhead named Kip, is staring at us through the glass door. He frowns at me, like, *what's going on?* and I flash him what I'm hoping is a reassuring smile.

"You knew she was here?" Kenji is saying. "You knew Nazeera was coming here, and you didn't think to tell me?"

"She flies out like every three months," says Winston, rubbing the back of his head. "You already knew that."

"Plus, you told us never to discuss her with you," I add. "You said you didn't want any details on Nazeera, ever—"

"You're not supposed to listen to me when I say shit like that," he hisses, peeking out from behind the doorway.

I know the moment he sees her again, because he stiffens and retreats, collapsing against the wall.

"Oh my God," he says, appearing and disappearing, his invisibility glitching. "I think I'm dying. Did she get more beautiful? How did she get more beautiful?"

"I think we should take him inside," says Winston, shooting me a look. "Grab his arm."

"Is she with a hot Arab dude?" Kenji says, jerking out of reach. He peeks into the street again, then falls back, his eyes squeezing shut. "Wait, don't tell me. I don't want to know. I can't compete with those dudes. Those dudes are just built different. Oh God, I can't feel my legs."

A bell jingles overhead and we look up.

"Hey," says Kip, pushing open the front door in his apron. "You kids okay? What's going on?" He jerks a thumb behind him. "People are getting worried."

"Sorry, Kip," Winston says. "Everything's fine."

"Then what's with him?" he says, nodding at Kenji, who's stopped glitching only to begin sliding down the wall.

"Nazeera is here," I say.

Kip's face falls. He looks from me to Winston to Kenji and back again. "He didn't know? She comes through like every three months."

"I forgot," Kenji says, groaning into his hands.

"That's okay," says Kip, regrouping. "You'll be okay. She'll be gone in about a week, right?"

Winston grimaces.

"Two weeks?" says Kip.

"She's staying for the birth," I explain, glancing warily at Kenji. "She wants to be here for Juliette."

"No return flight planned," Winston adds.

Kenji makes a pitiful, keening sound.

"Aw, kid," Kip says softly, his eyes pulling together. "We've all been there. We'll get through this." He throws an arm over Kenji's shoulder, patting him on the back as he leads him into the diner. They walk inside to a clamor of concern and questions, but Kip waves the people down.

"Nazeera is here," he explains. "For the birth."

The crowd inhales collectively, then dissolves into therapeutic, universal sounds of comfort.

"Someone get my boy some waffles," says Kip, pushing Kenji into the crowd. "And ice cream."

"And chocolate chips?" says Kenji, looking up.

"And chocolate chips," says Kip.

"What about me?" asks Winston, following them inside. "I'm also depressed. I also like chocolate chips—"

I'm quietly laughing, about to cross the threshold into a cloud of warm sugar, when I feel a hand on my shoulder. Startled, I turn around.

It's Ian.

Ian Sanchez, lead psychotherapist at the rehab facility and old friend of the family. He looks pissed.

"Shit," I say, alarmed. "Shit, what'd she do now?"

# ROSABELLE

## CHAPTER 31

"I didn't do it," I say quietly.

Agatha is staring at me, arms crossed. "You have motive."

I stare into the middle distance, the vivid greens of the room blurring around me as the bright, earthy scents of plant life fill my nose. This place surprised me when I walked in. I didn't expect solitary confinement to be so beautiful.

Of course, they don't call this solitary confinement.

This is the Emotional Garden, where the delinquents are sent to think about what they've done. It's not a large space, but every inch of it is covered in hanging vines and vegetation, with a domed, windowed ceiling decanting marbled light across mounds of moss and wild grass. There's a desk and chair in the middle of the room, wooden legs like roots planted directly into the dirt, and we're supposed to sit here for hours, writing down regrets and reflections in our journals. As per the rules, I'm not wearing shoes or socks.

Clara would love it here.

I hate it.

"Rosabelle," she says sternly. "Someone ransacked his room while he was in recovery. Turned it upside down. What I want to know is this: How did you get inside? There was no indication that the lock had been tampered with."

I look up at her, then look away.

"Do you realize what a privilege it is to be here?" she's saying, shifting her weight. "If you're not careful, you might end up in a high-security prison—"

"Great," I say softly. "Transfer me."

She visibly tenses, then uncrosses and recrosses her arms. "The fact that you haven't been kicked out yet is frankly unbelievable. The waitlist to get into this facility is *yearslong*. Did you know that? Do you have any idea how lucky you are to have access to the resources we provide?"

I'm staring, fascinated, at the tight curl of a tender shoot: the terrified coil of youth, the clench of uncertainty. The young vine will be coaxed into life by the promise of light, unfurling each day toward the unknown, grasping for a path until a hand darts out, grabs it by the stalk, and snaps it in half—

"Now, I don't know what kind of strings you pulled to jump the line," Agatha is saying, "but we're only tolerating your behavior here because the orders to admit you came from way above my head. If you don't get your act right, I will petition to have you removed. There are a lot of people who believe in this program. People who dedicate their lives to this program. You've been here less than two days and you've already *killed* someone, then raided his room—"

"I didn't do it."

"What have you been doing in here for three hours?" she says. "Did you even write in your journal?"

I blink very slowly. My journal is sitting on the desk, still in its sleeve.

"You haven't written anything?" she says, stunned. She swipes my journal from the desk, sees the unbroken seal on the sleeve, and appears to burst a blood vessel. I sit back inside myself as she shouts, watching as she tosses my book in front of me. Her words mute and warp, losing shape as I disconnect from time. I listen to the sounds of my own breathing, clasp my hands and trace their lines.

For hours I've been watching the light dance and change in this room, using my time to sort through the mental files I've made on every person I've encountered in the facility. I've classified all parties by perceived threat and possible utility, but so far none have stood out to me in any marked way except James. Well, him and Leon.

Someone has ransacked Leon's room, and it wasn't me.

*Pay attention.*

I've turned it over and over: Is it possible someone was searching his room for the vial? If so, two new possibilities arise: either Leon is the double agent I'm looking for, or he's the unlucky caretaker of the object. The former theory falls apart when held up against logic: it seems unlikely The Reestablishment would entrust the vial to someone of unsound mind. Of course, the incident with Leon could be nothing more than an unrelated distraction. Still—

*If you're smart enough, you'll see it coming.*

Theories rise and dissolve, like air bubbles.

In my head I underline a picture of Leon's face, adding a question mark next to his name.

*Important? Or idiot?*

Pinned to the imaginary corkboard next to him is an image of James, his face circled and starred, notes scribbled furiously in the margins—

*Key to infiltrating Anderson family*

*Terrifying and dangerous*

*Notorious bloodline*

*Lulls enemies into false sense of security*

*Do not underestimate*

—with this last note underlined several times.

The truth is, the drama with Leon is probably little more than a domestic dispute between inmates. It seems far more likely, given everything I've been through thus far, that James is my true mark.

I draw breath at the thought.

Heat singes my skin, an uncategorized fear forcing me violently back into my body.

"That's right," says Agatha, and I look at her.

She's misunderstood my reaction.

"You *should* be ashamed of yourself," she's saying. "Honestly, it's refreshing to see that you're even capable of remorse. I was starting to think you didn't feel bad about killing Leon at all."

"I didn't kill him," I say, remembering. "He's not dead."

"You know exactly what I mean—"

My eyes unfocus.

James had been so calm. He didn't shout or ask questions. He didn't even seem mad. He just looked at me, then walked around the table and reached for Leon, and when he put his bare hands on Leon's bleeding throat, I thought maybe he'd decided to snap his neck, put him out of his misery. Instead, he spoke calmly into Leon's ear, telling him he was going to be all right, and then held him until he stopped convulsing.

I watched, stunned, my unspooling mind wandering in a dangerous direction—

I wondered then whether James could heal Clara.

I'd dismissed the thought by the time he stepped away from Leon. Someone had already called for the medics. We were swarmed. James, I reasoned, would never meet my sister. He'd no doubt be dead by the time I saw her again.

Meanwhile, Leon had fallen asleep.

"He passed out," James explained to the responders, his hands slick with blood. "We have to get him into recovery as soon as possible, but he'll be all right."

Only after everyone had cleared out did James turn to look at me. He wiped his hands on a stack of napkins, the blood sticky, sticking; paper tearing. He sighed, shook his head.

"Rosabelle," he'd said softly.

I swore I felt the earth move. His voice, low and steady, slid inside of me, circled my dead heart and squeezed, pumping blood to my veins with a force I'd never felt before. I couldn't look away from him. I had no idea what he was about to say to me, how he might condemn me.

"Are you okay?" he said.

And I liquefied.

*Are you okay?*

*Rosa, are you okay?*

"Hey." Agatha was snapping her fingers at me. "Did you hear what I said? What's wrong with you?"

*Rosa, what's wrong?*

*Nothing*, I'd said, scrubbing my hands in the sink. I was scrubbing them raw. They were red and stinging. My eyes were burning.

*Why do you keep washing your hands?* Clara asked. *Why won't you come read to me?*

*I have to wash them, Clara. I have to wash them first.*

*But you've been washing forever, Rosa. Aren't they clean now?*

*No.*

"Excuse me? Are you listening to me?"

The door slams open and I jerk up at the sound, my ears ringing.

James rushes into the room.

# ROSABELLE

## CHAPTER 32

He looks like he ran here.

His face is pinker than normal, his bronze hair windswept, his eyes bright and arresting. Every time I see him it becomes more difficult to see him.

When our eyes meet, I hold my breath.

His absence is beginning to leave an impression on me. I can already feel my nervous system quieting in his presence, the screams of the world stamping out into soft noise. I don't like this feeling. I don't like that I look forward to seeing him, that I've been waiting for him to come back, that I've almost finished counting the scatter of freckles across the bridge of his nose.

Seven.

"Rosabelle," he says, shaking his head. "What did you—"

"I didn't."

He stills, staring at me. He looks from me to Agatha, then behind him, at Ian, who's glowering.

"Okay. Well." James exhales, shoves his hands in his pockets. He looks at the other two. "She says she didn't do it. So unless you've got proof—"

Agatha and Ian explode.

I watch, unhearing, as they argue with him, blood

rushing to my head. Time seems to draw out and bend, double back and blur. Why is he defending me? How does he know I'm not lying?

"Because," he says to Agatha, his voice piercing my haze. His voice, I realize, always returns me to my body. "She's not afraid of you. If she'd done it, she'd admit it."

"How do you know that?" Ian and I ask at the same time.

James looks from me to Ian. "I don't know," he says, glancing at me again. "I can just tell."

Ian studies me stonily as he considers this.

James exhales. "Hey, don't forget to run those labs, okay?" He says this to Agatha. "I listed everything in my report. There was something off with that guy yesterday."

"Let me be absolutely clear," says Agatha, bristling. "Every one of our patients has been through a rigorous mental and physical vetting process, and Leon was no exception. There's only ever been one exception, and she's sitting right there." Agatha narrows her eyes at me. "Leon has been known to have issues with lucidity in the past, but that is to be expected from someone with his challenging history, and he shows progress every day. I can assure you that there was no alcohol in his system—"

"I know what I saw," James says with finality. "His eyes were unnaturally dilated. His speech was slightly slurred—"

"Maybe she drugged him," says Ian.

"Ian," Agatha cries, offended. "We run a tight ship around here. We would know if she'd brought drugs onto the premises—"

"Look," James says, sounding suddenly tired, "until you have proof to support accusations against her, this is unproductive. She's not the first person to lash out at another patient, and since we can't prove that she was trying to kill Leon—"

"I was," I say. "I was trying to kill him."

"That isn't helpful, Rosabelle," he says, each word clipped.

"Let's meet later," he says to the others. "Ian, don't you have a session right now?"

Ian glances at his watch and mutters an oath, and by the time he and Agatha trail out of the room—flashing me dirty looks—a soft chime rings several times.

James offers me a grim smile.

"Time to go, troublemaker," he says. He keeps his face stern, but his eyes are light with private humor. "You have a midmorning session on radical gratitude to get to."

"Okay," I say. But I don't move.

My heartbeat slows as I stare at him, my limbs softening. I feel liquid when I look at him for long enough, like I might come loose from my bones. I like it. I like this silence.

I feel safe in this silence.

"Why do you always look at me like that?" he says, the light fading from his eyes.

"Look at you like what?"

He holds my gaze, his chest lifting slightly as he breathes. I catch the movement in his throat, then linger on the column of his neck, the sharp line of his jaw. I drag my eyes up to his mouth—

He exhales suddenly, looks down. "Nothing," he says. "Never mind."

I like his hair.

It looks soft. It seems to glitter in the refracted light of the domed ceiling, touches of gold glinting among the brown.

I like his eyes.

His pupils have contracted in the morning glow, shades of blue now rendered with greater subtlety, lighter irises circled by a ring of dark. His lashes are long and thick and when he turns away from me I study the outline of his profile, the contained power in his body. He shifts his weight. He's wearing a faded denim jacket with a fleece collar. There's a bright, kite-shaped pin on the pocket.

"What are you thinking," he says, looking away from me, "when you get quiet like that?"

"Nothing."

He exhales a harsh laugh. "Sure. Okay."

"Why is there a kite-shaped pin on your pocket?"

He turns to face me immediately, surprise coloring his expression. "You're asking *me* a question?"

Heat, that familiar, horrible heat: I feel it burning on the crests of my cheeks. "No."

"No?"

"No," I say, this time with forced indifference. "I'm withdrawing my question."

"No way," he says, smiling now. "You've already spoken it into the world. You can't take it back."

"You don't make the rules."

"How about a deal?" he says. "If you start answering more of my questions, maybe I'll answer some of yours."

I shake my head, panic threatening.

I already have to live with the enormous mistake I made the other day, exposing myself and my inspection of him in a childish burst of anger. I'd been unbalanced by the sheer force of James's attention, his easy smiles and laughter. No one but Clara ever smiles at me with sincerity. I'd been subjected to the dizzying power of his charm for hours by that point, and I was feeling frustrated and reactive. I spoke too much without thinking.

Never again.

I force myself to break away now, to gather up my journal and clear my mind before I say or do something irreparable—when I'm suddenly, uncomfortably aware of the moss between my toes. I realize I don't know what they did with my shoes.

"They're outside the door," he says.

I look up like I've been slapped.

"Your shoes," he says, unprompted. "They're outside. In a little cubby with your name on it."

"I didn't say anything about wanting my shoes."

"I know," he says.

"How did you—"

"Because," he says. "You just looked at your feet, and then looked around. I did the math. It's not complicated."

I'm looking at him and coming loose again. I have a new dream: I'd like to be neatly folded, set aside in a slant of light, and allowed to collect dust.

James, I realize, makes me feel like I can rest.

It's a hysterical, dangerous thought. As if I might ever be allowed to untie these ropes, unlock these chains.

I'm going to go home.

I'm going to go home, collect Clara, try to avoid marrying Sebastian, and spend the rest of my life withering into ash. I was trained from childhood for life as an executioner. It was what my parents wanted for me; more than that, it was the only career path I was allowed. For as long as I can remember, every psychological evaluation and aptitude test agreed: the child appears to be dead inside.

There was something wrong with me, something broken, some meaningful reason why I never laughed the way other children did, never smiled at strangers. Why I never cried when they sliced me open over and over and over again, trying to feed my mind to a machine.

I would not be a scientist or a doctor. Not a mother or a soldier. I would grow up to be an efficient killer. An excellent asset to the regime. At the height of The Reestablishment's power, I never imagined my skills would be so enthusiastically desired, but now that we lack the robust military of a bygone era, mercenaries are more important than ever.

Spies, assassins, executioners. We've been forced to downsize our kill capacity, designing missions with surgical precision and efficiency.

This is all my life is worth. And I decided long ago to sacrifice my dead body so that Clara might live.

"By the way," says James, interrupting my reverie. "If you're going to pretend to go through the motions, you need to work on the details. You carry that notebook around but you never carry a pen. You're not fooling anyone."

I don't know what prompts me to say it. I'm not sure I'm thinking at all when I say, softly—

"I've been fooling people all my life. You're the only one paying attention."

# JAMES

## CHAPTER 33

"Let me ask you something," I say, dropping into the velvet armchair. I sink into the plush fabric, the weight of the day dragging me down. "Is it normal for a girl to just stare at you a lot and not say anything? And if it's not normal, does that, like, mean something?"

Warner looks up at me from the darkened window, his eyes narrowing.

"Right," I say on an exhale. "I forgot who I was talking to. Staring at people and not speaking is *your* thing, isn't it?"

Warner doesn't take the bait.

He says, "A cold-blooded mercenary—loyal to The Reestablishment—is essentially imprisoned in a rehabilitation facility, where she's forced against her will to participate in excruciating group therapy sessions followed by hours of invasive questioning, and you're hoping I'm going to tell you that her silent, unyielding stare is an indication that she's in love with you?"

I slump backward, letting my head hang off the edge. The world flips upside down and I squeeze my eyes shut. "Well," I say, "when you put it like that."

A cool breeze pushes through the room. Crickets chirp steadily in the distant night. Low light warms the cozy space, the lamp on the side table casting a gentle glow over Juliette, who's sitting up in bed, rubbing her eyes. A book is split open on her bump.

"Are we talking about Rosabelle?" she says.

"You're tired, love," Warner says softly. "James and I can discuss this elsewhere. You should sleep."

"No," she says, even as she tilts back, closing her eyes against the headboard. "I want to know what's happening." She stifles a yawn, then turns to me. "Did she get in trouble again today?"

"Uh—" I glance at Warner, who's gone rigid. "Yeah," I say, sighing in defeat. "Yeah, she did."

It's been ten days.

Ten days of endless Rosabelle. Gorgeous Rosabelle. *Infuriating* Rosabelle. She's been sent to the Emotional Garden six times. Just today she received another official censure. I'd left to use the bathroom for all of five minutes, and by the time I got back, the group session was in chaos.

Rosabelle had Jing in a sleeper hold.

One of the sponsors was shouting, "She's using him as a shield!"; Ian was saying, "This is not how we solve to resolve!"; and by the time I pushed through the crowd to get to her, Jing had passed out. I watched, stunned, as he slid out of her arms into a heap on the floor. Rosabelle startled when she saw me, stepping away from Jing like a child caught stealing a snack.

"What are you doing?" I'd said, horrified. "Rosabelle, c'mon, we've talked about this—"

"I was trying to help," she'd said.

I nearly rocked back on my heels in astonishment, and she just looked at me with those blinking cat eyes and said she was encouraging Jing to give Elias his slippers back. The explanation was so absurd I almost didn't believe her until a grizzled older man came barreling through a moment later, tackle-hugging her gleefully from behind.

I'm exhausted.

If she's not driving me up a wall she's driving me insane. Sometimes all she does is look at me. I never know what to do when she does this, so I just sit there as she stares, her eyes raking over every inch of me, wondering what the hell she's thinking and knowing she'll never tell me. Sometimes she won't speak for so long the silence begins to make me sweat. I wake up thinking about her. I fall asleep thinking about her. I accidentally brushed against her going through a doorway and the way my body reacted you'd think she'd pinned me to the wall and offered to unzip my pants. I had to leave the building just to get some air. I've started dreaming about her. I wake up in the middle of the night overheated and out of my mind. I've had trouble sleeping all my life—but this might be the worst sleep I've had in years.

"Maybe we should take you off this assignment," says Warner, stepping away from the window.

"What?" I sit up. "Why?"

"I'm not sure you can handle it."

I bristle, and the lie is automatic: "I can handle it."

"What did you discuss with her today?"

I swallow and sit back, glancing around the room, shopping for time. Today I watched her braid her hair. Braid and unbraid it. Braid and unbraid it.

I asked about her parents. She looked at me.

I asked about her sister. She looked at me.

I asked about her ex-fiancé. She looked at me.

I'd finally crossed my arms and said, "Are you going to do this forever? Seriously? You're just going to sit there and stare at me and give me nothing? What's your favorite color, Rosabelle? Can you tell me your favorite color? Or is that some kind of highly protected trade secret you can't speak into the world for fear of inciting a new war?" and then she *laughed* at me, and then I had a stroke. I actually felt the blood drain from my face. My hands went hot, then clammy.

It was a soft, musical sound I'd never heard from her. Hell, I'd never even seen her smile.

She was still smiling when she looked at me after that, the gentle expression lingering on her face.

My fucking soul left my body.

I'd always thought she was gorgeous, but I had no idea what I was missing. The way her eyes lit up, the way her nose wrinkled. She's been eating more every day, looking healthier, growing only more radiant.

"*Wow,*" I'd whispered, gaping at her like an idiot discovering his hands for the first time. And then, realizing I'd said the word out loud, I reached inside myself and put my fist through my brain.

"Have you actually lost your mind?" says Warner, his

anger so sharp it slaps me back to the present.

I'm not entirely sure how much of my emotional turbulence he's picking up on right now, but the look on his face is telling me it's probably a lot.

"You know," I say, pointing at him. "It's interesting. There's something about the way she always has her guard up that actually reminds me of you."

Warner's face goes neutral at that. A clear sign he's hiding his own emotional response. "Excuse me?"

Juliette makes a *hum* of interest.

"Like, obviously you guys are different people," I clarify. "But I know the real you, because I've lived with you for so long. I know that the face you put on for the world isn't the one you wear when you feel safe. She gives off that same vibe. Sometimes I don't get a lot of answers out of her, but then she'll look at me and I swear I can *see* her." I turn away. "Like the real Rosabelle is a girl living inside a fortress inside a fortress inside a fortress inside a fortress. But the walls are so thick no one can hear her screaming."

When I finally look up, I discover Warner is watching me. Juliette is watching me.

"What?" I say.

"You care for her," says Warner.

"No, I don't," I lie.

"You do," says Juliette, her eyes going soft. "Oh, James."

"This is an unfortunate development," says Warner, turning toward the window.

"It's not like that," I lie again, fighting for redemption.

"It's just that sometimes I get the sense that she's, like, genuinely scared. Or nervous. Or just *human.* Sometimes I really get the feeling she would walk away from The Reestablishment if she thought there was a way out. And for the record, I don't think she's cold-blooded—"

"Kenji might be able to handle it," Warner says to Juliette. "Or Samuel."

Juliette shakes her head. "They're both overloaded right now, and Samuel doesn't have the clearance."

"Hugo might be ready," says Warner.

"Oh, Hugo," says Juliette sleepily.

*"Hey,"* I say angrily. "You said I had eight weeks. It's only been ten days—"

"It might be a good entry point, give him a chance to prove himself," says Warner. "Then again, if we're wrong, he could prove to be a liability—"

"I'd like to see Hugo in action," Juliette says. "He's been in a holding pattern for long enough—"

"Fine," I say, throwing up my hands. "You want hard data? Fine. She told me her mother's name was Anna. She says her parents are dead. She's twenty years old. Her sister is seven years younger than her. She has no other siblings. You already know about the wedding invitation; she was engaged to a guy named Sebastian back on the island, and she told me when I first met her that it's not happening anymore. It's possible they were matched together by their parents, which might explain why she was able to walk away from the situation so easily. It also meshes with the theory that she was born into a wealthy, high-ranking family, because, as you know"—I look up—"betrothals were a common practice among The Reestablishment elite, and the very fact that she was on the Ark at all indicates she enjoyed a rarefied level of privilege—"

"When did her parents die?" Warner asks, cutting me off.

"I don't know."

"Which sector did she live in?"

"I don't know."

"Have you been able to gather any more information on the Nexus? How it works? Who controls it?"

"No."

"Why does she have a scar on the inside of her forearm?"

"I don't know—"

"Where did her bruises come from?"

"I don't know."

"Why wasn't she informed of your identity before she killed you?"

"I don't know!"

"Then what *do* you know?"

"I know that she's right-handed? She recently discovered she doesn't like tomatoes? Direct sunlight sometimes makes her sneeze?"

Juliette yawns again, shifting against the headboard.

"Ten days," says Warner. "Ten days you've been with her and this is all you've uncovered."

"You told me to talk to her," I hit back. "You told me to act like we believe she's here for a chance at a new life. You told me to ask her normal questions with no hostility. How am I supposed to interrogate her when I was explicitly told not to interrogate her?"

"It's called *finesse,*" says Warner, a muscle ticking in his jaw. "Maybe I should do it myself."

"No," I practically shout. "It's not safe for any of you to have direct exposure to her. Besides, you already have ten billion things to manage. Don't take me off the assignment. C'mon, bro. This is bullshit. She already knows me—"

"Shut up for a second."

I'm ready to protest, but then Warner crosses the room to Juliette, gathering her into his arms with a tenderness he exhibits with no one else. I watch, my anger deflating, as he helps settle her into bed, adjusting her head, drawing her hair away from her eyes. He positions extra pillows around her body, closes up her book, places it on the nightstand, and then draws the blanket up around her shoulders.

She murmurs a thank-you to him, and he kisses her forehead, the tender exchange making me restless, like I need to exit my body. Growing up with these two has ruined me for regular relationships. I want what they have.

Warner looks up at me as the thought crosses my mind, studying me as if I'd spoken the words out loud.

"Has she asked you any more questions lately?" Juliette asks, sliding a hand under her pillow.

"Sort of," I say, the fight leaving my body. "She doesn't ask a lot of questions about me, personally. But she's been asking some questions about what our world looks like. She was confused about my watch"—I hold it up as proof—"the regular use of pen and paper, the touches of analog tech everywhere." I hesitate. "She did ask a really specific question about the light in the Emotional Garden." I tilt my head, remembering. "She wanted to know if it was real."

Warner stiffens.

"Oh, she's planning to escape," Juliette says, stifling another yawn. "She must be expecting contact soon."

"What?" I frown. "What do you mean?"

"Use your head," Warner says quietly. "She's asking practical questions about tech and society because she's preparing for engagement in foreign territory. She wants to know whether the light is real because—"

And then it hits me. Hard. I slump back in my chair, feeling stupid. "Because she's trying to figure out whether the building is underground."

A sudden, shrill alarm rings softly through the room, and Warner stands up, sliding the receiver out of his pocket. He unfolds the razor-thin metal, and Kenji's voice projects immediately into the room—

"Hey man, I know it's super late and you're supposed to be offline right now, but Maya told Agatha to tell Ian who called *me* to say that they're all worried something weird is going down in the hall outside Rosabelle's bedroom—"

I bolt upright, nearly knocking into Warner. "What does that mean?"

Warner looks at me, annoyed.

"I don't know, man," says Kenji. "But Ian says that Maya

says your girlfriend is talking to Leon about— Oh, *shit*."

The line goes quiet. Kenji's just breathing.

"What?" we all say at the same time.

"James, get your ass over there," he says, all traces of humor gone from his voice. "Maya just sent me some footage from the hallway cams."

"Okay, I'm leaving now— I'll be right there— Is she trying to kill him again?"

"No," says Kenji, subdued. "I think this dude might be trying to kill *her*."

# ROSABELLE

## CHAPTER 34

The knock at my door comes in the night.

My eyes open, but my body is calm. It's been ten days since I arrived at the facility, and I'm still no closer to a lead on the vial. In the end, Leon proved to be nothing more than a distraction; I haven't seen him since the incident. I considered launching a covert sweep of his room just to be certain, but he's locked himself inside since the day I killed him, citing me as the reason he refuses to emerge, not even for meals. I'm not sure how they're feeding him.

Agatha and Ian officially hate me.

I've kept my focus on James, instead, watching him for signs, grasping for meaning in small details. Ultimately I'm at the mercy of another agent, waiting to be contacted by someone who has to find a way to reach me; if they fail, I will fail. There are only four days left. Lately I spend my nights staring up at the ceiling, holding on to the sides of my bed as my head spins.

James has poisoned me.

He's in my veins. I'm sick with weight of him, sick at the sight of him. His voice haunts me; his presence disarms me. His face surfaces every time I close my eyes, so I try not to close them. I try not to think about his hands or his laugh or the way he quietly sighs, sometimes, when he looks at me. I try not to linger over a startling, terrifying desire to touch him. To be touched by him. Mostly I think about the guillotine that is my place of rest.

When the knock comes again, the interruption is almost a relief. I reach under my pillow for the butterknife I snuck into my room, holding it loosely as I pad, barefoot, to the door.

I wait, listening. Not breathing.

The knock comes a third time, and with it, a voice: "Rosybelle? Rosy-rose, are you awake?"

I flip the butterknife in my hand and unlatch the door, swinging it open. Leon is standing in the dim light.

"Can I help you?" I say to him.

"I got your note," he says, looking unsteady.

I analyze his dilated eyes more closely, wondering at James's assessment of his lucidity. I assumed Leon was terrified to be near me, so this burst of enthusiasm is a confusing surprise.

"What note?" I ask.

"I forgive you, Rosy," he says, stage-whispering. "I know you didn't mean to hurt me."

"Leon," I say firmly. "What note? What are you talking about?"

He unfolds a piece of paper, skimming it. "You said you've been looking for somewhere to rest your head, for a home that will last forever. You said you would die for me. You described the depths you would go to for me. You said that if I want something, I just have to ask for it." He looks up at me when he's done, eyes dopey and unfocused.

I tighten my hand around the weapon. There's definitely something wrong with him.

"Can I have that note, please?"

"No," he says, crushing it to his chest. "I'm going to keep it forever, Rosy. I just wanted you to know"—he shakes his head, hard—"I had to tell you to your face, so you could see it in my eyes: I don't like you at all."

This actually stuns me.

"I have a wife," he whispers, his eyes going wide. "And you are very beautiful, Rosabelle No-last-name, but my wife is much more beautiful than you, and I know in my heart that we aren't meant to be together because I don't like you at all. I love someone else, and I'll love her forever, and she is so much better than you in every way"—he lowers his voice—"and I know that this is very sad for you."

"Leon."

"Yes, Rosy?"

"Where is your wife?"

He shakes his head again, this time so hard his hair flops around. "I don't know," he says, leaning into me. "Do you know? Did he tell you where they took her?"

"Who? Who took her from you?"

"You *do* know," he says. "You *do* know who took her,

because it's happened to you, too." And then he starts crying, his face crumpling. "Oh, Rosy, can you feel it happening again?"

I take a breath. At first I thought maybe Leon had simply lost his mind, but now I'm starting to worry. "Feel what happening?"

He looks around, shoulders tight, the tears stopping as suddenly as they started. "I can feel it happening again, Rosybelle. You can feel it, too."

"Leon."

"Yes?"

"Please give me that note."

"No," he says loudly. Angrily. "It's mine. You said you've been looking for somewhere to rest your head, for a home that will last forever. You said you would die for me. You described the depths you would go to for me. You said that if I want something, I just have to ask for it."

"Leon—" I try again, reaching for the paper.

"No!" He whips away wildly, breathing fast. "You said you've been looking for somewhere to rest your head, for a home that will last forever. You said you would die for me. You described the depths you would go to for me. You said that if I want something, I just have to ask for it."

*Pay attention.*

Intuition tells me to take a cautious step back.

Leon straightens, his forehead smoothing, his shoulders drawing back. He seems to slot into his body, growing back into himself, the sharp lines of his face catching shadows. His eyes gleam like flat coins and I clench the butterknife a little tighter.

"You're not the only one here," he says, smiling. "You're not the only one."

"What does that mean?"

"It means you're not special," he snaps at me. "And if you don't do it, someone else will."

*Pay attention.*

*If you're smart enough, you'll see it coming.*

"Do what?" I say, hoping to guide him with my voice to remain calm. "I need you to give me more information—"

His eyes die out without warning, shoulders hunching, tears streaming down his face again. He looks around, blinking fast. "Can you feel it, Rosybelle? Can you feel it happening again?"

My instincts are at war: Kill him or keep him talking?

I decide he might still prove useful.

"Leon," I say. "How long has your wife been missing?"

"I don't know!" he says, and grabs my arms. "Where did they take her?"

I command myself not to react to this physical contact, forcing myself to look into his wild eyes. He's clearly incapable of coherence.

"Leon," I say again. "Please give me that note."

"No!" he cries, backing away from me. "It's mine. You said you've been looking for somewhere to rest your head, for a home that will last forever. You said you would die for me. You described the depths you would go to for me. You said that if I want something, I just have to ask for it."

"I'm asking for it right now," I say, fighting my anger. "Give it to me—"

"You can't take it!" he says. "You can't take anything else away from me!"

"I didn't take anything from you. I wasn't the one who went through your things." I glance up and down the quiet hall, my instincts now screaming. "Leon," I say, trying to meet his eyes. "Listen to me. I wasn't the one who ransacked your room, and I didn't write that note. I think someone is trying to frame me—"

"Don't worry, Rosy," he says softly, turning the crumpled paper around to show me. "I know you didn't do it."

The page is blank.

Leon laughs, then goes limp, his arms hanging heavily by his sides. "Why would you go through my things? You don't even know where I hid it." He leans toward me, and I watch, horrified, as a slinky black skin appears and disappears across his eyes. Then, whispering: "I didn't want to find it, Rosabelle. He made me find it."

Now, a spike of true fear impales me.

I'm trying to stay calm. Trying to keep my breathing even. But a terrifying thought is gathering steam in my head, disparate strokes of color coming together to form a disturbing picture.

"Who made you find it?" I ask.

"Nosy Rosy!" Leon shouts, his head lolling sideways. "My beautiful rose, I'll give you a little earth, Rosabelle, let me look inside you, Rosabelle, Rosabelle, Rosabelle—"

Finally I snap.

I grab a fistful of his shirt violently, pressing the butterknife to his throat. "Start answering my questions," I say. "Or this time when I kill you, I'll make sure no one will be here to save you."

His eyes widen. He looks suddenly panicked. "But I brought you a drink of earth," he says. "I'm a big boy, Rosy, I made it all by myself." He reaches into his pocket and retrieves a glass vial, the glinting receptacle filled with darkness. "Klaus made me find it," he says, and then he's crying again, his shoulders collapsing. "Klaus wanted you to have it. He made me leave my room. He made me do it, Rosy, I didn't want to—"

My right hand trembles and I let go of him, shaking the tremors loose from my fist before taking the proffered vial. My heart is racing dangerously fast. The glass is warm against my skin.

"Goodbye, my beautiful rose. Goodbye. Goodbye. They took your father the way they took my wife, remember? Can you feel it happening again, Rosy?"

Shock rattles through me. "What? What are you talking about?" I shake him slightly. "Leon? Leon, where's Klaus?"

"Klaus?" He breathes the word, his voice changing,

his back straightening. The black skin crawls over his eyes again. “Klaus is here.”

I stifle a shudder, containing my horror. “Where?”

Leon grabs me by the throat and lifts me off my feet.

# ROSABELLE

## CHAPTER 35

I fight back a scream.

I already know better than to kill him. I know, even as spots crowd my vision, that Leon is gone, that killing his host body will only delay the inevitable. Somehow, I'm being punished, and I need to pay attention.

I don't know how this is happening.

I don't know why his eyes flash black instead of blue. I don't know how Klaus has managed to override Leon's mind; I didn't know it was possible for Klaus to have this kind of control from a great distance. I only know that I'm losing oxygen, struggling to see straight. He pushes me into my room, slamming my back against the interior wall. My eyes flutter as the butterknife falls, with a dull thud, from my hand.

"Phase three is now complete," he says.

He lets go of me without warning, and I collapse to the floor, slamming my head against the edge of the dresser, pain exploding behind my eyes. I look up, the room surging around me. I watch Leon close my door, turn on the lights, then flip the lock. I gasp for breath, massaging my throat.

"I wonder what time it is," I rasp, repeating the words I was instructed to speak.

"Late," he says, his voice low. "I heard you had questions, Rosabelle."

I try to swallow. "What do I do with the vial?"

"You drink it," he says.

"What will it do?"

Leon blinks, the inky film floating and retreating across his eyes. "Clear the way for the final three phases of the mission."

This renders me still. Fear is now unfolding within me at a rate I can't overcome.

"Look what they did to us," Leon is saying, gesturing around the room. "Look at what they took from us. Look what they did when they were allowed to think for themselves. They, like you, think they can escape control. Leon, too, thought he could escape us. He was the first scientist to taste the earth—to experience the power of his own invention—but he decided, too late, that he didn't like Klaus. He performed merciless experiments on himself, trying and failing to undo the gene edit. Don't be like Leon," he says. "Leon tried to fight the future, and look what happened. Nothing good can come of the masses ruling themselves. Only chaos. War. *Anarchy.*"

"So you're testing this vial on me," I whisper, "to see if you can control me better than you controlled Leon."

"Control you?" Leon frowns, his muddied eyes affecting confusion. He bends down to my level, then taps my head like I'm a toy he's turning off. "Have you not figured out yet why you're here?"

I stare at him as he stands, my heart hammering against my ribs.

"Rosabelle Wolff, you've been sent here to die. Klaus looked into your mind and saw weakness unworthy of our greater mission. Your father was weak. Your mother was weak. Your sister was weak. You are a disgrace. You entertain near-traitorous thoughts about your nation, you resent the only man willing to marry you, and your everyday actions are motivated by the welfare of a diseased child whose existence only drains our resources. Your mind has been found wanting—and your life, as a result, is no longer worth sustaining. Your only benefit to us will be in your final sacrifice, should you choose to accept it."

This revelation batters me in waves, shattering the planes of my body like sheets of glass, leaving me in ribbons.

"You said— You promised me that if I completed my mission you would set me and my sister free—"

"Death is freedom. Should you choose to accept your final sacrifice, we will reward you by killing Clara swiftly. If you reject the final sacrifice, we will keep her alive for ten years, each day enduring greater tortures than the day before."

The room is spinning around me. Suddenly I can't breathe, can't see straight—

"You will dig your own grave, Rosabelle. You will drink the vial and bury yourself alive. Your body will decompose within twenty-four hours, the results of which will ignite an undetectable explosion that will radiate the land at unprecedented levels, effectively cauterizing all within a hundred-mile radius. The rebels' preternatural powers will disappear. Within six months, their bodies will succumb to the gene edit, allowing us control over them without further bloodshed or strife. This is the magnitude of our mercy."

"Why do I need to bury myself alive?"

"Your decomposing body will require fusion with a classical element; of the four, earth with earth is the most powerful."

I'm out of my mind, a collapsed star, a black hole, then nothing, nothing—

*You're not the only one,* Leon had said to me. *You're not the only one here.*

"You're doing this everywhere, aren't you?" I gasp. "All over The New Republic. I'm not the only one—"

"You have eight weeks to accomplish this task. Should you choose to reject this mission, you will be replaced, promptly assassinated, and your sister will suffer the consequences."

"What are the last three phases of the mission?" I manage to ask.

"Death, destruction, and rebirth."

"What does that mean?"

In response Leon unhinges without warning, his head hanging forward from his neck hanging forward from his body, his limbs locked in positions so unnatural I back away from him with a strangled sound. Leon is hyperventilating uncontrollably. He finally falls to his knees and claws at his head in a frenzied panic, and by the time he starts screaming I already know how it's going to end.

I throw my arms up over my face, the vial still clenched in my fist, bracing myself as he screams and screams until the lights come on in the hall, the sounds of footsteps thundering toward us. The handles on the dresser drawers begin rattling, the ground shuddering beneath me, fists pounding relentlessly against my door. I hear muted voices and cries, the clatter and snick of a lock tumbling. By the time Agatha slams open my bedroom door in a crazed panic, Leon has self-immolated.

I draw my hands away from my face and it seems to take years. Blood has spattered across the scene, smearing everything. I am numb as I survey the aftermath: gone are his eyes, his nose, his mouth. Leon has been eviscerated from the inside, flesh and blood pushed out of open orifices. My stomach heaves.

I double over.

I hear Agatha scream, and then the room is swarmed—faces and limbs blurring together and I'm stumbling upright, realizing too late how this looks: Leon, brutally murdered inside my bedroom, entrails still exhaling from his body as blood stains the carpet beneath us. I stand over him, my face wiped of emotion—me, his murderer, the person who's already tried to kill him once. Jaws are slack with horror, eyes wide and accusing. Even I can understand the ease with which they form their conclusions. Soon, hands are reaching, rushing at me. Crazed expressions, gasps of urgency, someone shouting *get the manacles* and I remember, with a start, Agatha's promise to melt my mouth off my face.

I realize then that I have no choice.

I tuck the vial in my pocket and fumble for the butter-knife on the floor and Agatha shouts *She's got a weapon!* and I dive out of the way of an electric lasso, crashing into the mirror hanging behind the bathroom door. Glass shatters around me and I don't hesitate: I whip a shard at the woman's throat—Deepti, her name is Deepti—and listen for impact, then scramble to my feet as she releases a guttural, choking cry. Agatha launches herself at me in a rage and I make use of her momentum, flipping her over my head, dropping to one knee, and burying the knife in her chest.

I feel a buzz of awareness as I yank the dull blade free, the hum of an unexpected quiet falling over the room. I look up, slowly, at the stunned sea of familiar faces, then the blood on my hands, the look of frozen astonishment on Agatha's face. Jing is crying. Elias has covered his mouth in horror. Aya has wet herself. Ian is sagging against the wall, looking like he might throw up. I'm miles and miles away from my mind when James finally bursts into the room, and the look on his face as he takes it all in—when he turns and stares at me with a wordless, shattering, breathtaking disappointment—

It actually kills me.

I feel it: my extremities go numb; my heart slows inside my body. My bones give out and I slump to the ground, my head hitting the wet carpet. I stare up at the recessed lights as they dim and flare, pushing everything out of focus. I turn my neck and the effort is exhausting; I blink and it lasts a century. Hands handle me roughly, strip the butterknife out of my fist. I don't want to fight anymore. I don't want to kill anymore. I don't want to be this person anymore. I don't want to live in this body anymore—

You've been dead inside for years, I remind myself.

Die, I tell myself.

*Die.*

My eyes roll back inside my head, my heart turns to stone in my chest. I feel my mind disconnecting. My chest stops moving. I'm aware, somehow, that I'm no longer breathing, no longer feeling. My skin is a rubber suit, sloshing with liquid.

*Die, Rosabelle,* I tell myself.

*Die.*

And this time, I do.

# ROSABELLE

## CHAPTER 36

*In my dreams, everything is soft.*

*The harsh edges of the world are blunted, my face cradled by clouds. My body seems suspended in water, my hair freed from its utilitarian knot, silky lengths cascading down my back. I am a body still becoming, untouched by tragedy. In my dreams I am safe; I have a strong hand to hold; a door to lock against the dark; a trusted ear into which I whisper my fears. In my dreams I am patient and kind; I have room in my heart for more pain than my own. I am not afraid to smile at strangers. I have never witnessed death. In my dreams sunlight glazes my skin; gentle wind caresses my limbs; Clara's laughter makes me smile.*

*She is running.*

*In my dreams, she's always running.*

My heart restarts with an electric jolt.

*"Then try it again," barks Soledad, his voice booming inside of me. "What do you mean there's no brain activity?"*

*"Sir, we've tried to implant the chip several times now, but we can't get her to connect—"*

*"That's bullshit," he cries. "Try it again."*

Alarms blare, hands handling me, stripping me. Cold metal and flashes of light.

*"We did it exactly as you asked," says someone nervously. "We tried it again—this year without any anesthetic, just as you instructed—"*

*"Then why isn't she moving?" he says. "Shouldn't she be screaming?"*

*"Yes, sir. That would be the normal reaction, sir. Yes."*

*"What the hell is wrong with her? Is it possible she still has a mutative gene interfering with the process?"*

*"It's hard to know. We've administered the gene-editing therapy several times now; at this point she should have no residual mutations, had there been any to begin with."*

*"This is unbelievable. Billions spent on research, and you can't give me a solid reason why there's one person on this island who can't be brought online?"*

Cool water, warm water, more hands on my body.

*"It's been two years of trying," says Sebastian. "She's had plenty of time to recover between attempts. I'm sorry, sir—she promised me it would work this time. She promised me it wouldn't happen again—"*

*"I'm sick of this," Soledad says angrily. "It's been years of bullshit excuses. I want a real explanation—"*

*"Her body is exhibiting some kind of resistance," says a voice I*

*don't recognize. "We've tried it a number of different ways now. No matter what we do, by the time we get everything online it just stops working. The tech is being rejected."*

*"That's impossible," he says. "The program is flawless. It's been tested in a thousand ways—"*

*"We don't know why it's happening," says the voice, terrified now. "In order to bring her online, the mind has to be active. For some reason, we can't get a signal."*

*"What the hell does that mean?" Soledad demands. "Her brain just isn't working?"*

*"Yes, sir. Her brain waves are nonresponsive."*

*"How?" I hear the moment his anger becomes suspicion. I hear it from lifetimes away, as if I'm suspended from the sun. "You're saying her body assumes a vegetative state at will?"*

*"Yes, sir. As far as the program is concerned, she appears to be dead inside."*

It occurs to me that I am naked.

My flesh is pressed against cold metal, a coarse sheet pulled up to my neck. My nerves awaken, like antennae unfurling. My skin seems to soften, my bones to harden. Sound returns to me slowly and scattered: the buzz of electricity, the drag of a footstep, the jangle and clatter of steel, the scrape of tools, sharpening.

Then his voice: a miracle.

"I can't believe she's really dead. This is crazy. Are you sure there was no heartbeat? Shouldn't we be absolutely sure before we do this? Because there's no logical reason why she should be dead right now—"

A woman says, "She suffered a bad blow to the head at some point in the night. Sometimes the symptoms of a brain hemorrhage are hard to spot."

I'm on a gurney, I realize, wheeling through space. I feel every bump and rattle of the wheels, the cold bite of metal against my skin. Footsteps pound the floor around me, pound in my head. My heart is beating so slowly it seems to drag. I feel ancient, held together by cobwebs.

"Wait," James is saying. "Hey— Wait— Can you just hang on for a second—"

The gurney comes to a sudden, violent halt. My body sloshes. My teeth rattle.

"Let it go, James," says a cold male voice I've never heard before. "I want the autopsy performed without delay."

*Autopsy.*

I must be in the morgue.

"You're just going to cut her open?" James is saying. "You're not even going to try—"

"Look," the woman says, her voice brisk. "There's nothing we can do to help her. She's already dead. We're thinking she died at least thirty minutes ago. No amount of healing is going to bring her back to—"

My eyes open slowly, the effort like prizing an orange peel from its flesh. My fingers curl by micrometers under the starchy sheet, my lungs expanding a degree at a time.

*"Fucking zombie,"* someone screams.

My eyes tear as light and color flood my vision. I blink

several times before my sight settles, images layering and focusing. A man with jet-black eyes and matching hair is looking down at me, gaping.

"Oh my God," he says, clasping his chest. "She just gave me a heart attack. Oh my God, I can't breathe—"

Standing beside him is James. Twice.

Two Jameses.

I blink and the images do not reconcile; instead, they sharpen, the differences between them becoming clearer. Different hair, different eyes. One James is older than the other James: his face sharper, harder, fewer laugh lines around his eyes. Same nose, same jawline, no freckles.

I prefer the freckles.

I like the touch of sun on his skin, the way his mouth animates easily, as if he's always hoping to smile.

Except now.

Right now, neither James looks pleased to see me. In fact, they wear similar expressions of fury. And then, of course, as my mind sorts itself out, it becomes obvious to me that the second James, the one with golden hair and green eyes, isn't James at all.

This, I realize, must be the older brother.

Aaron Warner Anderson.

Even now, with my senses on simmer, a flash of trepidation moves through me. The stories about the eldest Anderson brother are legendary, even on the Ark.

"Rosabelle?" James says cautiously. "Can you hear me?"

I try to open my mouth, but the effort to unseal my lips is too much. I've been dead, I think, for too long.

"I don't understand," says the woman just out of my sightline. She sounds breathless with fear. "She had no pulse. There was no heartbeat, no brain activity—"

"I think we should stick her in the fridge," says the man with the black hair. He has an impish look, somehow charming even as he insults me. "Give her some time to finish dying off."

James frowns. "What are you talking about?"

"This is probably some kind of glitch, right?" he explains. "This is like when a worm keeps worming even when it's split in half."

"Kenji—"

I make a note: the black-haired man is named Kenji.

"What?" he says, gesturing to me. "Look at her. She's barely even moving. This is, like, actual zombie behavior. I vote we put a bullet through her head just to be safe."

James, I notice, doesn't dismiss this suggestion; he only looks resigned. It occurs to me then that I've lost even the idea of him. James will never again be a place of rest for me. His eyes will never again warm in my direction.

He sees me now for what I really am.

*Your father was weak. Your mother was weak. Your sister was weak.*

*You're a disgrace.*

The pain of this realization is so acute it draws a

tortured sound from my throat.

"Oh, shit," says Kenji. "I think she's trying to say something—"

The burst of battered emotion has a counterintuitive effect, the flood of cortisol and epinephrine restarting my body, propelling my heart and lungs, flooding oxygen to my brain.

"Never mind," Kenji says, waving a hand. "False alarm."

I manage to lift my head slightly, and three things catch my eye in quick succession: the lab coat hanging from the wall, the vial of earth sitting on a steel counter, and the exit to my right. I settle back down, my mind spinning out scenarios, preparing for eventualities. I make a mental list of the kinds of tools I might find in a morgue, things that might double as weapons: bone saw; chisel; hammer; brain knife; rib shears—

If I'm going to do this, I'll only have one chance.

"Soooo, what's the plan?" asks Kenji. "Are we going to just stand here and stare at her? Because I don't—"

Warner holds up a hand, and the room falls silent.

He inspects me with a lethal calm that sends a pulse of renewed fear through my body. I blink coolly, keeping my face impassive, but he's looking straight into my eyes when he says, "Lock down the building, she's going to run—"

# ROSABELLE

## CHAPTER 37

I pull the sheet with me as I roll off the table and into a tumble, tripping only slightly as I rip the coat off its hook, whipping it around my body before swiping the vial from the counter, dropping it in my pocket. Warner and Kenji pull guns on me immediately, and I dive out of the way, shots ringing off steel surfaces. Chaos explodes: someone pulls an alarm, an automated voice screeching a security alert through speakers, James shouting my name. The unidentified woman screams, then drops to the floor, body crawling toward the exit. Kenji shouts angrily at James to get Warner out of the room, and I manage to duck behind a counter to catch my breath, buttoning my open coat as I strain to hear Warner's response, but his quiet words are buried in the blare of sirens. Whatever he says only makes Kenji angrier.

"If anyone is going to die tonight, it's not going to be you," he's shouting. "That kid is not going to grow up without a father. James, I swear to God, if you don't get him out of here I will shoot you in the face myself—"

I dart past a supply cart, swiping an armful of tools as another gunshot whizzes past my head. The door swings open before slamming shut, and suddenly it's me and Kenji, and my heart is beating in my throat. I have no idea what I'm up against. He, like the other rebels, might have some unstoppable preternatural power.

Still, somehow, my hands are calm.

"The building is shut down, Rosabelle," says Kenji casually.

I hear his footsteps, circling.

"Why don't you come out with your hands up so I can get a straight shot at your heart? Make sure you stay dead this time."

I dive behind another counter, throwing a brain knife at Kenji before launching myself behind a nearby cabinet. I hear his explosive, muttered curse when the knife makes contact, but there's no time to experience relief.

My small victory only infuriates him.

He shoots at me more aggressively, the ricocheting sounds of metal all but shattering my eardrums as I run, barefoot, whipping a chisel at his chest as I go. He grabs a steel tray at the last second, using it as a shield to deflect the blow, and the ringing reverberation hasn't even stopped before he's unloading rounds at my head again. I duck, forced to take cover farther from the exit. Even with his injury Kenji is blocking the door with his body, refusing to give up his position.

I dart out from behind the cabinet, throwing the hammer as hard as I can, but this time—I don't see him. In the seconds the hammer hurtles toward the empty doorway, time seems to expand and slow down. I scan the area as if in slow motion, and when I can't catch a glimpse of him, I decide to make a run for the exit—but he suddenly materializes, like magic, whipping the tray in his hands like a baseball bat. Steel connects with steel, the deafening sound ringing in my teeth. The hammer launches back in my direction and it hits me in the ribs so hard I see sparks, the pain forcing me to cry out.

Grasping my side, I dive for cover.

"Feels good, doesn't it?" he says. Then: "What's in the vial, Rosabelle?"

My breaths are coming in harsher, the agony in my abdomen blooming. Kenji, apparently, can disappear.

This is bad.

If I don't dispatch him soon, he'll be able to come up on me from an angle I can't anticipate. The only leverage I have right now is his unwillingness to leave the exit uncovered. That means he's unlikely to go far.

Still, there's no way to be certain.

I take inventory of my three remaining weapons: a saw; a skull key; an empty syringe. A gun would be much better.

I take another beat to regroup, then risk a glance at Kenji from behind a steel rack. He shoots at me and I fall back just as a bullet whispers past my head.

"Do you have any idea," he says, speaking through audible discomfort, "how many people are going to be pissed off when they find out you put a knife in my leg? How am I going to walk to The Waffle's Waffles in the morning, Rosabelle?" He shoots at me again. "How am I supposed to feed the ducks at the fucking park, Rosabelle?" He fires at me again.

I listen to him shifting in the proceeding silence.

He's taking a moment to reload his gun, swapping out the magazine with a series of satisfying clicks, and I waste no time bolting behind a counter closer to the exit, whipping the skull key at his shooting arm. The chisel head of the instrument pierces his flesh with a satisfying *thwack*, and the gun clatters to the floor, spinning away from him.

"Son of a bitch," he cries.

I dive for the weapon, skidding sideways as I swipe it, then jump to my feet with difficulty, pivoting toward him. I'm breathing so hard my throat is dry, sticking as I swallow. I raise the gun to his face and he doesn't even flinch. He just looks at me. Looks at me and shakes his head, disappointed.

Another disappointment.

My every instinct screams at me to take him out: head, throat, heart. But the image of Agatha's face surges before me, reminding me—

I did everything The Reestablishment asked me to do.

I did what I thought I had to do, and in the end my sacrifices were worthless. My life, worthless. Darkness breeding darkness breeding darkness, all this blood on my hands giving birth to more bloodshed, the mutilation of my soul leading to the mutilation of others, my life gone up in flames only to set fire to the world.

I blame myself.

I thought it was smart to choose the lesser of two perceived evils. I thought I'd be rewarded for aligning myself with the obvious victor; I was naive enough to assume I might one day be offered immunity by a tyrannical regime. I took shelter in the arms of an open enemy, doing their bidding even as they starved and tortured my family—even as they slowly stripped their own people of humanity in the name of security. Cruelty rebranded as freedom, torture rebranded as justice, horrors exported to perpetuate horrors all in the interest of absolute control. An oblivious populace living in the palm of an all-powerful hand, easily crushed.

For all my efforts, Clara will never be safe.

I failed my sister. I failed myself. There's only one path left to set this right, and in order to fix things I need to be able to walk out of here alive. I need to get back home as soon as possible. That means I need to kill Kenji.

But I don't want to be this person anymore.

I don't want to live in fear of my hands, my head, the collapsed star that is my soul. I don't want to live every day only for the promise of death.

The problem is, I don't know how to stop being this person.

"I don't want to kill you," I say to him. "I just want to get out of here. I don't need your help to escape. I don't need anything from you. I just want you to let me leave. Let me leave so I don't have to kill you."

Kenji closes his eyes and sighs.

"All right, fine," he says. "You can come out now."

"What?" I hear the click before I understand, and my heart sinks as the cold barrel of a gun presses against the back of my head.

"Drop the weapon," James says quietly.

I let it slip from my fingers, and it falls to the floor with a resounding clatter. Kenji limps over to it, scoops it up with his good arm, and hauls himself over to me. Suddenly, I've got two guns to my head. Front and back.

"You got the manacles?" Kenji says to James.

I can feel him shake his head. "I've only got zip ties."

"That'll work for now."

I stand there, staring into the distance as James ties my hands behind my back, trying not to think about the feel of his skin or the warm, electric graze of his fingers against my wrists, so gentle with me even now. Of all the ways I dared to wonder what it might be like to touch him, I never thought it would happen like this.

Kenji pulls the glass cylinder from my pocket, holding it before my face with a knowing look.

"What's in the vial, Rosabelle?" he says. "Planning a massacre?"

My eyes close, horrors upon horrors crashing down around me. Images of Clara crowd my head. Reminders of a night still unprocessed, threats still unresolved.

No matter what I do, I lose.

"Warner is prepping a cell for her at supermax," says Kenji. "Can you handle getting her there? She's a flight risk. You're going to have to take the tunnels."

*Supermax.*

Maximum-security prison.

"Yes," James says darkly. "I can handle it."

The molten fury of his voice whispers across my skin, sending chills coursing through me. I still haven't seen his face. I have no idea what he's thinking.

"I'm calling for backup just to be safe," Kenji says.

"I don't need backup."

Kenji laughs, like this is absurd. "I'll make sure Samuel meets you underground. He'll bring the manacles."

James takes a tight breath. I can practically feel his irritation, even as he agrees. Then he says, "You going to be okay?" and for one delirious moment I think he's talking to me.

"I'll be fine," says Kenji. "Don't worry about me."

Kenji and James appear to be exchanging glances, communicating silently.

"All right, then, get her out of here," Kenji says, nudging my forehead with his gun as he steps back. I stumble slightly, and James slides a hand up to my waist, steadying me.

This brief contact nearly takes my breath away.

James draws the gun away from my head, the cool metal kissing my nape as he presses the barrel to my neck. He leans into my ear.

"I warned you," he says softly, and I stiffen, my heart

stopping. "I told you if you hurt my family you'd meet a very different version of me. Try anything with me tonight, and I will take you apart, Rosabelle. Do you understand? I will fucking destroy you. I don't care who you report to back home. Right now, you take orders from me."

His hand is still on my waist, his mouth so close to my skin. I don't even know what's happening to me anymore. I've been craving this kind of closeness with him for so long I can't tell the difference between pleasure and fear. My skin is hot, my head is hot. I can't catch my breath.

"Are we clear?" he asks, his whisper grazing my cheek.

I close my eyes, exhaling the word: "Yes."

# JAMES

## CHAPTER 38

This is an actual nightmare.

Hell on earth.

Worst day of my fucking life.

"Thank you," she says, the word echoing in the dimness. "You didn't have to do that."

I don't respond to this.

We'd been down here for all of five minutes before I realized she was barefoot. The tunnels are pretty clean—the polished concrete floors are fortified with steel panels—but we have at least a mile walk ahead of us, and I couldn't let her do this without shoes on. *Why* I couldn't let her walk a mile with no shoes on, I have no idea. The girl is every inch the backstabbing, cold-blooded mercenary everyone told me she was. I should probably get my head checked.

Instead, we went back.

Me, with a gun to her temple, going from nurse to medic on the floor, asking if someone had a pair of shoes—in her size—that they were willing to let her borrow. It was a literal comedy show. Absurd to an unbelievable level. I hated myself more in every second, and still, I couldn't stop. I kept thinking she was going to end up in prison with bloody, blistered feet. As if it matters. As if I should care.

I'm a raving lunatic.

At one point Kenji poked his head out of a recovery room and said, "What the hell are you still doing here?" and I gestured to Rosabelle and said, "She doesn't have any shoes," and he said, "She's not wearing any underwear, either, are you going to go around asking ladies to lend you their bras, too?" and I imagined, briefly, jumping off a bridge.

Now I'm here, holding a gun to Rosabelle's head and trying not to think about the fact that I've been having vivid, lucid dreams about this girl, trying for weeks to keep from so much as touching her by accident, and now here she is, practically in my arms, completely naked under that lab coat.

"James—"

"Don't talk to me."

My heart is racing so hard it's embarrassing me. I am an embarrassment to myself. My anger is out of control. My head is spinning, my emotions pinging from extreme to extreme. I saw evidence of her murderous sociopathy over and over again tonight. I saw the remains of an eviscerated man in her bedroom; I watched her nearly murder Kenji; I found a nefarious vial on her body; a plot foiled; plans made; and I still can't seem to shut off my feelings for her. It all happened so fast. The whiplash. I haven't had enough time to process, to kill the cancer she left in my heart. I feel sick. I feel literally, physically sick. The same day I hear her laugh for the first time I find her dripping in blood and entrails, surrounded by dead bodies. I can't think about it. I refuse to think about it.

*Fuck.*

I'm trying not to think about all kinds of things.

Deception. Betrayal.

The fact that she literally died before my eyes and then came back to life half an hour later.

"You know what I don't understand?" I say, laughing a little. I sound deranged even to myself. "I don't get how you're such a good actor. Being a talented mercenary is already a huge skill—but your theatrical skills are just on a whole different level. I can't believe I fell for it. All that stuff with the food, with your sister—"

I bring us to a sudden stop, something occurring to me. "Wait, do you even have a little sister? Or was that girl just a plant? Was any of the stuff you told me about yourself true? Should I just assume they were all lies?"

"James—"

"No. Don't *James* me. If you're going to say anything to me, make it the fucking truth." I turn her around, pin her to the wall, press the gun to her throat. "Who are you?" I ask her. "Who are you, really? I don't even know your real name."

When she stares up at me, I realize my mistake.

I haven't seen her face since the moment she pulled a gun on Kenji, and it was easier to live in my anger when I couldn't see her eyes. Now she's gazing up at me, soft and calm, with a sadness that feels so real it scares me. She looks wild and heartbroken and a little breathless, color high on her cheeks, eyes gleaming in the dim light. No walls, no shields. She's looked at me like this—totally and completely unguarded—only one other time. It was the day we met. Right before she killed me.

This was a bad idea.

Looking at her face was a bad idea. I want to turn her around, pretend this never happened, but now I can't stop thinking about all the places our bodies are touching, and it's making my head spin: my thigh brushing her bare leg; my hand on her waist. My fingers are pressing into soft flesh through her thin coat, my thumb almost grazing her navel. I lean into her unconsciously, moving no more than an inch, but when my hand slides across her hip she sinks back against the wall, her eyes closing on a sound so faint I think I've imagined it.

I want to hear it again.

I'm grappling with my self-control, still gathering my brain cells when she suddenly shifts under my hand, and my reflexive response is to keep her from running away: I step closer, gripping her more tightly, and this time she gasps, color flooding her skin. She blinks at me from under her lashes, her eyes heavy-lidded and glazed with hunger. The sight of her like this—the way she's looking at me with open, desperate desire—

I can't breathe.

My skin is too tight, these pants are too tight, my chest is ripping open. I want to taste her, tear open her coat and press my face to her skin. I want to come apart. I want her under my hands, want to breathe her in, want to know what she'd feel like in my arms with nothing between us. Just hours ago I'd have killed for this, for a moment like this.

"Don't look at me like that," I say, my voice like gravel.

She's staring at my mouth. She blinks up at me, her eyes clearing, returning. "Look at you like what?"

I can't take this.

I draw away from her and feel the loss immediately. My body is feverish, unsteady. I'm cursing myself, trying to pull myself together. I nudge her forward, one hand still on her waist, the other holding the gun to her neck.

My head is suddenly killing me.

My chest fucking hurts.

Our footsteps echo in the near darkness, orange light glowing at intervals. We've been walking in tortured silence for at least twenty minutes when she says my name again. She says it like a question.

"What?" I say, quieting my anger.

"Rosabelle is my real name. I didn't lie about that." She exhales. "My full name is Rosabelle Wolff. My family calls me Rosa."

For some reason, this admission clips me in the gut.

"And I do have a younger sister. Her name is Clara," she says, and her voice catches on the word.

I bring us to a stop.

We're holding still now, her back to my front, staring at nothing in the dim light of this tunnel, darkness narrowing in the distance. My heart is pounding so hard I feel lightheaded.

"My mother killed herself when I was ten," she says into the quiet. "Clara was three. I raised her on my own."

It takes me a second to realize I'm holding my breath. I've been pushing forever to get something real out of this girl. And now—

"Clara's been sick almost all her life. I don't know why. After my mother's death she was never the same. She cried nonstop for months. We never had enough food or firewood. Our cottage was always cold, always damp. Sometimes Clara was so hungry she'd chew the skin off her hands."

This nearly takes me out; I nearly lower the gun.

"Everything I've ever done," she says, her voice fading to a whisper, "has been for her. I realize that's not an excuse. I know I have no moral ground here. But doing my job meant I'd get the rations I needed to feed my sister." She hesitates. Breathes. "They used her to control me, and I knew it and I didn't care, even as their cruelty grew more apparent. They wouldn't give me medicine for her, not even when she started throwing up blood, and even when they did toss me scraps, the returns were diminishing. They'd give me less and less each time, always expecting more."

I shake my head. I feel like I'm at a breaking point. "Why are you telling me this? Why now?"

"I just—" She hesitates. "I just wanted to say I'm sorry."

I look away, swallowing. I don't know what to do with this girl. I don't know how I'm supposed to react to these words.

"Sorry for what?" I say, and I sound wrecked. "For

which part? For messing with my head? For coming into my life hoping to murder everyone I love? What's your end game, Rosabelle? What were you going to do with that vial? Are you still planning on trying to use it? Are you plotting another escape right now?"

"I haven't decided yet."

Now I'm fucking losing it. I laugh like an idiot, the sound echoing off the walls. "You're unbelievable. This is unbelievable. You haven't decided yet? And yet you expect me to just preemptively forgive you for whatever you're about to do—for anything you choose to do next—"

"Will you turn me around so I can see your face?"

"No," I nearly shout.

"Why not?"

"Because I can't look at you. If I look at you I'm going to do something stupid."

"James—"

*"Don't say my name."*

I feel her tense. Then her shoulders drop, her head falls. She seems so small and vulnerable and I hate it. I hate this. I hate that I'm pressing this gun to her neck. I hate that her hands are tied behind her back.

I hate that she's everything I hoped she wouldn't be.

# ROSABELLE

## CHAPTER 39

James swears softly under his breath.

We've come to a dead end.

After a series of circuitous turns through the labyrinthine tunnels, we've reached an inflection point. I look up at the towering ladder affixed to the wall, the exit door awaiting at the top. The tension in James's body is coming off him in waves.

"I forgot about this part," he says, shifting behind me.

It's the first time he's spoken to me in at least half an hour. His hands have been on my body for even longer, the heat and scent of him dimming my head, filling me with dizzying awareness. It doesn't seem to matter that he hates me; there's nothing I hate about him. He takes a breath, and I feel his unsteady exhale against my skin and I want to sink back against him. Feel the weight of his body around me, on top of me. Every time he touches me I wish he'd touch me again.

"I have to cut off your ties here so you can climb the ladder. Once we're at the top, I'll put on a fresh set. Do you understand?"

"Yes."

"Try to run," he says, leaning into my ear, "and I will kill you."

Somehow, I manage to breathe.

I hear him putting away his gun, then the slice of a knife unfolding, and then, moments later, the sharp tug of the ties before they come apart. He holds my wrists in one hand as he puts away his knife, and then he walks me to the base of the ladder like that, releasing me for only a second before grabbing a fistful of my coat, yanking me back against him.

I gasp.

Without my hands behind my back I can feel the press of his body against mine, hard and soft. So warm.

"I'm warning you," he says quietly. "You go up the ladder. Then the ties go back on."

"Okay."

He releases me. I don't move.

"What are you waiting for?" he says. "Go."

Still, I hesitate. "Can I just— Can I turn around for a second?"

"No."

Blood is rushing to my newly freed arms, my skin prickling as it awakens. Absently, I massage my wrists. "Please," I whisper. "This is important."

"If you have something to say, say it. You don't need to look at me."

"All right," I say, bracing myself. "I was going to ask, very politely, whether you might consider letting me go."

"What?" He stiffens behind me, then laughs, the harsh sound colored by disbelief. "Let you go where?"

"Back to the Ark."

Now he spins me around himself.

"Are you joking?" he says. The fiery lights cast a warm glow across his face, softening the harshness in his eyes. "Tell me you're joking, Rosabelle."

"I'm not joking."

This seems to hit him like a blow. "After everything you've done, you think you can just ask to be sent home? Pretend this never happened? Is that how you usually get out of these situations? You just ask, very politely?"

"That's not what I meant—"

"I don't even understand you," he says. "These people have been torturing you and your sister for years and you're just going to run back into their arms? You're going to do whatever they tell you to do for the rest of your life?"

"It's not what you think," I say desperately. "I have to go back because I need to fix things. I have a plan, but it's going to be complicated. Things are so much worse than you know, you don't understand—"

"Then help me understand," he says, his voice charged with feeling. "Tell me what's happening. Tell me what's going on—"

"I can't," I say.

"Why not?" he shoots back.

I'm shaking my head, trying to sort through my own

tangled thoughts. I made my decision to eliminate Klaus the moment he threatened to kill Clara.

It's the only solution to an impossible problem.

Klaus gave me eight weeks to destroy myself and, in the process, torpedo the epicenter of the resistance—which means I have eight weeks to get myself back to the island. Eight weeks to steal back the vial, find Klaus's tank, drink the earth, launch myself into the waters of his synthetic mind, and hope my decomposing body will detonate the explosion necessary to kill him. It's the only way to save Clara. It's the only way to spare the rest of the world a fate like Leon's. If I can take out Klaus before countless other agents launch their own attacks against The New Republic, I might be able to dismantle the entire system.

But I don't want anyone to know my plan, because I don't want anyone to try to stop me.

"I'm just— I'm not used to working with other people," I manage to get out. "I'm used to doing things on my own, and I don't know if I can trust your team—"

"Can you trust me?"

This question strikes me through the heart, rendering me silent. James steps somehow closer, his hands loose at his sides. No gun, no zip ties. He is, himself, the greatest weapon against my defenses. In his presence my shields warp, my heart slows, my fears quiet. In his presence my body yields to its original form: ice releasing under sunlight, returning to the sea.

"Rosabelle," he says. "Do you trust me?"

I look up into his eyes, astonishing myself when I say, softly, "Yes."

His eyes shut briefly as he exhales, and I watch him swallow as he looks at me, his eyes darkening with a look that leaves me breathless. I feel weak and euphoric this close to him, slightly intoxicated.

"If you trust me," he whispers, "we can fix this together. If you trust me, everything is simple."

"It's not simple," I say, shaking my head. "Infiltrating the Ark isn't easy. Their technological advancements are unparalleled. Their surveillance systems are like nothing else on earth—"

"I know, Rosabelle, I've been there. It's hard, but it's not impossible—"

*"No,"* I say sharply. "You don't understand. I know you think you escaped the island on your own, but it—"

"Oh, shit," James cries, grabbing me suddenly, spinning me away from the ladder. He pins my body against the wall, his back to my front. *Guarding me.*

I'm still trying to understand what's happening, my heart hammering, when over his shoulder I finally glimpse it—

The familiar laser line of a sniper.

# ROSABELLE

## CHAPTER 40

"You know we've got cameras down here, right?" calls a voice I've never heard before, echoing from above us.

"You can put away the scope, Samuel," James calls back. "Everything is fine."

There's a moment of hesitation. "You've been down here a long time, man. You sure you're okay?"

"Yeah," he says. "We're coming up right now."

"Great," says the guy named Samuel. "I'll wait."

James sighs, then turns to me, his eyes roving over my face in a quick, heated inspection. "You okay?" he asks quietly.

Two words, like a lead pipe to a pane of glass.

I'd like to curl up inside his shirt and rest. I want to be dropped in his pocket and left to sleep. I want to stand close to him just to be near him. Delusion has consumed me.

"I'm okay," I say.

He slides a hand around my waist like it's something we've always done, gently guiding me forward, ahead of him, toward the ladder. Then he lifts me into the air like it's nothing, holding me up until I find my footing on the rungs.

"You okay?" he asks again.

"I'm okay," I say.

As we approach the top I see the vague outline of a man looming overhead, boots thudding as he paces the landing. He watches me closely as I ascend, his rifle trained on my body at all times.

I pull myself up, deeply aware that I'm not wearing underwear as I disengage inelegantly from the ladder, bare legs scraping slightly against the concrete floor. I get to my feet and Samuel catches me by my collar, body-slamming me against the wall so hard the pain in my ribs flares suddenly back to life. Stars explode behind my eyes. He wrenches my arms behind my back.

I hear James shout "What the hell are you doing?" and Samuel laughs, confused, like the question is a joke, and by the time James hauls himself onto the landing I feel the cold slide of metal against my wrists, the *click* of bolts fitting together. I'm wearing a pair of heavy manacles that hum with controlled electricity and I feel the static in my teeth, the back of my knees. There's a metallic taste in my mouth rising by the minute, making me nauseous.

I capture the basics of Samuel's face as he pulls open the heavy exit door—brown skin, lighter brown eyes—then lose my footing as he shoves me into a blinding hallway, lights buzzing overhead. I stumble forward, unbalanced, and catch myself against a smooth, cold wall, my mind growing fuzzy. My tongue feels rough. Low-level electric currents are coursing through me, fizzing under my skin.

I push off the wall, still struggling with my feet when James rushes up behind us saying, "Hey, c'mon, that's not necessary—"

Samuel holds up a hand to slow him down.

"Bro, are you feeling okay?" he says, and I can hear the frown in his voice.

"What? Yeah, I'm fine—I'm just saying you don't have to handle her like that—"

"Like what?" Samuel laughs again. "Like a criminal? Like someone who literally disemboweled a man tonight?"

If James responds I can hardly hear it. I'm sinking into myself again, retreating inward, walls rebuilding. I try to push my mind free of this electric cage, but the static is inside my nose, then crackling in my throat, searing behind my eyes, blinding and *blinding*—

A strangled scream escapes me and I lose my footing again, slamming into another wall before falling to my knees.

*"Turn it down,"* James explodes. "Don't you see how small she is? You're overloading her body—"

The electricity retreats almost at once, returning me slowly to myself. I feel wrung out suddenly. My lungs tight, my mouth dry. My bones trembling.

Then hands on me, under me, and I'm in the air, my cheek against his chest, eyelids fluttering. My blood is fizzing, carbonated. I'm trying to wake up.

"What the fuck is wrong with you?" James is saying

angrily. “You were torturing her—”

“That was the default setting!” Samuel shoots back. “I’m treating her just like every other piece of shit who comes through here. You’re the one who’s clearly lost his mind. I came out there to help you—”

“I didn’t ask for your help,” he snaps. “Where the hell is Warner?”

“Put her down,” says a cold, familiar voice.

My eyes flicker open. Fear forces me back into my skin, adrenaline pushing my heart to work harder. James slides me carefully out of his arms, helping me stand, but he doesn’t remove his hand from my lower back. I look up into the bright, blinding light, my eyes tearing slightly. We’re at the edge of a common space, an interior quadrangle that anchors the multistory building. I count floors, stunned by the dimensions and the clean white lines. A few people mill about on every open level, moving from place to place.

“Step away from her,” says Warner, moving into my sightline. He’s looking at me, not James, when he says this, and the fury in his green eyes is so cold—so intensely palpable—I’m beginning to understand his reputation.

This man was raised by The Reestablishment. Forged in blood. Just like me.

James doesn’t move. “I need some time,” he says.

Warner turns toward his brother like a rising tide, the movement slow and powerful. “Excuse me?”

“I need more time. I have to talk to her.”

"Your days of talking to her are over. What happens to her from here on out is no longer your concern. Go home."

"What are you talking about—"

"Go home, James."

"Look, I know it's been a crazy night, but there are some developments I need to discuss with you—"

"Developments?" Warner echoes, astonished. "In the time it took you to walk her from a morgue to a penitentiary? Let me guess." Warner levels me with a look so black it borders on hatred. "She's opened up to you. Shown remorse. Given you just enough information to make you think you're special without telling you anything at all."

"Stop," James says angrily. "Don't do this. Everyone around here thinks they have me figured out—"

"I thought she told you her parents were dead."

At this, I inwardly flinch, and James stiffens beside me.

"Tell him," Warner says, addressing me directly for the first time. It surprises me how difficult it is to hold his undivided attention. There's a steel in him so severe it's disorienting. "Tell him the truth. Are your parents dead?"

I have no idea whether my father is still alive.

Still, the fact that Warner has somehow managed to figure out who I am—that he's managed to unearth unsavory details of my family history—does not come as a great surprise. After all, my father abandoned his family in order to pledge his allegiance to *him*.

To this man standing before me.

"My mother is dead," I say. "My father is dead to me."

This earns me something like a smile. "Take her away," Warner says. "Tell Hugo we'll begin in the morning."

I go suddenly still.

Warner is watching me for a reaction, and I realize only then that I've been expertly outmaneuvered.

*Hugo.*

I don't resist when I'm hauled away by rough hands, my mind surging with panic.

*Surveillance is security, Rosa. Only criminals need privacy.*

"Hey— Wait—"

*But, Papa, I don't want strangers to watch me all the time—that sounds awful—*

James takes a step toward me on instinct, falling back only when his brother claps him, hard, on the shoulder.

*Sometimes it doesn't matter what we want, Rosa. Sometimes we don't know what's best for us. Sometimes a child wants to touch the fire just to feel it burn. If we want to protect the child, we have to teach him to obey.*

I haven't seen my father in ten years.

*Hugo, sweetheart, can you ask Rosa to come here, please? She keeps ripping the blossoms off my roses—*

I look back at James as they take me away, my thoughts unspooling in alarm. His eyes are burning, ablaze with feeling, and I try to hold on to this image of him, committing the details to memory. I don't even think to struggle as I'm shoved forward, then dragged around a corner. This is not the time for action. There are dark days ahead of me. Long nights awaiting me. I need a place to rest my head, a place to sort my thoughts, a place to make my plans.

Prison will do just fine.

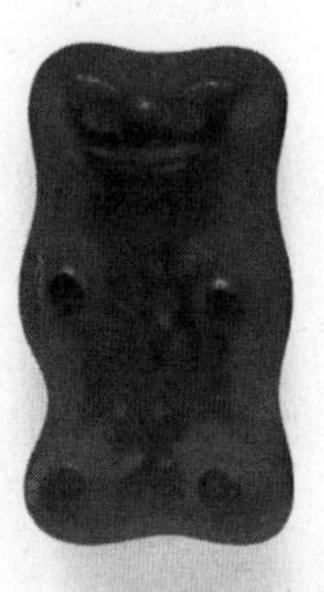

**James and Rosabelle's story continues in *Release Me*,**
**the breathtaking sequel to *Watch Me*.**

**SHATTER ME: SERIES TWO**
**BOOK TWO**

# WARNER

# 1

"Well?" I pivot slowly to face him, leaning one shoulder against a cold concrete wall. "Can you sense anything?"

Adam takes a tight breath.

"I don't know, man," he says. He shoves his hands in his pockets and shakes his head, exhaling. "I might need another minute. Something feels off."

I watch him shift his weight as his eyes track the vast window, assessing the stark scene beyond: Rosabelle Wolff is seated at a metal chair, unmoving, stiff as a stake in the ground as her estranged father, Hugo, attempts another ill-fated interrogation.

"Rosa," Hugo says desperately, his voice pitching higher. "Please—why won't you speak to me—?"

Every day has been a failure.

Every day Hugo's panic rises as the hours progress, his emotional instability spiking to near hysteria as Rosabelle grows only more remote. I've encouraged him several times to abandon the assignment, but now that he's seen her again after so many years apart, he's lost all objectivity. He's frantic for a spark of recognition—a moment of redemption—and he won't relent. I'd hoped his determination to connect with his daughter would give us a much-needed psychological advantage, but the unfortunate truth is that Hugo has become a liability. Worse, he's costing us time. Most days these sessions end in tears.

His, not hers.

I do my best, every day, to dissociate from his pain.

More concerning is that I haven't been able to get a read on Rosabelle in over a week. Her eyes are vacant, her energy cold. I've grown so accustomed to being flattened by the psychic torrent of other people that it's nearly disorienting to be confronted by her style of silence.

Rosabelle's emotional response is nonexistent.

In my life I've encountered one other person whose emotional state I couldn't fathom—and he's standing right next to me. My half brother Adam Kent Anderson. Only a year apart, we'd grown up never knowing the truth about each other or our family. For so long Adam and I had jettisoned our father's name from our lives; *Anderson* had once torn us apart. Our father had intentionally pit us against each other; in fact, we once sought to kill each other. But over the past decade we've learned to reclaim our shared name, slowly suturing ourselves back together. Me and my brothers, finally united under the same banner.

It was Ella who inspired this. Ella, who refused to be broken or branded by the story once written for her. It's what she taught me was possible when she took back the name Juliette.

She's known to the world as Juliette Ferrars.

She'll always be Ella to me.

I experience a stab of pain at the thought of her, tensing even as I try to ignore the blade of fear that's lately lodged itself between my lungs. A quickening in my blood chases every unguarded beat of my heart these days; my own feelings are so unstable I can't allow myself to experience them in full. The thought of losing her—or our unborn child—is more than my paper soul can survive. Even now I feel an encroaching tremor animate my body and I clench my fists in concert with my jaw, compartmentalizing my life the way I always do.

The way I have to.

"Hey," says Adam suddenly.

I realize only then, meeting his eyes, that he's been watching me.

"You okay?"

The lie comes out fast. "Yes."

"You sure?"

Adam's concern continues to surprise and disarm me, despite its consistency.

"I'm sure," I say, turning away, struggling to rebuild the walls in my mind.

"Hey," he says again. "Look at me for a second."

When I look up I feel the spike in his sympathy. More than that, I see it in the way he studies my face, then scans the rest of me, as if searching for open wounds.

"You want me to ask Alia to check on her?"

These words deliver me a disorienting injury.

I had no idea I was so obvious; I have no desire to be pitied. Still, my heart begins to pound, my fears threatening to bleed beyond their enclosure even as gratitude expands in me like static, bristling under my skin. That familiar blade pierces me again and I can't compartmentalize quickly enough; instead I retreat so far inside my mind I feel physically distant when I say, tonelessly, "Nazeera is with her now. But thank you."

Adam holds my gaze a beat longer; finally, he nods.

I once thought he was a brainless soldier.

I'd read him wrong, all those years ago. In fact, I couldn't read him at all. His interior quiet was never as complete nor as deafening as Rosabelle's; instead, his emotional cues came across as both vague and wooden, and I thought I had the latitude, as a result, to make the tragic assumption he was a garden-variety idiot. As it turns out, Adam has the uncommon ability to neutralize the preternatural powers of others—and he'd been unconsciously exercising a skill to shut me out. There was a time when he didn't even know how to unlatch this armor; now he rarely bothers to hide his emotions from me. He calls it *growth*.

I call it loud.

"So," Adam says, building toward a segue. He takes a breath as he returns his eyes to the interrogation. "You really think this girl is activating some kind of a shield?"

I step closer to the window, pulling up beside my brother. As my heart rate steadies, I feel the pager vibrate in my pocket, each buzz like a shot to the head. I glance at the notifications, scanning for emergencies and finding none for the moment. In my head I build the scaffolding for the work to come: I silently add things to my to-do list; draft responses to questions; sketch out solutions to problems; delegate responsibilities; attempt to anticipate the next pitfall. All this I'll set aside to manage later.

Right now I give Adam a cursory glance.

I thought I was dressed casually today, forgoing my

standard uniform for a leather field jacket, slacks, and boots; but Adam redefines the word *casual*. He's wearing a lightweight puffer jacket over an old hoodie and a pair of faded jeans, at least a day's stubble shadowing his jaw. He could use a haircut. His sneakers are scuffed and worn, and he's pulled his shoelaces so tightly the tongue and toe box are pinched, the sight of which so aggressively repulses me I have to force myself to look away. I spin my wedding ring around my finger. It costs me something to say nothing about his shoes.

Still, despite our outward differences, we share an uncanny moment of alignment: exhaling at the same time.

"I don't know if it's a shield," I admit, returning my eyes to Rosabelle.

There's a dim clang of metal as she sits up in her seat, her manacles knocking together, and Hugo, who's sunk to the ground in defeat, looks up at the sound.

"Rosa," says Hugo, his voice fraying as he repeats the same lines over and over. "Please. You have to believe me—I never would've left you. They forced me to leave you. Please, say something—"

I look at Adam, anchoring myself in the room.

"As you already know," I say to him, "we discovered last week that the mercenary has the unprecedented ability to die at will. It's possible she's able to shut off her mind by extension. But logic would insist that were she capable of such a thing, she might've activated this power earlier."

"And you don't think she has?"

"I don't know," I say again, more quietly this time. "I've never had an issue sensing her emotions, which leads me to assume for the moment that this is some new kind of power—something we haven't seen from her before."

Adam nods, even as he frowns. "And you think I might be able to disarm her. You think it's something she turns on and off."

"I don't know," I say for the third time. "I'm not ready to commit to absolutes yet. If you find that you're able to shut off her power, I might be able to understand its origins. I'm trying to determine whether this—whatever this is—is an internal power, activated from within, or an external power, generated remotely."

"Remotely?" Adam raises his eyebrows. "Like, you think The Reestablishment might've turned off the chip in her brain?"

"The problem is, there is no chip in her brain," I say, my mood darkening as I meet his eyes. "If there were, she'd be a lot easier to understand. All I know is that *this*"—I nod at the window—"is not her natural state. I know her to be capable of heightened emotion and brain activity, but her mind has been impenetrable since the moment of her incarceration. It's like nothing I've ever encountered."

"Really?" asks Adam, his surprise peaking. "Not even with me?"

I feel him throw up a shield between us to illustrate his point, and his shock quiets to a note of flat, anemic interest.

"No," I say, returning my eyes to the inmate. "Not even with you."

Rosabelle's silence is so complete she might as well be dead.

She wears no expression despite having been recently united with her father after more than ten years of separation. Occasionally she shifts in her seat, her shackled hands clasped behind her, and the sounds of metal ring softly through the room. Each time this happens Hugo seizes with a visibly painful hope, practically holding his breath at the thought that she might finally speak, but in eight days, she hasn't said a word. If it weren't for the human blink of her eyes, the rise and fall of her chest, the occasional rearrangement of herself in her chair—she might be mistaken for a machine.

Or a ghost.

There's something spectral about her. She's surprisingly slight, lacking in substance and color. She's almost porcelain white; her skin and hair leached of pigment. Even her eyes are desaturated—some kind of gray. Still, the pallor of her skin is secondary to the real issue, which is perceptible only in her presence: Rosabelle doesn't seem to belong here. She emanates an otherworldly resonance, as if she might've died in birth but was sentenced to life.

Looking at her for too long makes me uncomfortable.

Looking at her for too long takes me to dark places. In her I see shades of myself, and I don't like the comparison.

"She really hasn't said anything in a week?" Adam asks me, his voice dropping to a near whisper.

"Eight days," I say to him, shifting slightly. Fatigue is beginning to wear at my edges. I press the heel of my hand to my forehead in a vain attempt to dispel the building pressure. "And no. Not a word."

I know she's capable of volatility.

I got a clear read on her when she'd first regained consciousness upon arrival in The New Republic. She'd been so unwell that her heart had nearly flatlined; she was so unstable that she'd vomited. I've seen her eyes brighten with fear; I've seen her face animate with feeling; I've seen her cheeks flush with color. I was able to get a read on her even when she'd been lying in the morgue, freshly awoken from the dead. She'd seemed to be processing something like grief, of all things, which surprised me. I even got a read on her right before her incarceration, when she'd been able to hide neither her shock nor her chaotic feelings toward my younger brother. I knew my tactical maneuver had paid off when I felt her horror at reuniting with her father; and I didn't mistake her feelings then.

We should've seen results by now.

Without warning, I feel Adam relent to a crashing wave of disappointment. He gives up his position by the window and flops down in a hard chair, the metal legs scraping the concrete floor as he sighs. Right away, his knee starts bouncing. His body language alone shouts that he doesn't want to be here, but I can actually feel his anxiety building, nervous energy gathering in the room like a storm. It makes me restless. My chest tightens.

I already know what he's going to say.

I've known for several minutes now. I've been trying to resolve my own disappointment as I wait for him to tell me what's now obvious.

In the interim, I glance at the time.

These days have begun to take on a pattern. Hugo gave up

any proper efforts at interrogation about fifteen minutes ago; he's now sagging against the back wall, visibly distraught. I close my eyes a moment, trying to shut his escalating pain out of my head. Hugo is on track for a complete breakdown, which is usually how these sessions end.

"I'm sorry, man," Adam finally says. "I wish I could help, but it's like—I don't know how to explain it. It's like trying to catch a fish with my bare hands. Sometimes I think I've got something, but then it's gone, like I might be imagining it. If she has some kind of power or shield up, I don't think it's normal. I can't get a handle on it."

I manage to nod. My head is pounding. Adam's misplaced guilt is assaulting me. "Thank you for coming in anyway," I say to him. "I know you don't like involving yourself in these matters."

Adam doesn't disagree with me.

In fact, my words seem to give him tacit permission to surrender to his own discomfort, and suddenly I'm shotgunned by the weight of his unleashed aversion.

"It's so damn creepy in here," he says, looking around the enclosed space. "I don't know how you do this every day."

There's a sudden upsurge in Hugo's agony, and I nearly strain my neck trying to shake it off.

"You say that," I force out, "as if you think I enjoy being here."

"Don't you?" Adam asks.

I shoot him a dark look. He laughs.

"What?" he says, crossing his arms. "Isn't this, like, your natural habitat? I thought you liked—" Adam physically recoils, metal screeching through the room as he pushes back in his chair, nearly falling over. "Jesus, is he crying?"

I glance at Hugo, and the tension in my body coils tighter. "He's been having a hard time."

"You mean he does this regularly?"

"Most days," I say.

I steel myself before touching my fingers to the window to awaken the glass; a digital list of commands glow green, superimposed over the scene beyond. A melodic murmur echoes through the room.

"Good afternoon, General," says a smooth, disembodied voice. "Play back transcript?"

"Not now," I respond. "Prepare to end session. Page Samuel. Initiate security protocols for prisoner transfer."

"Yes, General."

"Upload today's transcript to my files upon termination of the session. But first, confirm that you've made note of every instance of sound and movement from Rosabelle Wolff today."

A rhythmic ping.

"Confirmed, General."

"Previous transcripts noted only dialogue—or lack thereof—from Rosabelle Wolff. Search through all previous recordings and update existing transcripts to include sound and movement from Rosabelle wherever applicable."

"Yes, General," says the voice. There's a pause, then another rhythmic ping. "Transcripts have been updated."

"Increase the voltage on Rosabelle's manacles to seventy-five percent," I say. "Reduce to forty-five percent when she's safely inside her cell."

"Yes, General. Increasing voltage now."

As always, Rosabelle evinces no reaction to the surge.

In eight days, she's displayed no evidence she even experiences pain. Now, as the manacles radiate what I know to be a breathtaking charge of electricity, she doesn't so much as draw audible breath. She waits patiently to be collected, as lifeless as a doll.

My jaw tightens.

If all this is a strategic effort on her part, I'm forced to admit it's effective. I'm beginning to lose my patience with these methods. I'm losing my patience with *her*.

I'd be tempted to pivot to a less humane approach to provoke a reaction, except that I've witnessed enough of her eccentricities to know that she can somehow deaden herself to suffering, even while maintaining consciousness. Weeks ago I made the deduction that physical torture would not be enough to compel her to speak. Psychological manipulation was my only recourse. I assumed her weakness for her sister would translate to a weakness for her father. Clearly, I was wrong. Clearly, she knows what she's doing.

And I have no idea what she's planning.

"Voltage increased, General. Session has now been terminated."

The lights in the interrogation room brighten to painful levels, a soft alarm chiming through the space. Hugo remains rooted to the floor, his knees pulled up to his chest like a child. He buries his face in his hands as the door unseals, guards storming inside.

Another day, another failure.

My anxiety ratchets only higher.

There's no doubt in my mind that Rosabelle is biding her time. She, like me, was built by The Reestablishment. Our type was bred on cruelty, custom-designed to survive the harshest conditions, trained to thrive as prisoners of war. The trouble is, I've never encountered anyone quite like her before. Not only is she apparently numb to external stimulus, but she's proven immune even to the tech we have that might've shut off her power.

Exposing her to Adam was a worst-case scenario.

I take a slow, even breath as a band of pressure seems to tighten around my skull. I have the ability to sense the emotions of others, but greater than that is my ability to draw upon any latent preternatural power. In a normal scenario I'd be able to take Rosabelle's power and use it against her.

Instead, dealing with her is like handling a dead battery.

Another melodic murmur sounds throughout the room. "Can I assist you with anything else, General?"

"Compile a separate file," I say, "highlighting all of Rosabelle's nonverbal responses over the past eight days. I want a day-over-day comparison."

"Compiling now, General."

"That's all for today."

There's a reverberating slam of a metal door as Rosabelle is safely escorted from the room. In my periphery, Adam startles. I clear all the prompts, ending the comms with another melodic ding.

Finally, reluctantly, I turn back to Adam.

All this time, I've felt him openly staring at me. I've felt his silent, hesitant, confused admiration.

It bothers me.

"Is it weird," he says, his smile growing as he studies me, "that I keep forgetting how fancy you are now?"

"Yes."

He laughs out loud. "It's cool that you're so humble about it."

"It's not a matter of humility," I say, bristling. "I oversee all branches of the military in The New Republic. You'd have to make an effort to forget what I do."

"I never said I forget what you do," he says. "I just keep forgetting your title."

I only stare at him, my impatience building.

"What?" he says. "It keeps changing. Doesn't it keep changing?"

"No."

Adam's frown deepens. "But you've had a couple of title changes, right?" He bounces his knee again and I snag on the sight of his unforgivable laces, the pinched toe box, the triple-knotted mess. The pounding in my head is only getting worse. I'm reminding myself to say nothing about his shoes, to keep my unsolicited advice to myself, when he adds, "I thought you were a chief commander of something. Or head of state. But the robot just called you General. I think it's fair to say it's a little confusing."

"It's not confusing," I say coldly. "Juliette is head of state. I'm general of defense."

"Can you remind me again how those jobs are different?"

"No."

"It *is* new, though, right? Weren't you recently promoted?"

"No."

I silence another series of incoming notifications on my pager, scrolling through at least a dozen urgent missives to glance at the few highlighted as priority—

**Nothing to report. Calm down. She's sleeping.**

**STOP FUCKING PAGING ME**

**Bro I think James is on his period**

**Inconclusive, sir. We'll need another extract from the vial in order to run a new set of trials**

I stretch my neck and clench the pager too tightly in my fist, trying to release the tension radiating through my shoulders. I fight to organize my thoughts, but there are too many things vying for my attention. My mind is like a faulty camera lens, hunting for focus and failing.

My head is overrun.

Hugo's soft cries are haunting me; echoes of Rosabelle's skittish movements continue to susurrate through my memory; the low buzz of overhead lights is compounding my headache; the bouncing of Adam's foot is starting to drive me insane.

I close my eyes. Open them.

*I miss my wife.*

*I want to go home.*

"Oh," Adam is saying, his frown deepening. "Maybe I'm thinking of Kenji? Did Kenji get a promotion?"

"Two years ago," I say, forcing myself to be present.

Adam's confusion is palpable and annoying. "Someone

got a promotion, though, right?" he says. "Why do I feel like someone got a promotion?"

"Maybe you're thinking of James," I say unkindly. Too sharply. "Who was recently *demoted*."

Adam sits back in his chair, one foot propped up on his knee. Bouncing. "Hey, whoa—I'm on your side in this, okay? I'm just as pissed off at James as you are."

"I doubt that."

"Okay," he says slowly. "Whatever. It's not a competition."

I can't seem to breathe deeply enough. This pounding in my skull is nearly blinding. I tell myself to return to center, to finish out this session, to focus only on the emergencies ahead of me. *Priorities.* Instead, I hear myself snap: "Your sneakers are too big for you."

Adam's head shoots up. "My what?"

"Your sneakers," I say, turning my eyes to the window. Hugo is sitting like a dead insect in the corner, collecting dust. As always, I'll need to manage this emotional fallout. "You shouldn't have to pull the laces that tightly. Get a smaller size."

Adam laughs, unamused. "Uh, I've been buying my own shoes all by myself for a long time, man. I think I know my shoe size."

I turn to face him. "Apparently not."

"What the hell is your problem?"

"I know how shoes are supposed to fit," I say, even as I wish I'd never spoken. I don't know why I brought this up. I don't know why I'm still talking. I wish I could take it back. "You shouldn't have to choke the laces in order for the shoes to stay on. If you have to strain the laces like that, then you've chosen the wrong fit for your foot—"

"You know," he says, cutting me off, "it's shit like this that makes people hate you. Why do you need to lecture me about my shoes? Let me choke my fucking laces if I want to. Why do you care?"

"Because someone has to care," I counter. "Someone has to know that there's a correct way of doing things. Why would you choose to do it wrong when there's a better way? Why insist on the path of ignorance simply because it's familiar? And why do you need to use profanity to emphasize your point? How many times have we talked about this?"

"You know what I love?" says Adam, crossing his arms.

I can feel his anger building now.

"I really, really love it when you, the reigning king of virtue, give me life advice."

I shake my head, looking away.

"Like, you could be shooting someone in the face," Adam goes on, "and if I walked by at that exact moment and said, *Holy shit, you just shot someone in the face!* you'd look at me like I was the one who did something wrong."

"I only shoot people when they deserve it," I point out. "Yet you feel the need to punctuate every other sentence with a vulgar epithet that only serves to diminish you in the process—"

"Wow," he says, feigning amazement. "You should be studied. I don't think I've ever met anyone more delusional in my life. Except maybe James, and we both know that's your fault."

"My fault?" I say, stiffening as I turn to face him. Fury radiates through my chest. *"My fault?"*

Adam scowls. "Yes, bro, fucking your fault—"

"If this situation is anyone's fault, it's yours," I say sharply. "You made him think it was okay to disrespect authority, to live arrogantly. You made him think it was okay to be reckless. You made him think it was acceptable to speak using the cheapest words language has to offer—"

*"Me?"* Adam makes a sound of disbelief. He uncrosses his legs; sits forward; finally stops bouncing. "Are you serious? If I had any influence over that kid I would've prevented him from turning into *you*—"

I physically recoil. "He's nothing like me."

"He's exactly like you!" Adam cries, throwing up his hands before rising to his feet. "You both occupy the same delusional landscape! He thinks he's some kind of superhero. He thinks he can go around murdering bad guys for a living. You made him believe he could grow up to become king of the fucking world—"

"I did no such thing—"

"Bullshit—"

"He never even listens to me," I argue. "I've spent ten years trying to teach him to be disciplined and thoughtful, and instead he's turned out to be entirely unmanageable—"

"I really thought it'd be good for him, you know?" Adam is saying. "I knew he'd seen some dark things. I could tell he was desperate to prove himself. Even as a kid he was doing dangerous shit, always nearly getting himself killed, and I was worried he'd end up hurting himself without an avenue to work out his anger. I thought training him would be productive. I thought he'd at least learn proper self-defense. I thought it would make his life safer. I thought he'd spend a few years working things out of his system and then he'd come to his senses, and instead he's lost his fucking mind and fallen for a psychopath—and all because of you—"

"You coddled him!" I counter. "You gave him too much positive reinforcement. You fed him too many lies about life. You didn't want him to be afraid of the world. You made him think he could be anything he wanted to be if he just believed in himself—"

"Oh yeah? Well, you fucking spoiled him," Adam shouts back. "You gave him whatever he wanted. You gave him a fancy title and too much power. You let him go everywhere with you. You let him see how people look at you and talk to you and shit their pants around you and he fucking loved every second of it. Hell, he even looks like you—"

"It's not my fault," I say, my voice rising dangerously, "that James decided to take the wealth of knowledge I gave him and use it to make bad decisions—"

"It sure as hell isn't my fault—"

"Yes, it is—"

"No, it isn't—"

"*You did this to him,*" we both say at the same time.

# ~~Her touch is lethal.~~
# Her touch is power.

DISCOVER THE *NEW YORK TIMES* BESTSELLING

SHATTER ME: SERIES ONE.

STORYTIDE
An Imprint of HarperCollins*Publishers*

epicreads.com

An epic, romantic fantasy series inspired by Persian mythology from #1 international bestselling author

# TAHEREH MAFI.

“Prepare to be destroyed.”

—Stephanie Garber, #1 *New York Times* bestselling author of the Caraval series

STORYTIDE
*An Imprint of* HarperCollins*Publishers*

epicreads.com